CRIME SCENE

He drove into the parking lot. It was just past seven and there weren't too many cars. Most were clustered in the prime spots by the front of the store. There was one car, just one, parked far at the other end of the lot. He could see from here that it was white, like theirs. He drove closer. A white Volvo station wagon. Like theirs. Closer. A 9VL. Like theirs. As he pulled up behind it, he saw their New York license plate and read their number.

He parked the SUV and jumped out. He walked around the station wagon, trying every door. . . .

"So you found it." Geary approached the Volvo. "So this is it."

Will nodded. "The groceries are still there."

Geary stepped closer and stuck his head into the back of the car. He made a face and pulled out. "I've smelled worse, unfortunately. I saw you checking the ground." He swung himself down to peer under the car. "Too bad it rained last night."

FIVE DAYS IN SUMMER

Kate Pepper

AN ONYX BOOK

ONYX
Published by New American Library, a division of
Penguin Group (USA) Inc., 375 Hudson Street,
New York, New York 10014, U.S.A.
Penguin Books Ltd, 80 Strand,
London WC2R 0RL, England
Penguin Books Australia Ltd, 250 Camberwell Road,
Camberwell, Victoria 3124, Australia
Penguin Books Canada Ltd, 10 Alcorn Avenue,
Toronto, Ontario, Canada M4V 3B2
Penguin Books (NZ), cnr Airborne and Rosedale Roads,
Albany, Auckland 1310, New Zealand

Penguin Books Ltd, Registered Offices:
80 Strand, London WC2R 0RL, England

First published by Onyx, an imprint of New American Library,
a division of Penguin Group (USA) Inc.

First Printing, July 2004
10 9 8 7 6 5 4 3 2 1

PUBLISHER'S NOTE
This is a work of fiction. Names, characters, places, and incidents either are
the product of the author's imagination or are used fictitiously, and any resem-
blance to actual persons, living or dead, business establishments, events, or
locales is entirely coincidental.

BOOKS ARE AVAILABLE AT QUANTITY DISCOUNTS WHEN USED TO PROMOTE
PRODUCTS OR SERVICES. FOR INFORMATION PLEASE WRITE TO PREMIUM MAR-
KETING DIVISION, PENGUIN GROUP (USA) INC., 375 HUDSON STREET, NEW YORK,
NEW YORK 10014.

For Oliver, Eli and Karenna

ACKNOWLEDGMENTS

With thanks to my agent, Matthew Bialer, whose skill, patience and generosity never failed. Special thanks to my mother, Gail Barrnett, whose careful reading of the manuscript, unflagging encouragement and willingness to babysit eased the writing process. Without the love, support, intelligence and humor of my husband, Oliver, I may never have set out on this one last try. Thank you for reading every word, over and over, and for sharing my feeling that this was an idea worth pursuing. And finally, appreciation and thanks to Kara Welsh and Claire Zion of New American Library, who welcomed this novel with such enthusiasm; and to Audrey LaFehr, who opened the door.

FIVE DAYS
IN SUMMER

PROLOGUE

Five syringes lined the bleach-clean counter. Five shots, five days. No food, no water, just total darkness and the sway of the ocean. She would sleep and wake, and when the blindfold finally came off, her eyes would be frozen open. If the muscle inhibitor worked as it had before, along with starvation, whatever was right in front of her would be visible, but that was all.

What she saw would terrify her.

He prepared the boat, cleaning every surface of the cabin until the long wooden benches gleamed; their cushions had been beaten of dust and the galley fixtures appeared never to have been touched by sea air. He'd had many boats over the years, but this one was his favorite; built for the river, it was tough enough to handle the fickle estuarial crosscurrents of the coastal inlets and bays.

The cabin stayed cool and damp despite the burning summer heat outside. A residual odor of mildew lingered even after the hatch had been left open all afternoon. He knew the smell would grow worse in the days ahead, and he hated it, but it would weave itself into her torment. The smell, the darkness, and damp coolness, the trickling away of life. It was all part of his plan.

He checked his supplies. A wreath of hose in the cabinet under one bench. Under the other, an axe, sharpened and oiled. Cooking oil on the blade made the cut cleaner. A little research, that was all it took to discover these things; and of course, practice. A butcher's knife. A paring knife. Scissors. Gardening shears. Long metal skewers. Bottles of purified water. Coiled rope.

The smaller items were in the single drawer under the galley counter. A swath of black fabric, folded neatly in the corner. Extra syringes. One hundred straight pins equidistantly piercing the soft fabric of a pincushion shaped like a bulbous strawberry. It was a ridiculous item he'd been unable to resist, just like something he'd once discovered in his mother's sewing box. He'd removed the hastily jammed pins and used the pincushion as a ball. Later that night, he was the pincushion. Eventually the scars were covered by chest hair.

The small, under-counter refrigerator was clean and cold. Glass vials of pancuronium and trifluoperazine were lined up on the top shelf like little soldiers..

He had waited seven years.

DAY ONE

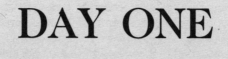

Chapter 1

Emily stepped back onto wet sand and looked out over Juniper Pond. A calm sky hovered over four acres of gleaming lake. Pines and lake grass roughened a shoreline that curved into secret places then reappeared. In a lifetime of summers here, there were parts of this lake she had rarely seen. She lifted a hand to shade her eyes against the afternoon sun and watched her middle child, Sam, lurch out of the water. He stood dripping at her side, scanning the shore with her.

"Why is it doing that?"

He pointed at what they had come to call the reaching tree. The old pine was anchored at a peculiar angle a few hundred yards away, just where the shoreline turned into a neighboring cove. Bent sharply at the base of its trunk, the tree seemed to reach with all its branches, like a bereft lover, toward the center of the pond.

"There must be something it needs," she said.

"Or wants." David, her eldest, glided into the shallow water.

"What does the tree want?" was always the question Emily, as a child, had asked her mother.

"I suppose it wants everything," was always Sarah's answer.

Emily decided on a new answer. "Maybe it wants to fly," she told her sons, and reached out to tousle Sam's wet hair a moment too late; he was already back in the water, chasing David, who had swum away.

A cloud shifted and the sun briefly vanished. Water lapped at Emily's toes. She ached to go back in and join her mother and children for a swim but she'd already delayed her trip to the grocery store too long. It had to be at least three o'clock. She was taking the kids home to New York tomorrow—the boys started school later in the week—and she wanted to leave the house stocked with food as a thanks to her mother.

Emily raised her arm to wave good-bye. A jangle of metal fell from her wrist; the clasp of her silver charm bracelet had come loose again. Snapping it shut, she called to Sarah, "Remind me to get my bracelet fixed."

"Careful not to let it fall into the water, dear," Sarah called back. She stood to her waist in the lake, with year-old Maxi squirming in her arms. The broad rim of Sarah's straw hat dappled Maxi's plump face in shadow and light.

Emily threw Maxi a kiss, and Maxi's lips smacked the air, kissing back. Emily smiled, Maxi clapped. And just as Emily's words "I love you" sailed across the water, Sam splashed in her direction, vying for attention as he struggled to swim.

"Sammie, control your strokes." Emily pointed at David. "Look."

David moved between surface and depth, a spray of water at his kick. He was just like she had been, in this very lake, at the age of eleven: a natural fish. Sam at seven was a fish out of water. The shopping could wait another five minutes. Emily strode into the lake and Sam threw himself into her arms, all soft skin and burgeoning muscles, nearly toppling her backward.

"Try it like this, sweetie."

She circled him, her arms rotating in the water, face pivoting back and forth for air. Sam jumped up and down, splashing, then stopped. David had swum to her side like a dolphin pup, perfectly mirroring her movements. Winking at David, she reached for Sam's hands and swam backward, pulling him along. He began to kick and splash and his natural glee returned to those chocolate eyes.

They splashed their way over to Sarah and Maxi, who reached her arms around Emily's shoulders. Emily held and kissed and squeezed her last baby. "Mama's going to the store, Grandma will take such good care of you."

"No!" The silky cheek buried in Emily's neck.

"Mommy will be right back. I love you. Take good care of Grandma while I'm gone."

"No!"

"Yes!" Sam lightly splashed Maxi, who splashed back, laughing.

"Careful of Maxi's ear infection," Emily said.

Sarah shifted Maxi out of Sam's spray, and he happily turned the waterworks on himself.

"Mom," David said. He'd slid next to her, coolly unnoticed. She pushed a strand of wet hair off his forehead. "Strawberry ice cream, okay?"

"Are we out of cones, too?"

"Yes," Sarah said over the splashing, "we are."

"I'll try to remember that."

"Better go, dear. Look at the sky."

From a distance, Emily could see that a group of clouds was approaching the sun; an unanticipated storm was coming. Her father used to quote the daily weather reports in the *Cape Cod Times* as reliably "cloudy, sunny, and dry, with rain." If she was lucky, she'd be home from the store before it started.

She waved good-bye to Sarah and the kids and walked through the grove of trees that separated the lake from the house, giving them privacy in both places. Once on the wide grass path, she was bathed in scorching sunlight. As she walked up to the house— a standard, weatherworn Cape clapboard with a porch off the back—she sensed a tingling excitement, as if she were escaping to a tropical vacation, or going for a spa day, or a movie at noon. There was always that same contradiction when she left the kids: the pang of loss, and the seductive possibilities. Maybe she'd pull into the drive-through at Starbucks along the way for an iced tea.

An iced tea. It took so little now to triumph over the day. Before kids, she'd toured the world as a cellist with the New York Philharmonic, sometimes visiting three different countries in a single week. As a young musician she had challenged herself to the fullest, or so she'd thought. Until falling in love with Will. Until motherhood. Now her work outside the home was a weekly music column for the *Observer*. She reviewed all kinds of music and could be as opinionated or ir-reverent as she wanted. It was the perfect job: Will got an evening to himself with the kids, free of her hovering, and she got out on the town and was paid for the pleasure.

Emily passed under the porch into cool, welcome shade. It was easier to enter the house by the down-stairs back door. She took a deep breath of the sweet honeysuckle that Sarah had trained to climb the tall supports up to the porch. Her mother's gardens were spectacular; everywhere you looked, in every direction over the three-acre property, something was blooming. Sarah's attentions to the gardens had strayed somewhat this summer, though, since Jonah's death. Emily sorely missed her father. The weeds, the shot lettuce, the overgrown grass, every dead blossom that had not been pinched back were ghosts of him.

Toys littered the downstairs common room. Emily kicked a path and went to her room, which since her childhood summers had been transformed into guest quarters. All her pretty colors had given way to neutrals, her adolescent posters stripped away. Over the bed was one of Sarah's paintings of Emily as a small girl, holding her father's hand, which entered the picture just at the edge of the frame. Between the windows were two photos: Emily on stage at Carnegie Hall and Jonah with his first vintage car.

Emily opened the bottom dresser drawer and remembered she was in the middle of laundry; most of their clothes were upstairs in the mudroom off the kitchen, churning away in the machine or waiting in a heap on the floor. She peeled off her bathing suit and put on the same underpants and khaki shorts she'd had on at lunch. Holding her blue shirt against her front, she went upstairs to the mudroom and looked through the unwashed piles for a bra. It seemed all her bras had gone in with the load of whites, which were currently mid-cycle. So that was it, she'd throw caution to the wind and go braless; if someone wanted to look, that was their problem. She slipped on her leather sandals and remembered her sunglasses before heading out the door.

It was Labor Day and traffic was thick on Route 151 all the way to Stop & Shop. Emily abandoned the idea of the iced tea. By the time she got her turn at the green arrow at the intersection, directing her into

the shopping center, all sensation of escape had evaporated with the heat; she would get it over with and go
home. She pulled their white Volvo wagon into the
only spot she could find at the far end of the crowded
lot. It looked as if everyone else who had seen the
distant clouds had run to the store to beat the rain.
She couldn't see the clouds anywhere now; the sky
was blue.

She followed her usual routine in the store and went
straight to the deli counter. They had a nifty new computer, as an alternative to the long line, and she touch-
screened in her order. She'd get just enough of her
mother's favorite cold cuts and sliced cheeses to take
her through the rest of the week alone. Sarah always
stayed on the Cape through the end of September
before returning to her own apartment in Manhattan,
and Emily had urged her to follow her normal schedule even though Jonah was gone. The deli's computer
screen spit out a receipt, instructing Emily to arrive
at the pickup counter in twenty minutes.

Turning into the vegetable aisle, she impulsively decided on corn for dinner with their grilled salmon. She
pulled up at the bin of fresh corn and waited for a
man who was carefully filling his bag. He seemed to
touch every ear of corn, even if just slightly, as if per-
forming some kind of ritual. She had never seen anything like it. He appeared to be in his fifties and had
pasty skin to match his white hair. A navy blue sailor's
cap that didn't fit well sat on top of his head. He wore
a white windbreaker, the only person in the whole
store outside of the butcher department wearing a
jacket on this hot summer day. When finally she
turned away to get some red peppers and stop wasting
time, he curtly spoke.

"That's it. I'm done."

His eyes flicked at her chest, then her face, then the

corn. Emily's bravado at going braless vanished in that instant. He touched three more ears of corn, then carefully placed his bag in his shopping cart and moved away. Back at home in Manhattan, she would have steeled herself in the gaze of another shopper and muttered, "Only in New York" with a shared laugh. But here on the Cape, in this crowded exurban store, she was alone, and this guy was weird in a most uninteresting way.

It took shucking a dozen ears of corn before she found six good ones, and by then, to her relief, the strange man was long gone. She pushed her way through the aisles. Extra tuna and peanut butter for sandwiches on the ride home tomorrow. Goldfish crackers for Maxi's snacks and entertainment. Those awful fruit rollups the boys loved so much. Juice boxes. Small water bottles. An extra can of Sarah's favorite loose tea, just in case she was running low.

Emily turned into the bread aisle in search of her mother's favorite loaf, and there he was, right in front of her: the corn man, slowly pushing his cart along with his eyes fixed forward. She moved straight past him and couldn't tell whether he had seen her. At the end of the aisle she found the bread she wanted with a sense of relief that was all out of proportion.

"Didn't you realize it was gone?"

An older woman with bleached blond hair and too much makeup stood next to Emily holding the silver charm bracelet in an open hand.

"I noticed you wearing it before because I have one too." The woman lifted her other wrist to show her own bracelet covered in twice as many charms as Emily's, all gold. "It slipped right into the corn bin. You're lucky I got there next. I've actually been following you."

Emily took her bracelet—a jackknifed swimmer, a

cello, a sword, a heart, three babies and a coin—and closed her fingers around it. She savored the cool silver against her palm. It had been a gift from Will after David's birth and she'd worn it every day.

"I don't know how I missed it," Emily said. "I didn't even realize it was gone."

"I treasure mine," the woman said.

"Just how many children do you have?" Emily had noticed that most of the many gold charms were babies.

"Four children, nine grandchildren. And counting." The woman winked. "Don't wear it until you've had it repaired."

"Good advice." Emily slipped the bracelet into her shorts pocket. "I've been putting off fixing the clasp. I guess this is my wake-up call."

"I've always said life is a series of close calls."

"You can say that again."

The women parted ways, and Emily figured this was why she'd had that sensation of foreboding just before. It wasn't the corn man. She had lost her favorite bracelet, the one she never took off, and didn't know it, at least consciously. It was impressive how the mind worked, understanding things even before they were apparent.

The cart was loaded and it was time to return to the deli to pick up her order. She pushed her way back, marveling at the sheer amount of stuff these megastores could offer. With its constrictions on space, the city had nothing even similar to this when it came to food. She stopped at a bin filled with pink, yellow and blue plastic cups. The sign said they were "magic cups" that would change color when a cold drink was poured in. She knew the kids would love them and bought two of each color.

She was almost at the deli counter when she saw him again. The corn man was back at the corn. Just when she noticed him, he looked up and saw her. He quickly looked down, and touched three ears of corn. She read the number on her deli receipt, picked up her cold cuts from the appropriate cubby, and detoured two aisles back so she wouldn't have to pass him to get to the checkout.

The feeling was back, just when she'd forgotten all about it. She checked for her charm bracelet in her pocket; it was still there.

Luckily the lines were not as long as when she'd arrived and she reached her cashier quickly. She unloaded her items onto the conveyor belt and bagged them herself as soon as they slid down the ramp. She was nearly done when she looked up and saw the corn man right behind her on line, his cart half full with nothing but corn. He placed it neatly onto the conveyor belt in groups of three. The teenage girl at the register, deeply tan with a ring on every finger, rolled her eyes at Emily. She rolled hers back. They waited in silence through the screechy buzz of the credit card connection and approval. Emily scrawled her signature on the receipt and hurried her cart toward the exit.

It was a relief to get outside, away from that bizarre man. She couldn't wait to get home. When she opened the back hatch of her car and stale heat blasted at her face, she knew she was ready for another swim. She could see herself in her red racing suit, plunging into the cool lake. She could hear the chaos of her children's laughter on the beach.

She was brought back to the moment by the crescendoing chimes of her cell phone. Digging through her purse, she found it, and answered.

"They accepted our offer!" It was Will.

"What offer?"

"The one I made on the house yesterday. I didn't want to tell you. It was a surprise."

"It *is* a surprise. Does that mean you got the job?"

"My third interview's set up for Wednesday."

"But, Will—"

"Honey, they don't see you three times if it isn't in the bag."

"I just think we should wait on the house until the job's definite. You know we can't afford—"

"Houses like that go in a day, Em. It's just an offer, the worst is we'll lose the promise money, but that's just a couple thousand dollars and it's worth the risk, don't you think so?"

"If you get the job, it will be."

"Don't worry, it's the cost of doing business." She heard his laugh and saw his handsome winking face and felt his confidence, his ability to bound forward. They had always landed on their feet.

"I know, Will, leap don't creep." She unloaded the bag of ice cream into a shaded area of the trunk.

"Stop worrying. Anyway we won't be fully committed until we have to sign a contract. By then we'll be sure."

"You know what?" Toilet paper and snacks. Milk and cold cuts. Magic cups. "I *am* sure. It's going to work out, I feel it." She knew how much he wanted that gorgeous house in Brooklyn Heights, with its wide rooms, fanciful turn-of-the-last-century details, space for everyone, and views of the East River curling around the southern tip of Manhattan.

"Upward and onward," he said. "Where are you?"

"In the parking lot at the grocery store. It's hot out here."

"Get home, sweetie. Kiss the kids. I've got to make

some calls before the dinner rush. The new manager still can't really handle it without me."

"What's on special tonight?" she asked as she always did, in the tone of the knock-knock jokes the boys told incessantly.

"If it's Monday—"

"It's fish."

They laughed and she slammed shut the trunk.

"All right, honey," she said, "I've got to get back to the house. Talk later."

He sent her a kiss through the phone, which meant he was uncharacteristically alone somewhere in the restaurant. Even if the Madison Square Café didn't hire him as its new executive director, she knew he'd still be happy in the busy swirl at Rolf's, just disappointed; it would mean, of course, turning away from the house.

She ended the call and dropped the phone back into her purse. A shadow passed over her and she looked up to the sky, expecting to see the clouds back in force. But just as her mind registered *blue,* an acrid cloth slammed over her face and she was overcome by darkness.

Chapter 2

The sweet smell of onions frying near midnight reminded Will of his bachelor days, when meals naturally fell out of sync and you never knew what came
next. Back then he ate most of his meals at whichever
restaurant he was working; as a striving actor free
meals and untaxed tips had baited him to the work of
survival. Now, his hankering for the stage dulled by
years on a wheel that had spun him nowhere, he understood the value of a good job with benefits and a
future, and the succor of a meal in the quiet of his
own home. Cooking here, in the family kitchen, was
nurture, not art; what he demanded of his chefs he
forgave in himself. He loved the sanctuary of cooking.
And though he missed Emily and the kids during their
long summer holidays, and joined them as often as
the restaurant could release him for two days or more,
there was nothing like the tranquility of an empty
kitchen and the sizzle of onions as they cleared then
began to brown. Jeans, cooking, music; he could stay
young forever this way. Tonight it was Louis Arm-
strong and Jack Teagarden melding their gritty voices
in "Rockin' Chair."

As he chopped the vegetables, the cooking and the
music and even the cold kitchen tiles on his bare feet

triggered a feeling he couldn't decipher. It had been that way as long as he could remember: sensations, sounds, smells almost connecting, but never quite, with a life that preceded memory. It was like an endless loop with a blank spot; and the blank spot was a single day, thirty-six years ago. He had lost his parents to a car crash just at the moment in his childhood when he might have known them beyond a flash of expression, a word swelled in volume, a scent resonating something exquisite sealed inside him. He was just four when they died; his sister, Caroline, was nine. Some days were volleys of déjà vu, thoughts that never crystallized and ultimately had the effect of an itch he couldn't reach. He had learned that if he stayed busy enough, most of the tempting sensations would pass over him unnoticed. He was left with an impression of floating. As a young man he had floated into Emily's arms and she had anchored him. As a father and husband he had come to appreciate more about his capacities than he had previously understood. Most of all, he learned that whatever his parents had given him, it must have been enough.

Will and Emily had lived together in this old two-bedroom apartment for sixteen years, before marriage, before children. They'd outgrown it years ago but only now would their income allow them to move, or at least soon it would; in two days he would know for sure. He saw himself signing the contract for the new job in neat precedence to the contract for the new house. His saw his new kitchen: a six-burner Viking cooktop, a double oven built into the wall, a built-in fridge, granite countertops, and custom-made cabinetry of a light wood, maybe birch. They would raise their children to adulthood in that house. When they were old, he and Emily would retire together to the Cape.

He grabbed a handful of string beans from the strainer, jostled them into a line on the cutting board and sliced the tips off one end, then the other. In a clear glass bowl he'd collected a rainbow of sliced carrots, red peppers and broccoli florets. He peeked under the lid at the pot of water he was heating for pasta; a boil was undulating but hadn't bubbled to the surface. He replaced the top and stirred the onions, then sat down to look at the morning newspaper while he waited to put the pasta in. The front section was full of the same old stories, politics at home and trouble abroad, and after a quick leaf through the second section he had read enough.

He put down the paper and reached over to press down the corner of Sam's monster drawing where the tape was coming loose from the wall. Better yet, he'd replace the tape; he'd been meaning to do it for months, but in the rush of life that consumed minutes like candy, it never got done. He got out the masking tape and went to work, repairing all the crooked and loose art: creatures and aliens by Sam; Escher-like transformations of fish into ninjas, and the like, by David; Maxi's scribbles; and Will's own cartoony sketches of the kids, hung at eye level to amuse them while they ate. He was just getting to the last drawing when the phone started ringing. It was late for someone to call.

He picked up the black receiver from its cradle on the counter. The caller ID screen told him the call was coming from Sarah's house. Emily phoning to say good night.

"You'd be so proud of me," he greeted her.

"Will?" It wasn't Emily. "Will, it's Sarah. I've been trying you for hours."

"I just got home a little while ago, I haven't checked

the machine. Why are you still up?" She usually went to bed at nine thirty.

"I should have your work number. Don't you have a cell phone too? I should have all your phone numbers. I should have a list with every phone number for both of you."

Will had not heard Sarah so distraught since just after Jonah's death, when she had focused on details to avoid noticing the glacial shift beneath her feet.

"Emily has all my numbers."

Silence.

"Sarah?"

"I don't know where she is."

The lid of the pasta pot began to shake above a rolling boil. Hot oil snapped out of the frying pan where the onions were starting to burn.

"What do you mean?"

"I don't know where she is."

"What time did she get back from shopping?"

He heard the whisper of Sarah's breath. "She didn't."

"But I talked to her. I called her on her cell phone, she was in the parking lot. She said she was on her way home."

"You spoke with her? Do you remember what time it was? The police—"

"You called the police?"

"Will dear, don't you think I should have?"

Of course she should have. It was just that the idea of Emily not arriving home made no sense. Emily was always home, and if she wasn't, he knew exactly where she was. She didn't keep secrets and she didn't like mystery.

If she wasn't home, she had to be somewhere.

"I'll call her cell phone," he said.

"I've been calling it all night, Will. She doesn't answer. That message comes on."

"What did you tell the police?"

"I told them she went to the Stop and Shop. That she usually gets home in about two hours. That she calls if she's going to be delayed. I told them all I know."

Will's body walked to the fridge and pulled the blue marker off the dry-erase board; his mind froze in place. Freeze-dancing, Sammie called the game they played in school. A contradiction in terms. An impossibility.

"Who did you talk to at the police?"

"Detective Al Snow. I have his number."

Will wrote the name and number on the crowded board, under his outsized WEDNESDAY 3:00 MADISON SQUARE, over Emily's *plan Val's baby shower early Nov.*, next to the partially rubbed-off caricature of the three children he had drawn stacked on each other's shoulders. David was on the bottom wearing his *gi*, eyes closed, standing on one leg, arms spread wide to demonstrate his balance; Sam was in the middle, loosely straddling David's neck, spouting talk bubbles; Maxi was on the top, squeezing Sam's head with her knees, grabbing a fistful of his hair with one hand, holding her velour bear in the other.

"Do the kids know?" Will heard the steadiness of his own voice and recalled the moment he learned about his parents' accident. He was chasing a basketball through the newly cut grass in his front yard—his father had mowed it just that morning—when Mrs. Simon from next door rushed across the driveway in her floral housedress and curled bluish hair. She was crying. When she picked him up he felt her tears sticky on his neck. The babysitter was in the yard with him and hadn't heard the phone ring. Caroline had been reading on her bed and had not gotten up to answer it.

"I pretended to talk to her on the phone," Sarah said. "I didn't know what to do."

"That's good, don't tell them. This is probably nothing, Sarah. She'll walk in the door the minute we hang up. But just in case . . ."

"You'll come, Will?"

Will had planned another long day at the restaurant tomorrow, so he could take time off for his interview on Wednesday, and most of the day Thursday to help get the boys to school in the morning and pick them up in the afternoon. It was a family tradition; the first day of every school year was a big deal, and he wouldn't miss it.

He drew a line with the blue marker between the stacked kids and the detective's name.

"I'll call the detective right now. Then I'll call you back. I'll let you know what's happening."

"I'll wait."

"Sarah, call me the minute she gets there."

"Of course."

Will hung up the phone with the certainty that Emily was alive. She had to be. It was simply not possible for his soul to be swallowed up twice.

Detective Al Snow answered on the third ring, in a pleasant voice, stating his own name in greeting: "Detective Snow, how can I help you?"

"This is Will Parker. I'm calling because—"

"Yes, Mr. Parker, I had a call from your mother."

"My mother-in-law. My wife's mother. It's about my wife."

"Mrs. Parker told me all about it."

"Mrs. Goodman called you. Mrs. Parker never came home."

The detective took a moment before speaking. "I'm

sorry, Mr. Parker. Yes, I have it written down right here."

"I'm calling because—"

"I understand," Detective Snow said in a tone that was mild but somehow firm, as if he had heard this all before. "I want you to know that nine times out of ten the missing party turns up. What I mean is, they turn out not to be missing at all."

"But it was eight hours ago," Will said, "and she was on her way home."

"I understand, Mr. Parker. I took the report. It's right here. She's filed missing."

"Filed?"

"It's an open report, Mr. Parker. Not filed like in the cabinet. We're looking into it."

Then why, Will's mind raced—as it hit him, really hit him, that Emily might have vanished—*are you sitting at your desk answering your phone? Talking to me?*

"Are the police out looking for my wife?"

"Yes, we are, Mr. Parker, as we speak. But I can't emphasize enough that these cases usually resolve themselves. That's what we always tell the family so you don't worry yourselves to death. That's why it's twenty-four hours before a person is officially missing."

Will didn't like the *but* or the *usually* or the *twenty-four hours*. He said good-bye to the detective and hung up the phone, called Sarah and told her he was coming. Then he called Thrifty Car Rental down the block and asked for whatever they could have available quickest. It was a top-of-the-line SUV, and he booked it, figuring they were cashing in on the tension in his voice. He didn't care. Even if he drove all night only to find Emily asleep in her bed, he had to go.

It took six minutes to turn off the stove, toss the

food either into the fridge or the garbage, pack the basics in a canvas bag, and lock up the apartment; two minutes in the elevator; and half a minute to sprint down the block and get ripped off by the night shift at Thrifty. He shoved his wallet into his back pocket, tossed the bag onto the passenger seat and sped down West End Avenue to the Ninety Sixth Street entrance to the Henry Hudson Parkway, heading north.

In twenty minutes, Will was speeding up the Hutchinson Parkway. He had all the windows open and the cool midnight summer air swooshed through the SUV, shifting its balance. He gripped the wheel to keep steady and reminded himself to breathe. When he felt tingling in both hands, he shook out one hand, then the other, and tried to drive with a looser hold. The mix of adrenaline and exhaustion made him queasy. The main thing was to stay awake. As he passed through the Bronx and into Westchester, the clusters of brick buildings and the glow of a city that never turned off gave way to complete darkness. Headlights brightened as the occasional car passed him then faded around a bend. Only when he could taste the silence beyond the road did he know he had covered some distance.

He got off at the first rest stop in Connecticut, stood impatiently on line to buy a cup of bitter fast-food coffee, dumped in some tepid half-and-half, and got back in the SUV. He drank the coffee with one hand and steered with the other. After a while he turned on the radio but couldn't concentrate. He tried to sing but his voice sounded thin and made him lonely. He pressed the accelerator and passed the speed limit. They said that if a person you loved was dead, you'd know it. Feel it. He had known his parents were gone that very first day. But he didn't feel Emily's absence.

As long as he had known her, he had sensed her with
him. She was with him now, in the back of the SUV.
He could feel the warmth of her breath on his neck
as she leaned forward to speak. He could feel the heat
of her body. There was no way this woman could just
disappear. When he pictured her, he saw her in her
well-worn *gi* cinched with her black belt, flipping
through the air to land on solid feet, then gliding out
of harm's way.

From the first time she twisted him to the mat at
the dojo, when he didn't even know her name, he was
convinced of her resources. He had never forgotten
that look on her face the first night they saw each
other and touched as aikido partners-of-the-moment:
focused and determined, summoning strength that had
to come from a place not quite physical. That night,
he thought her eyes were black, but it turned out they
were hazel. He thought she was tall, but she was only
five feet six. He thought she had short blond hair, but
unclipped it fell thickly past her shoulders. He thought
her skin was paper white, but it was brushed carelessly
with freckles. He assumed that under her *gi* was the
body of a fishwife, and he was the fish powerless in
her hands, slapped to the butcher block for carving.
But in fact she was lithe, a swimmer. He saw it as
soon as he hit the mat. Her practice pants were too
short and her ankles had the sexiest curve he'd ever
seen. Those were the dating years, and he had never
met a woman so unafraid to ignore his jokes when
they weren't funny, who understood when he was trying too hard and let it pass. He was no fool. He recognized her immediately. They were married within a
year.

Just below New Haven, he made the transition to
95 North. Normally traffic jammed at New Haven and

again in Rhode Island when you came into Providence, but not tonight. There were no rush-hour crowds, no families with bikes strapped to the backs of their minivans, no motor boats in tow, just trucks and a few strays like him. The air turned cold and he closed his windows, separating himself from the other drivers. Night driving had never unnerved him like rush-hour traffic; his parents had crashed on a highway, first thing on a clear April morning.

As he approached the Cape, it started to rain, then pour. His wipers could barely fight the torrent that slammed against the windshield. The deluge slowed him down as he crossed the Bourne Bridge. It was another twenty minutes to the first sign for Juniper Pond. The house was half a mile down Gooseberry Way, an unpaved road that ended in their private cul de sac. The modest house, a gentle slope down, and the lake. It was past four in the morning but the moon was bright enough for him to catch glimmers of water through the trees. There was complete silence. The rain had stopped as suddenly as it had started. The air was unspeakably sweet.

The house was dark except for a glow from the side where a kitchen window faced the woods. The garage door was rolled up, with only Sarah's car parked inside. Will walked through the garage and found the mudroom door unlocked.

Sarah met him halfway through the kitchen. The sight of her son-in-law was clearly a huge disappointment; he wasn't Emily. Sarah's eyes squeezed back tears, which she tried to hide with hands worn by years of effort. She was shaking. She still wore her wedding ring.

Will held her and she felt so frail in his arms. He rubbed her back and steeled himself against his own urge to cry. They had no real information, no reason to assume the worst. He would not react as if Emily were dead. She was missing. That was all they knew.

"Why don't you get some sleep, Sarah?"

"How can I? All I do is think."

"I'm going to the police station." Will engaged her eyes. "I need you to get some rest so you can take care of the kids."

"Oh, but, Will, I *can't* sleep."

"Do you have any of those sleeping pills left?"

She nodded.

"Take one now. They won't be up for a few hours. You'll be groggy but it's better than not sleeping at all."

"I'm glad you came."

Her eyes were so rimmed with red that it looked as if a blood vessel had actually broken. Emily was her only child. All she had left, except for her grandchildren—and Will. He knew Sarah had distrusted him when they first met. It was one thing for Emily to be a musician—Sarah herself was a painter—but it was too risky for Emily to love an actor. Aspiring actor. He had once overheard Sarah refer to him as a *waiter* with such antipathy that to this day he still strove for her approval, even though he sensed she had long since relinquished herself to a deep affection for him. He had come through as her daughter's husband and her grandchildren's father, and they both knew it. Years had passed; they were family now.

Will kissed Sarah's forehead. "I'm going to talk to Detective Snow. I'm going to find out what's happening. We're going to find her, Sarah. I promise."

"But, Will—"

"No, don't go there. You'll drive yourself crazy, Sarah, then she'll walk in the door. Don't do it. Okay?"

"I'll try to sleep." She kissed Will's cheek. "Have you eaten anything tonight?"

"I'll get something later. Don't tell the kids I was here. I'll think of what to say before I get back."

"Emily always knows when something's bothering one of the children," Sarah said.

Will nodded. "She does."

"I'm a mother, too, don't forget."

DAY TWO

Chapter 3

On the outside, it was one of the prettiest station houses John Geary had ever seen, especially in the peach light of six in the morning. Brick with New England white wooden trim. A vast green lawn separating it from Route 151. Surrounded by bountiful summer skies. He left his car in the visitors' parking lot out front and walked up the loopy stone path to the main entrance. It was only the second time he'd come to pilfer the Mashpee Police Department's files, too soon to park in the official lot in back.

The station lobby was as plain as the front was pretty. It was like being introduced to a beautiful woman, only to find out nothing much went on inside. When it came to buildings, the well-worn old faithfuls worked best. In all his years at the FBI's training campus at Quantico, Virginia, he'd learned the maze and savored his little basement office. It had held all his books and files accumulated over twenty-six years, and eventually a computer had linked him to the ever-evolving knowledge base of the Behavioral Science Unit. He'd entered as a middle-aged man, wrecked as a cop from the beat on Boston's south side, a doctorate in psychology fresh in his pocket. He'd founded the BSU and honed criminal profiling to a science.

Entered the years tunnel in his prime and came out the other end, old. What was retirement about, anyway? With his wife, Ruth, gone, it wasn't fun.

It was his old friend Roger Bell who had given him the idea to work on a book, researching and analyzing cold cases, trying to profile killers who had never been caught. It would keep his mind nimble, give him something to do. Bell had lured the Gearys here for retirement, then propped John up at Ruth's funeral; she'd died of a heart attack just a month after they'd moved into their new house. Bell promised to read the book before Geary embarrassed himself with publishers. It was the least he could do, enticing him to the Cape just to end up a sorry old widower.

Geary nodded to the front desk officer at the glass-and-stainless reception window. Her blue uniform was nice and neat but her shield was upside down and that caught his eye; must have been why she was at the front desk. A man about forty was slumped in one of the brown leatherette chairs that lined the wall facing the road. He looked agitated. The minute he saw Geary he jerked forward.

"Detective Snow?"

"Sorry, not your lucky day."

"I've been waiting for over an hour. He told me he'd be here."

"I'll tell you what," Geary said. "I'll check his desk and see if he's there."

"Thank you. Tell him Will Parker's waiting. Tell him I've been waiting—"

"Over an hour. Got it."

Parker was wearing blue jeans and a white shirt it looked like he'd slept in. Except that it looked more like he hadn't slept at all. His brown hair was as mussed as very short hair could get. He hadn't had a shave in at least twenty-four hours. Geary wondered what was on his mind but didn't stop to ask.

He hiked a left down the hall, past the records division, to the dispatch center. He'd been introduced to half the small staff the day before, and one of them, an officer who looked like a coed too young to be on the force, was typing into the computer in the report-writing room. Now that he thought of it, someone had said she was a detective. Hard to believe. Long dark hair pulled off her face by a headband. Too pretty for a cop.

"Morning!"

"Morning to you, too." Crisp voice. No smile. Must have been a habit picked up from too much getting leered at.

"Looking for Snow. Seen him?"

"He's out on a missing persons."

"Must be a relative out in the lobby. Guy's pretty eager to talk to Snow."

"I'll let him know if I see him."

Geary considered going back out to tell Mr. Parker but decided not to get involved. Snow would show up eventually.

He backtracked to records. Twenty years of case files were on computer, which meant that plenty of unsolved cases were still filed on paper. With his printout of cold cases from the Middleboro State Police up in Framingham, he'd been making his way slowly through the town stations throughout the Cape. He skimmed each file, looking for the most interesting ones.

Just half an hour into it, he was ready for a cup of coffee. Age worked him; sixty-eight and he needed not just trifocals but liquid stimulation to read for very long. He gathered up his papers and walked down the hall to the kitchen. It was a spare white room with a dropped ceiling. Wires from the wall clock and wall phone dangled down to the same outlet. A white formica counter separated the kitchenette from two round tables. Al Snow was sitting at one of them, eating cold eggs and slick buttered toast out of a molded foam container. He had brought his own diner coffee in a blue-and-white cup.

"Morning, Detective Snow."

"Morning, Mr. Geary."

Geary sucked down the spiky comeback that wanted to rip out of him. He was Dr. Geary or Special Agent Geary or Retired Special Agent Dr. Geary, but not *Mr.* Geary. He would never get used to that.

Snow shoveled a mound of scrambled eggs onto a triangle of toast. The long black fringe of his comb-over fell into the plate when he leaned over to take a bite. If he lost twenty pounds and accepted his baldness, he might have had better luck at the singles bars. He was a big bear of a man, all smiles and winks and *whatever*s, *whatareyougonnado*s, the kind of guy no one much minded having around. Affable, like a hat rack or an initialed hand towel. Not Geary's type.

The coffeepot was empty. Geary had a thought.

"What's the girl's name at the front desk?"

"Suellen, and she's no girl. She could be my mother."

"I guess you both look younger than your age."

Snow raised his wormy black eyebrows and smiled. "We're having a birthday cake for her Thursday, if you're here. Five o'clock."

"Mum's the word." Geary zipped his lips and pretended to throw away the key, mixing his metaphors and not giving a damn. "Think I'll just go check with Suellen about the coffee supply."

Out in the lobby, he leaned on the counter in front of the reception glass. "Any news about the coffee situation? Snow's in the kitchen and he sent me out to ask."

Parker was on his feet. "Detective Snow's here?"

"Excuse me?" Geary twisted around to look at the poor guy.

"Did you say Snow was in the kitchen?"

"I mentioned you were waiting, but I guess he's had a long night. Needs his cup of joe."

Suellen was a little older than Geary had noticed, now that he got a closer look. Plump and pleasant, with salt-and-pepper hair cut short. In the old days, there just weren't too many females to be seen at work; he still had trouble processing their presence.

"Well, there must be fifty bags of coffee in the cabinet just under the machine," Suellen said. "Here, I'll get a pot started."

"Stay where you are, my dear. Let an old hand take care of it."

Geary smiled his best one. Suellen shot one back. Nice lady. He missed Ruth.

"Nonsense, let me."

Suellen got up, tucked her blue shirt into her blue pants, adjusted her holster, even straightened the upside-down badge. She buzzed another officer to come mind the front desk, then went her own interior route in the direction of the kitchen.

Geary turned and walked slowly down the hall. In the moments the reception desk was unattended, there was no one to stop Parker from following him. He could tell this guy wasn't someone who would wait around to get Snowed on.

The kitchen door was open. Suellen already had the water poured into the machine and was dumping a bag of grounds into the filter. "There you go, Al."

Snow looked up from the rim of his paper coffee cup, lifted to his lips. "Excuse me?"

"Here's your fresh pot. You must be beat after that night shift. Though how you'll sleep on all that caffeine, I certainly can't tell."

Suellen left the kitchen through the interior door that led to the front office and her desk.

Geary went straight to the coffeepot, to wait for it to brew and to watch the show.

"Detective Snow?" Parker asked.

Snow put down his coffee and stood up. He had to be six feet three and a good two hundred pounds. "How can I help you?"

"I'm Will Parker. I've been waiting for you." He was straining to keep his voice polite. "Didn't they tell you I was here?"

Snow shook his head. Here came the Snow job. "I've been out looking for your wife, Mr. Parker. I just got back."

"I've been here almost an hour," Parker said. "I don't understand how this could have happened, how she could just disappear—"

"Mr. Parker, why don't you sit down?" Snow pulled out a chair and held on to the back until Parker had settled in. Then he went around the counter and took one of the brown mugs from the wall cabinet.

"How do you take your coffee?" Snow asked.

Parker twisted around, forehead tight as a fist. "Milk."

Snow pulled out the glass pot and let the coffee drip right into the mug until it was three-quarters full. Then he added a splash of milk and carried it around the counter. He set the steaming mug in front of Parker, who took a sip and seemed to have to force it down. He set the mug back on the table.

Snow got started, flipping open his pad, uncapping his pen, even giving the tip a little lick. Geary listened as Snow spun out all the right questions and jotted down the answers. When he got to, "Your wife ever disappear before?" Parker had enough.

"Of course not," Parker said. "How can a person be missing twice?"

Snow shrugged. "Some people can't stay put."

Parker leaned back. "Not Emily. She's never run away and she never would. She's not capable of leaving the children."

"Tell me about the children." Snow twirled his pen between his thumb and pointer.

"We have two boys, eleven and seven. And Maxi's just one."

"Most mothers don't walk out on their kids." Snow nodded. "But they do walk out on their husbands and sometimes the kids get left behind."

"Detective Snow." Parker stood up and scraped his chair under the table. "We're wasting time with this. Please."

"I'm sorry"—Snow smiled; he actually smiled—"but it's procedure. Have to do it."

Procedure, sure. This guy was a do-nothing piece of work—Geary had seen it a hundred times. Bottom line: Snow should have been out looking for the woman, finding traces of her at the place she was last seen, following threads. Any thread. Even invisible ones. When Geary was on the job, they used to say it took a magician to conjure a missing person back into the world from inside a black hole. They called it the vanishing point, the place you stepped into by mistake, and vanished. There were no *procedures* in the rule book for that one.

"Your wife stressed out, by any chance?" Snow asked.

"Of course she's stressed out," Parker answered. "She lives in the twenty-first century. Aren't you?"

"Not really." Snow glanced at his notes. "Can I call you Bill?"

"It's Will." Parker forced a smile but it didn't work. He looked a day past exhausted.

Geary took a mug from the cabinet and poured himself some coffee. He leaned over the counter drinking it and kept his ears open. His interest was piqued and he wasn't sure why. It wasn't just that a woman was missing; it was something else.

"What do we do now?" Parker asked.

"Roll call's at eight," Snow said. "I'll be off duty but your wife's case will be presented. We could use a photo, Will. Something that gives a good idea of how your wife looks. We'll fax the photo to every station house on the Cape and to Middleboro, that's the state headquarters."

"Then?"

"We keep looking. Sometimes someone calls in with a lead. Maybe someone saw something."

"What did they tell you at the grocery store?"

Snow thought too long; Geary could tell he hadn't bothered to go. Obviously Snow had decided to see if she would turn up on her own. Geary had seen it too often. And then it was too late.

"Nothing out of the usual," Snow said. "No one remembered her."

"I'll call my mother-in-law and ask her to fax over a picture of Emily," Parker said. "What's the fax number?"

Snow had to go find it. While he was gone, Geary couldn't help saying something. "Don't mean to pry—"

"I didn't catch your name?" Parker let his edgy tone spill onto Geary. The young ones did that sometimes, figured you were too old to notice or would forget it happened. They needed a punching bag and it was you.

"Dr. John Geary, retired special agent with the FBI." Geary waited for it to sink in.

"Excuse me, Dr. Geary. But if you're retired, why are you here?"

"Same reason you're here. Looking for people who disappeared. I'm writing a book."

Parker nodded. He stood and fished in his pocket for his cell phone. "Where did he go?"

"Snow's a slow walker. Give him a minute."

Parker paced to the window, where the venetian blinds were pulled all the way up. Traffic on Route 151. A white sun pulling into a baby blue sky.

"If I were you," Geary said, slipping in this one coin on the chance it might start Parker's motor, "I'd go to the grocery store myself. I wouldn't wait for a snowball to roll up a hill."

Parker laughed.

Geary liked him.

Snow returned with the girl with long dark hair. Geary let out a little snort but luckily no one heard. He went back to the coffeemaker, poured himself another cup, and stayed just long enough to hear Snow introduce her.

"This is Detective Amy Cardoza. She's on shift for the rest of the day. She'll take care of the photo and she'll present your wife's case at roll call."

Amy stepped forward to shake Parker's hand. She was younger than he was, maybe thirty, smooth skin, no tan, nice eyes.

"We're going to do our best to find your wife," Amy said. Her gaze shifted rapidly to Snow, then back to Parker. "I know this is frustrating for you."

Parker seemed to appreciate the acknowledgment. "I'll need that fax number."

Amy handed him a Post-it note with the number on it. "There's a phone on the wall. When you're done I'd like to ask you a few more questions."

Parker turned his back to them, flipped open his cell phone and pushed two buttons.

Geary walked out of the room. He had something he needed to do.

Geary drove the seventeen minutes back to his house at Cotuit Bay Shores. It was a nice little post-and-beam prefab just right for a retired couple. That was what the broker had said. Not too big, not too small. Cozy. A screened-in summer porch. Fully winterized. All the amenities. What sold them in the end was that there was a groundskeeper who took care of the whole community for a small annual fee. John and Ruth were done with cleaning gutters and shoveling snow. And Roger Bell's house was just two dead ends away.

Geary pulled into the driveway but not the garage. He'd only be home a few minutes. He unlocked the front door and went straight to his desk in an alcove off the living room. It was a mess but he had a system; he knew where everything was. The file he wanted was from the Woods Hole precinct. It was on the left side of the desk, between an oversized street atlas and a copy of Ruth's last diary: a half-filled book of blank pages with a pale green cover on which she had sketched a sprig of dill, her favorite herb. He had never read the diary and never would, but he liked to keep it near him.

There wasn't much in the manila folder, just a few cold cases from over the years, but one in particular made him think of Emily Parker. On top of the file was a yellowed copy of a report from the local paper.

Shocking Discovery Under Wharf

Woods Hole, Massachusetts. September 13, 1994.

A severed arm was discovered Monday when three seven-year-old boys were scraping barnacles from beneath the dock near Stony Beach. One of the boys, Brian Lee, thought he saw a circle of dark rocks in the wet sand. A collector of rocks and shells, Brian went to investigate, and made the discovery of five fingertips protruding just above the sand. The boys immediately notified a passerby, who called the police. The police retrieved the arm, and the area surrounding the docks was sectioned off by investigators. While it has not been confirmed, some believe the arm may belong to Chance Winfrey, age seven, a resident of Brewster. Chance has been missing since Friday, following the disappearance of his mother, Janice, the previous Monday.

Geary read the article then skimmed through the file. The boy's arm had been knifed off at the joint. The day after the arm was found, Janice Winfrey turned up, alive, stretched out on a bench outside the Woods Hole Aquarium. She was starved, dehydrated and delirious. Two weeks in the hospital stabilized her vitals but her mind never came back. The file hadn't been notated since the case was marked closed, two years after the boy's arm turned up at the beach. The rest of his body was never found. One of the strangest things about this case was that there was only one clue, a footprint in the sand that had outlasted the tide. The cops did a Cinderella but it was never successfully matched.

Geary reread the article. Then it hit him. The Winfrey kid's arm was found on the tenth of September. His mother went missing a week before, on a Monday.

Monday, September third.

The son's arm turned up seven days after the mother disappeared.

Geary opened Ruth's desk calendar—the gardens of Monet, recent months starkly blank—and checked today's date. It was September fourth.

That meant Janice Winfrey disappeared seven years ago yesterday. Exactly seven years before Emily Parker vanished from a parking lot.

And Emily Parker had two young sons.

Geary's brain did a flip.

He picked up his cordless phone from where it was lying next to its base, but when he pressed TALK there was nothing. Damn battery. He cradled it and went to the kitchen. He didn't like to use the creamy white princess phone on the counter because it reminded him of Ruth, stretching the extra-long coil so she could talk while she cooked. She wouldn't have a cordless phone, she liked dancing with this one. He lifted the handset and dialed Roger Bell from memory.

"Good morning, John."

"Caller ID, you're not that smart, Bell."

Bell's grainy voice chuckled.

"I'm calling for a reason."

"Did you stub your toe getting out of bed again?"

"Hardy har har. Don't make me laugh this early. I'll burst a hemorrhoid and you're the only doctor I'd let fix it."

"Now, John, you know I delve best into the bowels of the mind."

"Yeah, I know, and mine's a cesspool. Can we be serious for a minute? And don't say—"

"I *was* being serious."

"Now listen to me, Roger. I might have a case. A repeater."

"Oh?"

"From the cold files. Something that might match a new missing persons. I've got a strong hunch about this and I want to brief you on it later if you have time."

"Not on anyone's payroll, I'd wager."

"Roger, I tagged you as a consult onto my cases for years. This one you'll do for the book."

"Of course I will," Bell said. "Have you had breakfast?"

"I ate at five. I've got something I need to do right now. I'll fill you in at lunch, high noon, Lizzy's Diner."

"Noon, then."

Geary hung up, opened the fridge and took a long swig of orange juice from the carton. For the first time in his life, this was something he could do without annoying someone; but after all that waiting, it really wasn't so much fun. He used the palm of his hand to wipe a dribble of juice off his chin and put the carton back in the fridge. There wasn't much in there to eat.

Seemed like he could use some groceries. Maybe he'd try that big new Super Stop & Shop across from the Mashpee Commons. If Emily Parker shopped there, it was good enough for him.

Chapter 4

The police station coffee had fried Will's nerves, and now, as he drove up 151 to the Mashpee rotary, he had to take yawning breaths to keep steady. He gripped the steering wheel so hard his palms burned. Sweat trickled down his back and bled a wet stripe down his shirt. Emily had to be somewhere, didn't she? She didn't go shopping, then vaporize. Did she? He counted four deep breaths as he waited at the red light intersecting the Mashpee Commons and the new shopping center just across the street. The kids would be waking up by now. He hoped Sarah could pull herself together. He would check in on them later, reassure them. At the green arrow, he turned left and drove past a yellow clapboard drive-through bank, a liquor store and a high-end kitchen design center. Just around the corner was the Stop & Shop. People ambled from the parking lot into the store, and out with their overstuffed carts, as if it was a normal early morning. He envied them the simplicity of their shopping. Just yesterday, Emily had been one of them. She had gone into the store, and come out; that much he knew.

He drove into the parking lot. It was just past seven and there weren't too many cars. Most were clustered in the prime spots by the front of the store. There was one car, just one, parked far at the other end of the lot. He could see from here that it was white, like theirs. He drove closer. A white Volvo station wagon. Like theirs. Closer. A 9VL. Like theirs. As he pulled up behind it, he saw their New York license plate and read their number.

He parked the SUV and jumped out. He walked around the station wagon, trying every door; each was locked. Drops from last night's rain clung to the white paint. The sun was inching up the early-morning sky, and before long the car would be dry.

In the backseat he saw Maxi's baby seat, stained from juice bottles and snacks. The black-and-white beanbag cat he'd given her earlier in the summer was slumped over one armrest. The pink thread that had been the mouth had been snagged out. One blue eye had been browned over with chocolate. On the middle part of the seat were two small Ziploc bags with the dregs of a popcorn snack. There was another Ziploc filled with Sam's holographic Pokemon cards; he carried them around in case he met new kids at the playground or the store or the ice cream parlor or any of the countless places Emily took them. In the net bag strapped to the back of the driver's seat was a paperback of *The Lion, the Witch and the Wardrobe,* which David had finished reading on the drive up to the Cape a few weeks ago. In the cup holder next to the driver's seat was a half-drunk bottle of spring water, fogged on the inside.

He could see that her keys were not in the ignition. He used his own keys to open the driver's-side door so he could check around her seat and was hit by a stench of ruined food. The groceries. They were still in the car.

The back hatch lifted effortlessly on its hydraulic

hinges. The smell was worse here, where the food was piled. A gallon of milk had soured in the heat, cheese had putrefied and pink ice cream had oozed out of an overturned bag onto the camel-colored upholstery. The smell was nauseating, and the implication of the smell was worse. He swallowed hard and stepped back. His instinct was to take all the food and dump it into the nearest trash. But would it be evidence? Evidence of her having been here, if nothing else.

He surveyed the area around the car, bending down to see under the chassis. There was nothing there, not a drip of oil, no keys, no stranger to capture and maul in revenge. Under the car was only the wet shadow of a rainy night that had passed.

Hunched by the ground, Will heard a car drive up and park in a spot nearby. He stood and saw the driver's door open on a brown sedan. John Geary stepped out and Will wasn't that surprised; a retired cop, trying to keep busy. He was creased and rumpled, half bald with a halo of curly white weeds in need of a trim. Though he wore a wedding ring, no one had bothered to tell him to change his pants, which were stained around the pockets.

"So you found it." Geary approached the Volvo. "So this is it."

Will nodded. "The groceries are still there."

Geary stepped closer and stuck his head into the back of the car. He made a face and pulled out. "I've smelled worse, unfortunately. I saw you checking the ground." He swung himself down to peer under the car. "Too bad it rained last night."

"I was driving in it. I could hardly see." Will pictured Emily drowning, submerged by the force of the heavy rain. He saw her eyes close, her mouth open, a spray of bubbles carrying away her breath. He shook his head and the image scattered like unwanted dust.

"The rain won't help forensics," Geary said. "Anyway he probably didn't touch the car. He probably waited until she finished loading up her stuff and locked the trunk."

"He?"

Geary's old walnut face considered Will. "Ninety-nine times out of a hundred, it's a he. Been inside the store?"

Will liked Geary well enough—the old man seemed harmless—but he didn't like his certainty, the *he*. Geary's assumptions were already conjuring pictures Will's mind couldn't hold. "I'm going in now," Will said, and turned to walk away.

"Hold it a minute." Geary nearly dove into the putrid-smelling back end of the Volvo. He poked through the bags until he found the long, white receipt. He scanned the top and then the bottom. His rheumy blue eyes lifted to Will. "Cashier number eight."

It was a smart move and Will was thankful, but when Geary tried to hand him the receipt, he shook his head. He had the information he hadn't known he needed; he didn't want the piece of paper. He wasn't sure why but he didn't want to touch it.

Geary nodded but didn't smile; his eyes just sat on Will and waited. Finally, he spoke. "I could help you, you know."

Had a stranger offered help to Emily yesterday? Help getting the groceries into the car? *I could help you, you know.* Had it started as simply as that?

"I don't know," Will said. *Let me hold you*, Mrs. Simon had whispered into his four-year-old ear. "I'll think about it."

Will turned and walked across the parking lot. He didn't look but he could feel Geary watching his back. His sweaty shirt stuck to his skin. He was grateful for the blast of dry, cool air when the store's automatic doors slid open. It was a strange time of morning in the store, a junction of sleepless exhaustion and early-bird energy. A small group hovered at the tiny coffee bar, sharing a daily transition. Will felt a covetous pang for the simple normality of ritual. Breakfast in the morning with the family, helping get the boys off to school, playing with Maxi while Emily showered, then back to the restaurant for another long day and late night.

He walked past dozens of nested shopping carts and stopped when he saw what appeared to be an endless row of cashiers. The closest one was numbered twenty-one. He walked along the exit ends of the checkout counters until he reached number eight. The light on the signpost was off; the checkout was closed. It was a dead end. But at a dead end, you didn't turn off your motor, you turned around and looked for the next road out.

Fifteen feet back, toward the main entrance, Will spotted a counter built into the wall with a window and a sign above it reading INFORMATION. It seemed the obvious place to start.

He went to the window and rang the little bell on the silver-and-pink-speckled Formica counter. No one came at first, so he rang again. He glanced around at the cashiers near him and none seemed to notice that he was standing there. He rang the bell again, four times, hard.

This time, a young man emerged from a back room. He wore a starched white short-sleeved shirt with a blue-and-red-striped tie that stopped short of his last button. A name tag pinned above his shirt pocket announced him as TODD, MANAGER. He couldn't have been more than twenty-five years old.

Todd smiled to reveal two tracks of braces. He leaned into the counter. "What can I do for you, sir?"

"My wife shopped here yesterday," Will said.

Todd nodded and smiled.

"And she never came home."

Todd's smile began to melt.

"She was last seen here."

"Are you sure she shopped *here*—at *this* Super Stop and Shop? We have other outlets all around the Cape. And there's a Shaw's over at the Commons."

"This is where she always shops," Will said. "The receipt says she was at checkout number eight. Can I find out who worked there yesterday afternoon?"

Todd took a moment to consider the request. "Well, I don't really see why not. Hold on a minute." He disappeared into the back room and quickly returned. "That would have been Pam."

"Is she here now?"

"No, she's off today."

"I'd like to talk to her."

"I can't give out personal information on my employees." The smile, thick with silver. "I'm sorry. Policy."

"She may have been the last person to see my wife. I'd really like to talk to her."

"Well, sir, there's just not much more I can do for you. Have you tried the police?"

"Is there a supervisor I could talk to?"

"I *am* the supervisor."

Will felt old, graduated into middle age not incrementally by marriage or fatherhood or professional accomplishment but abruptly and unexpectedly by Todd, Manager.

"Is there anything else I can help you with?" Todd cheerily offered, that shiny smile shutting down any hope of information.

"No." Will started to walk away, then turned back to give Todd a little advice—he wasn't sure what, something about lightening up, being a person and not a job. Or maybe just to vent his frustration at an easy target. But then, off to the side, Will saw Geary coming around the bank of shopping carts. The old man's determination suggested the worst, and Will intuitively recoiled. He spun around and passed the wrong way through the first unoccupied checkout he saw, straight into the belly of the store.

The aisles were long and wide, shelves densely packed with everything made under the American sun and beyond, pale green floors buffed to a glossy shine. He wove up one and down the next, feeling overwhelmed by choices he normally made with ease. His fool's errand struck him hard. In looking for Emily, he was worse than lost; he didn't know what his choices were, and even if he had, he wouldn't know where to begin.

At the end of the aisle, he turned left. He had to go somewhere, he was afraid to keep still.

Maybe, if he kept moving, kept looking, she would materialize right here, right now, at the cocoa, comparing brands. She would look at him and her light, freckled face would open in a loving smile. She might wink at the fun of his having left haute cuisine to someone else so he could join her more mundane task at the grocery store. "Which one"—she would hold up two cans of powered chocolate—"do you think the kids would like best? Maxi would like this can with the bear, but David would like the good, dark chocolate. Sammie, I think, would like both." She would have been there all night, choosing cocoa for their children, suspended in the crystallized moment of that single choice. A winter drink for a summer day. She would be planning ahead. Emily would choose preparedness over sleep. How many mornings had he awakened to find her out of bed, getting something ready for someone? She would be pleased at having had a quiet breakfast before dawn.

But when he opened his eyes, she wasn't there. The deflation emptied him completely. His hands flew up to catch his face, and he stood there, alone in the massive store.

"Ovaltine," the voice said.

Will looked up. Geary.

"I've been drinking it my whole life and it hasn't changed one bit."

Will drew a breath and then another. He felt the oxygen reach his brain.

"I'm almost thirty years with the FBI, ten on the beat. When someone treats me like an irritating old loser because I'm retired, it gets me." He slapped his chest. "I wasn't filler for some title. I'm right here, on or off payroll." He kept his eyes steady on Will while he reached over and took a large can of Ovaltine off the shelf, then lowered his eyes to read the label. "Some things never change." He looked up at Will, unsmiling. "Don't be an idiot."

Will got the point. "Checkout eight's closed," he said. "The manager's useless."

"People in these jobs, they juggle their shifts all the time. Come on, we'll ask around."

Will followed Geary, the receipt trailing out of the old man's dirty pocket.

At checkout six, a generously proportioned woman with blond hair and bare, tattoo-covered arms was ringing up the last customer on her line. They waited until she finished bagging the groceries and the customer had left.

"Morning, Darlene!" Geary said.

Will just then noticed the plastic name tag pinned to the shoulder strap of Darlene's yellow tank top.

"Morning, Dick."

"Close. It's John. And this is Will, twin brother of Willy. So you practically hit it on the head, Darlene."

She suppressed a smile and looked Geary up and down. She clearly did not like what she saw.

"What can I do for you gentlemen?"

Geary took the receipt out of his pocket, then dug deeper for his wallet.

"Darlene, I'm FBI." He flipped open his worn black wallet too fast for her to notice that his ID was expired.

Her meticulously tweezed eyebrows arched.

"We're looking for someone. She shopped here yesterday, checked out at number eight."

Darlene looked over the receipt, then directly at Will.

"I saw you talking to Todd."

"He's kind of a jerk, if you ask me." Will forced a conspiratorial smile.

Darlene winked. "You sure got that one right!" She lowered her voice. "I wasn't here yesterday afternoon, but Tariq was. He's at number one. See him?"

Tariq was a slightly built teenager, clean cut with wire-rimmed glasses, apparently trying to defy his respectable appearance by wearing a silver hoop in his lower lip. Geary took the boy through a similar introductory routine that Will was beginning to understand had been used many times before and worked like grease on a lock.

"Pam was on eight yesterday afternoon." Tariq's tongue nudged the lip-ring as if trying to displace it. "She worked a double shift to midnight. But I think Susannah worked the afternoon shift with her yesterday. She's right over there at three. They're best friends. I hate them."

"Thank you, son." Geary nodded. "If you don't mind my asking, how do you brush your teeth with that thing?"

"Is that, like, part of the investigation?"

Geary smiled. "Not exactly."

"I don't feel a thing." Tariq nodded rapidly. "I don't even know it's there."

Will followed Geary to checkout three. All of six minutes had passed, and they had found someone who might have seen Emily.

Susannah was deeply tan, with peroxide hair in a short bowl cut and electric blue mascara. She let her customer wait while she studied the time clock information at the bottom of the receipt. She nodded sharply, then turned to continue ringing up items with her scanner as she spoke. "Pam came over to me just after that and we went on break. She said she was a little weirded out by a guy on her line so she shut down a couple minutes early. We're not supposed to do that, but, you know." She turned to look from Geary to Will. "Did something happen or something?"

"Maybe," Geary said. "That's what we're trying to find out."

"So anyway, Pam, she told me there was like this lady who was kind of rushing her, and she didn't like it, but then she figured maybe the lady wanted to get away from that guy right behind her. Pam said he kept touching things, like, over and over." Susannah rolled her eyes as she quickly scanned bar codes, punching in the occasional item that wouldn't read.

"Did you see the woman?" Will asked as calmly as he could, refusing his desire to shout, beg, cry.

"Nah, she was gone by then. But I saw the guy. Pam showed me."

"Can you describe him?" Geary asked. "Whatever you can remember."

"I've seen him before. He shops here like every Monday afternoon. I know because I'm usually on shift then. He's like totally *regular*. Okay so he's pretty old. I mean not as old as you—sorry—he's maybe fifty. He's got white hair and this really white skin, like he doesn't get into the sun. He's always wearing this blue cap with a twisty little rope on the front and a little visor thing."

"Some kind of sailing cap?" Geary asked.

Susannah shrugged. "And he's always wearing the same white jacket. We call him Mr. White." She rolled her eyes. "I was surprised yesterday because I actually saw him talking to someone. Usually he's just like this weird loner guy."

"Can you remember who he was talking to?" Will asked, hoping it wouldn't be Emily.

"It was a lady, older than him, but—"

"Not as old as me?" Geary smiled.

Susannah's eyes flickered in embarrassment. "That's not what I mean, really. She was just more like a grandma. But she had blond hair. She had this big gold charm bracelet. I think she was pissed at the guy."

"When was that, Susannah? While the first lady you didn't see was checking out?"

Susannah shook her head and her straight bright hair swayed at her ears. "Later, after he was finished checking out too."

"So the first lady was gone, the one we're looking for, and he was here in the store arguing with the blond-haired beauty queen?"

Susannah laughed. "Pam'll love that one! They weren't arguing together, like, she was just kind of letting him have it."

"And what did he do?" Geary asked.

"He just listened. He didn't really even look at her. Then he pushed his cart out of the store. She waited a second then left too. Now that I think of it, she didn't have a cart."

"Did he have a lot of groceries?"

"Not really. Just a whole bunch of corn on the cob. It was on sale yesterday, a dollar a dozen."

Geary nodded. "Anything else you can remember?"

Susannah was now bagging her customer's groceries. "Not really. He was like regular height, regular weight, just mainly on the older side and all white and weird."

"How can I get in touch with Pam?" Geary asked. "She might remember something else."

Susannah's eyes flashed to Geary; it took her a split second to decide to trust him with her friend's number. She jotted it on an old receipt someone had left behind and handed it over.

"I'll tell her I talked to you."

"Thanks." Geary winked.

Susannah winked back and started scanning the groceries of her next customer.

Will and Geary walked past the checkouts, through the automatic doors and into the clear morning light.

"Borrow that phone of yours?" Geary asked.

Will handed him the slender, folded phone. Geary turned it over in his hand and figured out how to flip it open. Then he handed it back.

"You dial."

Will dialed each number as Geary read them off the crumbled receipt, then gave back the phone. From the way Geary's eyes rolled up, it was clear he'd reached a machine. His message was wordy but got the point across. He left his home number for Pam to call him back.

They moved under the shade of a broad awning.

"How are we going to find Emily?" Will asked.

"We? You mean you and the Mashpee PD?"

"Do you think I should call in the state police?"

"Not just yet. They're good, but they'll file it too. A missing persons gets a blast of attention up front, then dries up fast. Unless there's money involved, or it's a kid."

Will's eyes stayed on Geary's face. "What are you thinking?"

"I have a hunch. Was I part of that we, Will?"

"I'll hire you, I'll pay you whatever you want."

"I don't need money. I just want permission to use whatever I might find in my book."

"Your book—"

"Cold cases. Unsolved crimes. If my hunch is right, one of the nuts I found sleeping in a file cabinet might have done a little grocery shopping yesterday."

"Mr. White?"

"Maybe, maybe not. When they're not caught, we don't know who they are. That's the puzzle. My job was to build a lens to focus them, create the picture, then use it to find them. Behavioral profiling. We gather what we know and we go from there. You'd be surprised. It's a science. Eight out of ten times, it works."

"What about the other two times?"

Geary shook his head. "It's not a perfect science."

"Why yesterday? Why Emily?"

"If I'm right, it had to be yesterday. I don't know if it had to be Emily."

A tremor passed through Will. Wrong place, wrong time. An overlap of timing and misfortune, as arbitrary as good luck. "What am I supposed to do, Dr. Geary?"

"Give me a little time. Don't talk to anyone before

I have a chance to figure this out. The local police might leak it to the papers, and that might spook our guy."

"But wouldn't the publicity help us?" Will thought of all the television bulletins, faces flashing on the screen, a disembodied broadcaster's voice earnestly requesting information on the disappearance of a woman or man or child. And the strangely painful details: date of birth, weight, hair color, missing from what place on what day at what time.

"There's a right time and a wrong time to bring in the media," Geary said. "I'd like to discuss this with a criminologist I know, get his take on it. He's helped me crack a lot of nuts in the past."

"What if waiting makes it too late?"

"It's always a risk. But think about it, Will. You've got more to gain now than lose."

"How long?"

"I'll call you at three o'clock, three thirty at the latest. Give me until three thirty today before you talk to anyone."

They exchanged phone numbers and addresses, and walked together into the full sun.

"Go home and see your kids. Take a shower, eat something. I'll be in touch with you."

Will got into his rented SUV with its smell of sanitized smoke. He decided he would trust Geary. He had to do something; he just hoped it wouldn't be the worst mistake of his life.

Chapter 5

"Daisy, come off that dock!"

Marian had thought that at five years old her daughter would have the sense to keep away from danger. She was wrong. From birth, Daisy had shown little fear and with age became only more intrepid.

"Ted, go see what that girl picked up."

Ted jogged onto the short dock and crouched down next to Daisy.

"Hey, Daddy."

Marion couldn't help but smile. Daisy looked just like her father. Tall, skinny, their brown skin glistening with sunblock. Ted's red baseball cap, with the feather logo of his publishing company dead center on the forehead, cast a shadow over his face and onto Daisy's open hand.

"What do you have there, sweetie?"

"A bracelet. Look. Isn't it pretty?"

Ted turned to look at Marian. "It's a charm bracelet."

"Let me see it. And please, Daisy, come away from the edge."

Daisy and Ted walked onto the grassy bank where Marian had laid down a blanket so they could sit while they waited for her cousin Henry to arrive with his boat. He owned a chain of drugstores but couldn't bring himself to use a public dock; that cost money. He could have motored straight from Martha's Vineyard to Waquoit Bay but instead took the long way around to Popponesset Beach. Every summer for nine years now they'd made this wait at the unpaved end of Simons Narrow Road, with its tiny dock at an obscure little inlet for people who liked to think of themselves as insiders.

"Too rich to pay" is what Marian called Henry. If Daisy hadn't liked to ride in Henry's boat so much they would have just taken the ferry over.

But Henry was fun, Marian had to admit. Once they got to the other side, he'd get them to their houses in Oak Bluffs in an old golf cart with tattered white fringe along the top. It was tacky but Daisy had the time of her life. Once they installed themselves in the orange gingerbread house Grandma Peet had left Marian's mother, Henry would disappear into his pink gingerbread house, which he'd inherited from his mother. It was said that Grandma and Grandpa Peet had once owned half the houses around Wesleyan Grove and that it was they who had painted them each a different color. All Marian knew for sure was that the colors had become a tradition, even a tourist attraction, and no house had ever been repainted a different color since.

She had spent every summer of her childhood in that orange house, surrounded by an African-American intelligentsia unacknowledged by the broader world. It was a house where you talked and read books. To this day, there was no TV, and the radio had broken two summers ago. It was just a three-day trip this time, and Marian was so tired from the end-of-summer festival she'd just finished running as executive director of a nonprofit arts exchange in Boston that she planned to seal herself up and do nothing but rest. She had a copy of Helen Dewitt's *The Last Samurai* in her suitcase and she meant to read the whole thing. Ted and Daisy liked to busy themselves fishing at the pond.

Daisy's knees were already scratched, in contrast to the frilly pink sundress she'd insisted on wearing. If a dress didn't have a spin, she wouldn't wear it. This one had a spin *and* a ruffle and was as dainty as could be.

She held out her small palm to show Marian the bracelet. It was silver, a nice grade by the look of it. It must have belonged to a mother with its three babies; an interesting woman, Marian would guess, by the cello and the sword.

"Mommy, put it on me."

Daisy held out her thin wrist and handed her mother the bracelet.

"I don't know, honey. Maybe we should leave it in case the lady who lost it comes back to look."

"No, it's mine. I found it!"

"Honey, it doesn't work that way."

"Please, Mommy, can I just wear it a while?"

The putt of a motor got louder, and Ted started waving.

"It's Henry! Come on, girls, get ready. He's here!"

"Oh," Marian said, "why don't you wear it for now? We'll figure it out when we get off the Vineyard. Maybe there's a lost and found somewhere here on the Cape."

Ted carried their bags to Henry's boat, *Everlasting Love*. The bottom half had been newly painted a high-lacquer forest green, with the top half a blinding white. And there was Henry in his sun hat, denim cutoffs and rubber flip-flops. He wore his ear-to-ear smile and threw open his arms for Daisy.

Marian had just gotten the bracelet clasped on when Daisy flew toward the boat. She leapt over the two-foot gap between the dock and the slim starboard deck of *Everlasting Foolery*. Her scuffed white sandal landed squarely an inch from missing altogether and she catapulted herself into Uncle Henry's arms.

The silver charm bracelet promptly fell off her wrist and clattered down onto the deck.

"My bracelet!" Daisy shouted.

"Will you look at that." Henry picked it up. "I can fix that for you lickety-split, back at the house." He put the bracelet in the front pocket of his shorts.

Marian took Ted's hand and carefully stepped on board.

"It isn't hers," she told her cousin. "If you fix it, do it right. As soon as we get back to the Cape we're going to find its owner."

"That's right," Daisy said. "And that lady you'll be finding she'll be *me*."

Chapter 6

Emily felt the sway and swish of water. She felt herself buoyed by planks of damp wood. And the smell. Mildew. Salt air.

Her right side was numb. Her arms hurt, pulled behind her, bound at the wrists with what felt like heavy rope. Her legs were cinched at the ankles. Her skin stung from chafing. Had she fought?

She remembered putting the groceries into the car. She remembered looking up at the sky. Dizzy. Something pressed against her face, a burning smell in her nostrils.

Her eyes were blindfolded and she couldn't see. Not a speck of light. Her mouth was sealed by a thick band of tape that pulled at her skin.

Her underpants were wet. There was a stinging rash between her legs.

Her mind jumped backward and landed nowhere.

That sick stranger from the store had noticed her. He did this. She wanted to reach out of her bindings and kill him first. She was a black belt—she could do it. Or was she out of practice? It had been years.

Where was the bastard? Had he dumped her here for later?

What about the kids?

What time was it?

Maxi had an ear infection; she needed her medicine. *Let me out, I have to go.*

How many times had she promised Sam bad guys weren't real? David knew better but Sammie was still young enough.

She shouldn't have lied to her children.

She shouldn't have gone out without a bra.

She rolled her body to see if she could move, jostle off the bindings, find out if there was any give. He had bound her tightly but she managed to propel herself onto her back. Stuck. Hands crushed. She felt the warmth of blood flowing into her right side and a sharp tingling. She couldn't move. She lay on her back, feeling her arms and hands give way to numbness, as if some kind of electric parasite was shifting through her body. She tried to rock to her other side but it was useless.

A creak across the cabin.

Another creak. A footstep. Two.

Another step.

She could see him in her mind—the corn man, white jacket, white face, flickering eyes—and her stomach rose. Vomit lurched up her throat but couldn't get past the tape. She swallowed it down. Some of it backed up her nose and she felt the seizure of suffocation. She forced herself to swallow hard, keep swallowing. She visualized her trachea and stomach and willed them calm so she could swallow the rest. Then she blew her nose hard and the vomit in her sinuses spit out onto her face. The smell was horrible; she could hardly breathe.

He stopped walking.

Her muscles quickened against the bindings. She felt her skin tear as her wrists and ankles swiveled to find a weakness somewhere. He must have been a fisherman, good with knots.

She was his catch.

This wasn't happening.

He was walking again, slowly, walking toward her. He stopped inches away. Stood there. Was he watching her? Did he enjoy this?

She threw her stomach muscles into a spasm and propelled her body forward. She was sitting. If she could sit then she could find a way to stand. And if she could find a way to stand, she could hop. And if she could hop, she could use her head to poke around for a way out.

Except he was right there. Standing next to her. She could hear him breathing.

She couldn't allow herself to stay trapped here when her children needed her. Especially Maxi; just a baby; she needed her medicine.

She recalled the feeling from childhood dreams in which she could fly, summoned the feeling into her muscles and projected herself onto her knees.

His hand clamped onto her arm and squeezed so hard she felt he would break skin. He pushed her back to the floor like a rag doll.

Then she felt it: a sharp prick in her arm, a hot flow into her muscles.

If only, if only . . .

Her body floated away like a piece of wood, no longer a part of her. And in what felt like staunch objection, her mind turned hyperaware. She sensed everything without gravity; she was an unearthed mass.

The swoosh of movement, water pressing against the surge of the boat. She was moving. Going somewhere. Being taken.

Where was he taking her?

Chapter 7

The house was quiet, the sun barely up. All the children were still asleep. Through the windows Sarah could see splinters of light on the tranquil surface of the lake. In their later years, she and Jonah were often up at this hour, and would carry their tea to the beach. They would sit on matching green recliners, a small, rotted tree-stump table between them holding their mugs, and face the water. Together they would watch the sun begin its arc across the sky, pushing orange-rose light into the fading blue darkness, easing open the morning. They finished their tea, recalled their lives, and discussed their day. It had been Sarah's favorite way to start the morning.

She sat at her desk in the loft above the kitchen and looked at the picture of Emily she had faxed to the police station at Will's request. It had been taken when she was pregnant with Maxi and Emily's face was rounder than usual, but Sarah felt it captured her. Her face was angled away, looking at the boys pressed together on the couch as David read aloud to Sam. Her expression showed delight in their closeness, in David's lovingness toward Sam, then five, and in Sam's awe at the capabilities of his big brother. Sarah had been struck by the moment, and as her camera had by chance been on the counter next to where she stood, she had quickly turned it on and aimed it at her daughter. Emily's eyes had pivoted toward the camera just as Sarah snapped the shot. Her hazel, almond eyes. The eyes Sarah had gazed into when her newborn daughter was first brought to her, the eyes that over years had questioned and adored and accused. They were the eyes of pure love, purer even than her love for Jonah. Every mother knew, when she looked into the eyes of her first child, that until that moment she had not experienced the kind of true love that claimed you forever.

Sarah ran a fingertip over the slick photograph. Where was her baby now? What was she going through? Was she afraid? Was she in pain?

If only Emily hadn't gone shopping. They hadn't really needed anything.

Sarah couldn't wait through the morning doing nothing; she had to do something to help find Emily. There was a copy shop in the new set of stores next to Ricky's Market. She could call her neighbor Barbara as early as eight o'clock to ask if she could watch the boys. Maxi wouldn't be too much of a bother while Sarah made her copies.

She took a piece of plain white paper out of the fax machine and taped Emily's photo in the very center. In bold black marker across the top, she wrote MISS-ING. In the space below the photo she elaborated: Emily Parker, missing since the afternoon of Monday 9/3/01. *Last seen at Stop & Shop by the Mashpee Rotary. 39 yrs., 5' 6", 135 lbs., sandy blond hair, hazel eyes, freckled complexion.* Sarah wished she knew what Emily had been wearing, but she could at least describe her bracelet, which she only took off to shower and sleep. *Wearing silver charm bracelet with swimmer, cello, sword, coin, heart, three babies.*

She put the pen down and looked at her sign. When Jonah had died, after a short bout with cancer at the age of seventy-seven, his sudden absence had seemed impossible, but not wholly unexpected. This void, Emily's, was unreal. It couldn't be happening to her daughter, or to her, or to her grandchildren. Sarah had worked so hard all night to stave off tears for fear of waking the children and frightening herself even more than she already was. But now she couldn't stop them and they came in a flood. Her stomach ached she cried so hard, nearly choking on her breath as she struggled to hold it. One hollow wail escaped her and seemed to fill the entire house.

Moments later, she heard movement downstairs. Voices. The boys talking. The whining cry of Maxi as she roused from sleep.

Sarah wiped her face on the hem of her shirt, the same one she'd worn all day yesterday. She didn't want the children to see she hadn't gone to bed and so rushed down the stairs to her bedroom. She pulled back her covers, took off her clothes and threw on her summer robe. Cold water on her face helped dissolve anguish into mere exhaustion. As she toweled dry her face, the bathroom door burst open.

Sammie threw himself into her arms. "I'm hungry!"

"Morning, sweetie." She kissed the top of his sleep-rumpled hair. "Have you used the bathroom?"

He pulled down his pajama bottoms and peed in Sarah's toilet.

David then appeared in her doorway, holding one of those glittering Pokemon cards Sam so dearly prized.

"That's *mine*." Sam lunged at David's hand.

"I know it's yours, dufus. I found it on the floor. You should take care of your stuff."

"Give it to me!"

"Try asking *nicely*."

Sam wrestled David to the floor. Sarah was on her way over to pry apart their thrashing bodies when Maxi's crying escalated.

Grandmothers were not built to handle this much chaos.

"Stop that fighting."

She had raised one girl, an only child. Boys, and brothers, were out of her league.

"I said—"

Sam was strong but David was bigger and more agile; he easily pinned his little brother down. Sammie thrashed valiantly, but David was unmovable. *Unbendable.* How many times had they demonstrated their "unbendable arms" to a grandmother who was capable of pride at even their hiccups?

They would hold their arms straight, concentrate, and say, "Go on, Grandma. Try and bend it."

She never tried in earnest, certain she could easily buckle their elbows. "My goodness!" she would exclaim.

"No, really try!" David insisted.

Once, she really did try, and in fact could not budge that arm an iota.

They had learned this skill in the children's aikido classes at the dojo where Emily had met Will. They prided themselves on their plan to be a family of black belts. Will and Emily both had theirs, though since motherhood she'd fallen out of practice. He kept his skills up by teaching in the children's program on Saturday mornings, which also allowed him hands-on mentoring of his own sons.

"I thought aikido taught you to defend, not fight?" Sarah said. It was her last stand, and it worked.

David pulled away first and threw up his arms. Sam lay pinned beneath him, panting, his bright eyes

FIVE DAYS IN SUMMER

scheming. His hands flew up into David's armpits and David collapsed in laughter. The shiny card lay next to them, ignored.

Sarah hurried downstairs to the kids' room. Maxi was standing in her crib, gripping the railing, face soaked by tears. Sarah kicked the foot lever that lowered the side and lifted her baby's baby into her arms. Maxi was hot. Sarah stripped off her pajamas and opened a window. She decided to check the temperature and consider turning on the central air conditioning.

Maxi's eyes darted to the door.

"Mama Bae?" Mommy Baby. Maxi's special phrase for two essential halves of one existence.

Sarah felt a rush of relief and turned around to look, but the bedroom doorway was empty. No Mama Bae. No Emily.

"You'll see Mommy soon, sweetie. Let's go upstairs and see what we've got for your breakfast."

The tears started again in force, but at the same time the small body relaxed onto Sarah's shoulder. She hugged her grandbaby against her chest and stroked the wispy blond hair at her neck as she walked heavily up the stairs.

The boys were setting the table with bowls and spoons for cereal. Sam took out all the boxes and lined them up on the counter while David brought the carton of milk to the table. Sarah stopped herself from reminding them that they didn't need to display all the choices at once and shouldn't leave the milk out in this heat.

"Bravo," she said. "What excellent helpers you two are."

The boys settled in at their places while Sarah prepared a bottle for Maxi.

Sam asked first. "Where's Mommy?"

"She didn't go to the movies, did she?" David asked.

Sarah wished she hadn't lied to them, but what could she say? *Mommy's disappeared. You may never see her again.*

"She went out already. She had an errand in Hyannis."

Sammie shrugged, and David just looked at her, considering her answer. Sarah was relieved when he didn't argue, though she hadn't a clue what she'd say when they found out Emily had never come home. She hoped Will got back soon; it was his place to explain it to them.

The boys finished their cereal and bolted from the table. Maxi was fussy, eating only half her rice cereal, occasionally glancing around and chirping, "Mama Bae."

Sarah phoned Barbara, who agreed to come by in twenty minutes. She told the boys to get their clothes on and busied herself getting dressed and preparing another bottle to bring in the car for Maxi. Still in his pajamas, Sam ran through the kitchen, pinched his sister on the shoulder and ran away laughing. Maxi cried strenuously. Sarah was still calming her down when the doorbell rang and Barbara issued her familiar "Yoo-hoo!" to signal her arrival.

Sarah made fifty color copies of her sign and bought a roll of tape. She had been wrong about Maxi being no bother; she cried and thrashed on Sarah's hip the whole time the copy machine whirred. Maxi tugged at her ear and Sarah remembered that she had failed to give Maxi her antibiotics. It was supposed to be twice a day and she hadn't given it even once. She promised herself to do better, remember more, notice everything. She would have to buck up and take good care of these children. She rocked Maxi on her hip and sang "Twinkle Twinkle Little Star" as Emily's face spewed out of the copier, over and over: MISSING MISSING MISSING.

She posted her first sign right there at the copy shop, one at Ricky's Market, a couple at the next grouping of stores. Two at Stop & Shop, one at each of the stores in the complex, and one at the drive-through bank facing the parking lot. It was already crowded with morning shoppers.

As it turned out, fifty copies didn't go very far. When she was through canvassing the Commons, she had only a few left. She drove up Route 28 to the Deer Crossing shopping center and posted the remaining signs. It was only ten thirty by the time she was done.

Maxi fell asleep just as Sarah pulled into the garage at home. The baby was exhausted and Sarah decided to let her have her nap in the car. Will's rental car was parked outside, and the talking, when she entered the house, would only wake Maxi if she was brought in.

Sarah went in through the mudroom, leaving the outside door open to hear Maxi if she woke. She didn't want to call out so close to the garage, so she crept in quietly. There was no sign of anyone. She checked the downstairs bedrooms, even the loft. No one. Maybe Barbara had taken the boys to her house. A quick call over was answered by Barbara, who said, "Will got back. Didn't know he was up Cape. He looked bad, Sarah."

"Do you know where they are?"

"Not a clue. He asked me where *you* were. What's going on?"

"I'll explain later. Don't take it personally, dear. We're having a hard day."

"And it's only just morning. Well . . ."

Sarah thanked Barbara and was finally able to usher her off the phone.

The beach. Maybe he'd taken them for a swim.

She flung open the porch door and hurried down the steps to the back gardens, along the grassy road that led to the grove of trees, and finally to the clearing opposite their small, private beach.

She had been right and she had been wrong. They were all three wearing their bathing suits—the morning had grown hot—but they weren't swimming.

Will stood in front of the boys, heels to shore. The boys stood side by side in front of him, facing the water. They were practicing their aikido. Will moved with a powerful grace, concentrated so fully on the moment that he didn't see Sarah at first. The boys' movements mirrored his. The slowly pivoting bodies, the sudden expulsion of an arm, its gentle drifting down. Then the same movement in the other direction, eyes focused ahead, responding to nothing, as if seeing inwardly. Their control was breathtaking. They were like swallows moving on an invisible pulse of air. It was one of the most beautiful things Sarah had ever seen, a moment she knew would stay with her. All three of them, even Sam, appeared as light as feathers yet bursting with strength.

When the movement ended, Will's eyes flicked up to see Sarah. He nodded, then continued.

"Balance," he told his sons. "Keep your weight *underside*."

The boys stood facing each other, set their legs apart so their feet dug into the sand, and pressed their hands against each other's as they leaned reciprocally into the space between them. Sammie appeared to be trying to push David over, as he resisted, a little annoyed.

"You're going for balance, not trying to overpower each other," Will said.

Sam eased up and met David's equilibrium.

Now Will's eyes settled fully on Sarah. She waved.

"Where's Maxi?" he asked.

"I left her sleeping in the car."

Sarah immediately realized her mistake. Emily was always correcting her mother's old-time habits, like leaving babies alone in untended yards or letting them stay outside a store while you went in. It was true that Emily had never left Maxi alone to nap in the crib while they were at the beach; certainly the car was a worse transgression. Sarah thought of her acres as home and had always felt safe within their perimeters. But she should know better than that, especially now.

Will shot by her, running quickly up toward the house.

Left alone on the beach, mentorless, the peaceful mood of the boys' practice instantly transformed to fight. Faces intent, they pressed harder against each other's hands. David moved so quickly, Sarah couldn't see exactly what he did, but Sam's body sharply twisted and he landed facedown in the sand with an arm bent behind his back. David leaned over him, his forehead bristling with drops of sweat, holding his sixty-five-pound brother down with one hand.

"David!" Sarah called.

He released Sam, who scrambled up and wiped the sand off his face.

"I'm telling Dad!"

Sam took off into the grove of trees, laughing. David ran after him, his face gleeful, shouting, "Go ahead, tell him. I'll really give it to you!"

How was it Emily had described this most peaceful of martial arts? "The art of love." "The way of harmony." "Learning to care for your attacker."

Sarah hurried up to the house, not worried about the boys' behavior so much as Maxi. She hoped Will had found her blissfully asleep, no worse for Sarah's lack of judgment. But if not, if he had found her weeping in her seat, begging for release, Sarah would take full responsibility for her error. No explanations and no excuses. Whatever Will wanted to say to her, she would simply listen and then apologize profusely.

She entered the kitchen and found Will standing there with his baby in his arms. He looked over at Sarah and smiled. So she had her reprieve. Maxi was thrilled to see her father. Sarah could imagine what Will was feeling: the soft plush body against his skin, the tight little arms around his neck, the exuberant smile. This man needed his family as much as they needed him. It had taken years for Sarah to understand that Will was a rare breed of father, as Jonah had been. She had mistakenly judged Will early on; and now, around this latest bend, she needed him more than she ever could have predicted.

Little was said as Sarah put together an early lunch of turkey sandwiches and cantaloupe. She was desperate to speak with Will, but it would have to wait, suspended, as the children's needs were met.

Maxi fussed again as Will tried to feed her. She kept turning her head away and pulling on her ear.

"How's she doing with that ear infection?" Will asked Sarah.

"I'm not sure. She's still fighting it off, I think."

"She's getting her medicine?"

"Of course."

Sarah couldn't bring herself to admit that she had completely forgotten the medicine. She would sneak it to the baby after lunch, when Will stepped away. It would be less than a lie, just a harmless omission. They were both so ragged from lack of sleep.

When Will took the boys into the living room to talk with them, presumably about Emily's disappearance, Sarah seized the chance to get Maxi her antibiotics. The calibrated medicine dropper was still in the sink from yesterday morning. Sarah was washing it out with hot soapy water when the phone rang. She turned off the faucet and answered it.

"I'm calling about the 'missing' sign," a man's voice said.

"Have you seen her?" Sarah felt a coil of hope.

"No."

Will appeared beside the phone, his expression keen. Sarah shook her head, and he deflated.

"Who is it?" Will whispered.

Sarah shrugged.

"Is it the police?"

She shrugged again.

He reached out for the phone. "May I?"

"Will, wait, I need to tell you something—"

But he took the phone out of her hand and pressed it to his ear. "This is Will Parker."

Sarah watched his face lose color, then blaze red.

"Please don't print anything. Give us a day to try and find her before he gets scared. He could run and take her with him." He listened briefly before his voice rose. "I don't know *who he*. I don't know anything. That's why you can't do this. Do you understand me? Do not do this! *Please*." He slammed down the phone. "That was Eric Smith from the *Cape Cod Times*." Sarah had never seen Will so angry; he had never dared reproach her in the past. "He saw a sign. What sign, Sarah?"

She explained. Maxi was still strapped in her high chair and her crying grew frantic as Will's voice rose. The boys came into the kitchen, drawn by the noise, and stood there watching.

"I promised I wouldn't tell the press! Sarah—why?"

"Will, I'm sorry, I didn't know—"

"You should have waited till I got back. Why didn't you wait?"

She tried to be compliant, to absorb the moment, but finally she just couldn't. She had done what she had needed to. She had believed in it. She would never have done anything to hurt their prospects of finding Emily.

"She is my daughter, Will. *My daughter*."

He turned around and looked at his boys.

"Dad," David said in a low, steady tone.

"Go outside, both of you. Now."

Sam ran out, but David just stood there and stared at his father.

"Now."

David slowly turned and walked away. The front screen door squealed open then banged shut.

Sarah stood and waited as Will, who had always seemed buoyed by good humor, searched his mind for something to say. She had never felt so exposed in front of him; but it wasn't just him, it was everything.

He began to shake his head, and when he closed his eyes, lines deepened across his face. Sarah was just deciding to walk the three steps over to comfort him—he was her son-in-law, nearly her own child—when the front door screeched open.

"Dad!" It was David, back in the house. "The police are outside."

Chapter 8

Detective Amy Cardoza pulled up to the Parker home just before one o'clock. It had been a long morning. Police Chief Kaminer had heard about the new missing persons case and ordered Snow to hang around for roll call before going home to sleep off the night shift. That worried Amy more than a little. She had just ranked as detective after three years on patrol and she needed to be partnered in her new department. Snow's partner had just retired. Amy had hoped Kaminer would shuffle the deck, break up another team that everyone knew was stale, but now it didn't look that way. Kaminer had ordered Snow back to the station house by three and the obvious assumption was that he was being put back on days. Amy could see it coming, and it wasn't pretty.

She and Snow had worse than no connection; both their families had long, conflicting histories on the Cape. His family came in on the *Mayflower,* landed in Plymouth and settled on the Cape. Hers followed the same route, except they arrived a hundred years later on whaling ships from Portugal, long enough after the English to seem like intruders. Her father was the first of his family to leave the Cape in nearly two centuries, when he married an Irish summer stock actress and moved with her up to Boston to join her massive family. Amy and her two younger sisters all had their mother's creamy skin and their father's pitch-black hair and brown eyes. Their father had jokingly called them his "Portugish Flowers." He told them they were true Americans and expected them to study law, medicine, finance, whatever it took to continue the long process of assimilation. He taught them to think of Cape Cod as nothing more than a hometown he'd left behind; it was never to be their destination.

Amy stunned her family by enrolling in the police academy, then accepting an assignment on the Cape. She learned quickly why her father had left: here, the Portuguese had a long history of interracial marriage with blacks and had come to share their perceived status as second-class citizens, especially in the eyes of the lily-white locals like the Snows. To the bluebloods, they were like the summer people—perpetual outsiders whose presence was tolerated only because it kept the economy afloat.

She knew that Snow had detested her name before he even met her. He had ignored her all her years on patrol. And now she had had the audacity to join his rank.

All the cops joked that Kaminer was bored and liked a good chicken fight. Well, if he partnered her with Snow, Amy was going to make sure that didn't happen. She was going to transcend the obstacles and become the best detective they had ever seen.

Two boys were standing in front of the Parker house, throwing rocks down the road and marking their landing point with chalk. The younger one was putting a lot more energy into the game than the older one, who noticed the squad car first and bolted into the house. Amy was still waiting to be assigned an unmarked car, and she had a hunch Kaminer planned for her to share Snow's.

She pulled up in front of a lush summer garden bordered by hand-laid stones, got out of the car and smiled at the young boy.

"I thought you were going to be a policeman."

"I am, sort of. I'm a detective."

"Where's your uniform?"

Her linen pants and tailored blue T-shirt were clearly a disappointment to him.

"Detectives wear regular clothes."

"Do you catch bad guys like the police?"

Amy nodded. "I try to."

"My mommy got lost, I think." He walked up to the squad car and peered inside. She couldn't tell if he was looking for his mother or admiring all the gear and gizmos in the front of the cruiser.

"Ever ride in one?" she asked him.

He shook his head.

"Well, maybe another day you could get a ride."

"How about now?"

"I'm a little busy right now." Amy smiled. "Anyway, you'd need permission from one of your parents. You know that, right?"

He nodded.

From inside the house, Amy heard voices getting louder, nearly shouting. "Hey, is your daddy home, or your grandma?"

Will Parker just then pushed open the screen door at the front of the house. "Detective! I see you've met Sam."

Amy smiled at Sam. "Yes, I have. Everything okay in there?"

"Sam," Will said, "go downstairs with David. The grown-ups need to talk."

Sam ran into the house.

"Nice gardens."

"My mother-in-law, Sarah, has a green thumb."

"I'd say so."

"Any news, Detective?"

"No. But the phone's been ringing. It seems some-one put up a sign?"

Will nodded. "Sarah. We were just discussing it."

"Discussing," Amy said.

"This is new to us. We don't know what we're sup-posed to do."

"There's nothing wrong with a sign."

Sarah appeared at the screen door, Maxi on her hip. "So it wasn't a mistake?" She pushed open the door and joined them on the slate path. Amy noticed the dark rings under Sarah's eyes, her fragile skin.

"Anything that can help us do our job is welcome. We could have given you a few tips about what to put on it, but the main thing is to work according to proce-dure or the system can fail."

"We just want to find Emily." Sarah tucked a wisp of the baby's hair behind her small ear.

Amy suppressed an urge to reach out and stroke the little girl's cheek. "So do we."

"I went to the grocery store this morning," Will said. "The car was there, and I asked around—"

"I know. I just came from there."

"It *rained* last night." It sounded more like an accu-sation than a statement, as if she had personally or-dered the weather conditions to blight the survival prospects of his wife. But Amy knew better than to take this family's agitation personally.

"Mr. Parker, I have a forensics team over there right now. The car's going into impound. We're going to look over every square inch of it with a microscope."

"When?"

"Today. It's happening now."

"Why did it take so long?"

The truth was, if Amy had been on night shift, she would have gone then. But Snow saw things differently; if a wife disappeared, he figured she had taken off, much as his own wife had, and would turn up if she wanted to, as his wife had opted not to.

"Procedure," she answered. "There's a twenty-four-hour protocol in adult—"

"Did anyone talk to the people working in the store? Did you talk to them?"

"Yes, I did. And I know you and John Geary got there first."

"Did you find out about Mr. White?"

Amy kept her voice calm. "Mr. Parker, it would be better if you let us handle this. We found out about this Mr. White character and we're going to check him out. We know your wife didn't run any other errands. None of the other local shops saw her yesterday. We'll get a preliminary report from forensics later this afternoon. Believe me, we're on the case. Let us do our work."

"What should I do?" It was part plea and part comment.

"You should both try to get some rest," Amy said. "No one can think straight when they're sleep deprived. It'll help put things into perspective."

Will shook his head. "I'm pretty much out of perspective right now."

"Maybe she's right, Will," Sarah said. "We can take turns watching the children."

"This one alone must be a handful." Amy smiled at the baby. "How much do the older kids know?"

"I'm not sure," Will said. "Obviously Emily's not here."

"Well, then they know everything. You might not

believe this, but I've seen all kinds of outcomes to these cases. Sometimes they do just turn up, with all sorts of explanations." It was an exaggeration, but she never told families the truth at first: that missing persons cases rarely concluded happily.

"John Geary's helping me." Will said it fast, like a confession. "I asked him to."

"I'm not convinced that's the best move," Amy said. "Geary has a . . . history."

"He said he was on top at the FBI, behavioral science. He seems to have experience."

"Oh, he's got experience all right. And he doesn't lie about his credentials. He was right there at the top. But it's complicated—"

"If he can help find her—"

"Just be careful, Mr. Parker. John Geary doesn't do everything by the book."

One of the other detectives had done a little digging when Geary first appeared at the station house, touting his credentials like peacock feathers. Amy had been as interested as everyone else to learn that Geary had faced a pretty serious sexual harassment charge halfway into his long career at Quantico. In the end, the case was dropped, largely on the basis of a psychological review that said Geary wasn't remotely capable of breaking the law. It seemed to Amy that personal transgression laws were seen differently by different generations of men and women, which was why the harassment laws had been passed in the first place, to stop jerks from playing with women who were just trying to do their jobs.

"I'd like to look around, if you don't mind."

"Of course," Sarah said. "Come in."

Amy followed them inside. It was a lovely house, strewn with toys and filled with antiques, Oriental rugs and the spattering of nautical lore that was inevitable in nearly all Cape homes. The walls were crowded with original paintings, mostly figurative, a few abstract.

"Someone collect art?" Amy asked.

"I'm a painter," Sarah answered. "Used to be. I haven't painted since my husband died."

"I'm sorry."

"It was just last winter." Sarah bent down to pick up a plastic sword that was lying across their path.

Amy looked around; the rest of the place was consistent with her first impression. It was a family, not atypical, just on the other side of chaos. Nothing in particular caught her interest until she got to the kitchen, where she immediately noticed the floor. It was wood, like the rest of the flooring in the house, but the color was uneven. A rectangle in the center, covering nearly the entire surface, was much lighter than the edges, which were darker and scuffed. She made a note of it, with a question mark she was able to cross off moments later when she passed through a laundry room and stepped into the garage.

On one side of the two-car garage was a gold Ford Taurus station wagon, and on the other side were all sorts of gardening tools and equipment. But what interested Amy most was the rolled-up rug standing in the corner.

"Was that rug in the kitchen?" Amy asked.

"It's just an old thing," Sarah said. "I was planning to take it to the dump."

"Can we unroll it?"

"Emily's gone," Will said, "and you want to spend time looking at Sarah's rug?"

"I'd like to, yes."

Taking the baby from Sarah's arms, Will went into

the house through the laundry room. He let the screen door bounce noisily shut behind him. Sarah stood in the garage, staring at the rug.

"I knocked the rest of our pizza onto the floor last night when I was getting Maxi some juice." Sarah squeezed shut her eyes. "I've always hated that rug but my husband had to have it—in the kitchen, no less. I had the boys roll it up with me. Honestly, Detective, I was happy for the distraction. Waiting for Emily was more than I could handle."

"Mrs. Goodman—"

"She isn't here," Sarah nearly cried. "That's the problem. She's *gone*."

This was the first time Amy had confronted a family in anguish without the armor of her uniform, and she felt naked. But she knew her job. She reminded herself that fear was disorienting. They didn't have the answers about Emily Parker's whereabouts, but Amy had been trained in the questions. "It's a matter of procedure," she said, "to search the home."

When Amy got back to the station house, Suellen handed her a stack of phone messages.

"That's the most calls I've gotten since I was promoted."

Suellen offered her crooked smile. "Honey, it hasn't been that long."

There were twelve messages in all, nine of them in response to Sarah Goodman's sign. Amy detoured to the kitchen to pour herself a cup of coffee, then sat down at her old desk in the report-writing room in the patrol division; she was still waiting for her desk assignment in the detectives division. She started dialing.

Right off the bat, most of the messages didn't pan

out. The information was off-key or just plain flat. But two of the conversations interested her.

One was a guy who must have had kids, because Amy heard them in the background. He sounded like someone who had plenty better to do than spend his time pulling the chain of his local police department. He told her he'd been returning movies at the video store the day before, and when he drove around to park at the grocery store to run in for a quick shop, he'd noticed something that caught his attention. He saw a man with white hair and pale skin driving away in an old silver Buick Skylark. He said that a lady was with him, blond hair, but that was all he could see, except that she didn't look too happy. When he saw the Missing sign he'd decided to call. Luckily the caller remembered a partial license plate number. Amy wrote it down and read it back to him to confirm.

The other call was from a man who refused to give his name. Amy didn't like that, but she listened as he described an older white-haired man with a younger blond-haired companion driving out of the parking lot at just the time Emily Parker went missing. But this Mr. White was driving a vintage Ford with dealer plates; it was the color of "salmon coral reef." *Funny description,* Amy thought, but she got the point.

There were two Mr. Whites.

Chapter 9

The neon sign in the window of Lizzy's Boxcar Diner flashed EAT HEAVY. Geary pulled his car into the parking lot and looked around for Bell's blue Nissan: nowhere in sight. Armed with a newspaper from one of the vending machines out front, Geary went inside. He took a booth by a window, ordered a tuna melt on rye, pushed aside the skinny blue glass vase with its one red carnation, and unfolded his newspaper to start the wait. In the decades they'd known each other, not once had Bell gotten anywhere on time. Geary had seen the man walk in late to meetings, trials, classes, even FBI conferences when they had to catch some psycho whose personal time clock said he had to strike again in maybe two minutes.

Geary read the front page of the *Cape Cod Times*. Some pilot whales had beached themselves off Wellfleet. A nine-year-old boy had been hit by a car while riding his bicycle in Yarmouth and was in critical condition in a Boston hospital. The schools were getting ready for the new year. And a big photo front and center told just how the locals felt about the Labor Day exodus of the summer folk: departing vacationers jammed in traffic along Route 6 were treated to hand-scrawled banners telling them to *Get Lost; Good Rid-*

dance; I'll Take Your Money, You Run; Come Again But Don't Stay Too Long. Geary didn't like it; he was still a newcomer and he sided with the people who had saved all year to afford the ridiculous summer prices on the Cape. The article under the picture was by one Eric Smith, who made no bones about how happy everyone was to see the locusts leave behind their "big coin."

Big coin. Geary felt his ire surface. He had thought the price he'd paid for his house was a little steep, but he hadn't figured the locals were laughing behind his back.

"Ah, the annual lovefest." It was Bell's deep voice, booming into Geary's airspace. "They love to see the summer people go home."

Geary looked up. "Why do I feel like summer people? I live here."

"You're a *washashore,* John. A step up."

"Doesn't make me feel too welcome."

"You pick and choose your friends here," Bell said, "like anywhere else."

Bell folded himself into the other side of the booth. He was over six feet tall with long thin legs, a bloated middle and the ruddy complexion of someone who had refused sunblock his entire life and now paid by wearing a map on his face. His closely cropped salty hair ringed a bald head hit hard by the sun. His tight goatee still had more pepper than salt. One eyebrow grew white and wild over a deep brown eye; the other eye was blind, hidden under an eye patch. Purple, to match his shirt. Geary shook his head and chuckled at the sight of his old friend. He could never get over the man's audacity in having his own eye patches made so he could coordinate them with his clothes.

Geary's tuna melt arrived. He folded the newspaper twice and tucked it behind the napkin holder. Bell ordered his grilled chicken on a Caesar salad without consulting the menu.

Geary spoke through a mouthful of tuna. "I thought college starts at the end of August these days."

"We start after Labor Day." Bell's voice was measured but loud, and as usual, heads spun to see who had made all the racket.

"That would make it . . . today?"

"Precisely."

"For once I'm glad you're the irresponsible asshole you are, Roger."

"My first class is Monday. The school can handle registration without me. I'll be there by the end of the week. I'm tenured, my friend, a privilege not available in government service."

"So we work our butts off while you do whatever the hell you want and rake in the pay."

"And benefits."

"Not to mention summers off."

"Great minds need room to wander." Bell leaned back against the sparkly turquoise banquette. "If memory serves, you did well by my personal expertise."

What a master of the universe. Bell brought out that old invoice every time they got together, waved it in Geary's face to remind him he not only owed big time, but interest was accumulating. It had started as a joke, their personal wink, but Bell hadn't let up all these years. Geary was getting a little tired of it but he played along. *Without the professional testimony of the brilliant Dr. Bell, John Geary would have been painfully, totally and officially censured by the FBI. Dismantled. Destroyed.*

Worse, Ruth would have known he had lied to her.

"Without you . . ." Geary shook his head.

"I've made a decision, John. I'm taking early retirement this spring. I'm going to winterize my house and join you here permanently. I'll edit your book for you. Full credit, of course."

"And a full cut of the advance?" Geary laughed. So that was why his old friend had pushed so hard for him to do a book when it was no secret he didn't like to write. When Geary had finished his dissertation, he and Ruth had thrown a party and he never looked back. The longest things he'd written since then were profiles, filled with FBI shorthand meant to focus a picture of a killer, not develop style. Maybe Bell was getting tired in his advanced age. Or was it payback time? He could see it now: Geary would do all the legwork and suffer through the first draft, then Bell would polish it up and share the credit—and the money. It stank, but Geary liked it. Bell had written whole books by choice, and one of them, *The Hate-Filled Mind,* had even popped onto the bestseller list. So they could double their money with his pain-in-the-ass name. The big personality and the big head. Stick a crown on it and you've got your king.

"Think again, John. I'm sure you'll reach the same conclusion. Retired, all alone." He broke out his over-sized, yellow-toothed smile. "We'll need each other. You'll see."

The waitress brought over Bell's salad and he dug in.

"I've got a title for our book," Geary said.

"Do tell."

"Head in the Dunes."

Bell's eyebrow twitched. "Interesting. Explain."

Geary filled Bell in on the Emily Parker case.

"People go missing all the time," Geary finished. "Women, mothers. But here's the hitch. Exactly, I mean exactly to the day seven years ago, a woman named Janice Winfrey goes missing from Woods Hole. Five days later, her son disappears. His arm washes up on shore, the rest of him they never find. The mother turns up naked outside the aquarium."

"Dead, I presume."

Geary shook his head. "Alive. But mentally detached. Unable to speak, can't even focus her eyes."

"And now?"

"Don't know. The thing is, she couldn't say what happened."

"I take it this case was never solved, and your Mrs. Parker has a son?"

"Two."

"And is she the only woman with a son, or two or three, who has been reported missing on the anniversary of Mrs. Winfrey's disappearance?"

"No, that's the point. Listen to this. Santa Monica, California, September nineteenth, 1973, the dismembered head of a child is found in the dunes. No clues, no case."

"Mother?"

"Head wasn't identified at the time so I can't say. But we can get the locals to pull the head and order a DNA check, see if it matches with a mother who went missing around that time, go from there. If the locals won't do it, I'll go to the state."

"And if they refuse to humor you?"

Geary smiled. "I'll get the feds to reinstate me. Piece of cake."

"We'll see. It's a sketchy connection you're making, John. It's almost thirty years ago."

"September tenth, 1980, Baton Rouge, Louisiana. A child's arm is found floating in a swamp. Mother went missing September third, found dead."

"Mutilated?"

"Not one bit."

"Interesting."

"September eighth, 1987, Fleetwood, New York.

The body of a boy is found at a playground, dead three hours, tops. His mother went missing September third."

Bell was listening.

"Watch the pattern," Geary said. "Mom on the third, the kid later. This fresh kill puts the kids' deaths at five days."

"And the first boy you told me about?"

"Chance Winfrey, age seven, 1994. Do you see?"

"Every seven years." Bell's eye stayed on Geary. "September third. Five days later, a child."

"I'm thinking they're all boys."

"Why?"

"To fit a pattern," Geary said. "This guy's organized. It's all planned out, to the day, to the year. Maybe he even chooses his victims in advance. What do you think?"

"Possibly. That could explain the geographical diversity. He chooses location by target, goes in for the job, out when his work is done."

"Our man was a frequent flier."

"Before they even started giving away miles." Bell smirked. "I'd call that bad planning."

"I called my pal Tom at VICAP this morning, he checked the database and came up with names connected to date and type of crime. He's cross-referencing the system and calling me back. Right now all I have are these newspaper articles I was able to pull off the Internet."

Geary slid a file folder across the Formica table to Bell. He opened it and read. When he was finished, he looked more sober than he'd been in years, and he didn't drink. Geary had known the articles would nail him.

"I'd say you're right," Bell said. "We've got a repeater."

"How do you see him, based on what we know now?"

Bell pursed his lips. "He's antisocial."

"I'll say."

"A psychopath. Not psychotic. A true psychotic could not plot out such a complex series of crimes. I'll be interested to see the forensics on each case. In my experience, the more organized a criminal, the less evidence they leave. And I wonder if our man here is working to perfect his craft."

"Perfect? How?" Geary pushed his plate away; he'd lost his appetite.

"Seven years ago, the mother was found alive. I'd like to know about the other mothers. Were they found? Dead? Alive? In what state of consciousness? Were any of them able to describe what happened?"

"I'm checking to see if the local offices have done any follow-up on these cases. I'll also check the bureau."

"It sounds like he kills the children, period."

"He doesn't just kill them."

"No. He dismembers them."

"More like torture."

Bell nodded. "But with the mothers, he's searching for an answer."

"Controlling the outcome by controlling the way he leaves the mother?"

"Possibly."

"Can you give him an age, Roger?"

"My math skills are out of practice." He worked his salad.

"I've already done the math, but I want your assessment first."

"Typically this kind of pathology brews for years, then blossoms in the late twenties. Adding up the seven-year periods, wouldn't that put him in his mid-fifties?"

"Bingo." Geary nodded. "What else?"

"He's white. Educated. I'd guess he's good at cross-word puzzles, chess, games of strategy."

"What's his line of work?"

Bell thought. "Professional, certainly. Probably white collar. He has the facility to hide his victims and control when and where he presents them. That takes not only ingenuity, but means."

"He isn't poor."

"No, though possibly not wealthy. He's searching for something. I'd consider that he could be building his own puzzle. A head, a torso, an arm, another arm."

"That leaves two legs." Geary wanted to vomit. Maybe retirement had softened him; he'd seen some pretty gruesome crime scenes in his day and had learned to keep a good distance. But children? He'd never get used to that.

"Yes. The first leg now, and the second one in seven more years. Then I presume he'll be finished."

"With his masterwork. In his mind, what makes him special?"

"There's the question. He's trying to tell us something, and so far no one has listened. No one has even heard."

"And it had to be me who heard this psycho, when I'm supposed to be enjoying retirement."

"He may wish to be caught, John. If so, he would make sure he was heard, but he's subtle and whoever heard him would have trained ears. So yes, in a way, it did have to be you. What I don't see is why your VICAP didn't identify the pattern before."

"I have the same question." The FBI's Violent

Criminal Apprehension Program was the first place local law enforcement went when they had an unsolved violent crime. Every crime of this nature was supposed to end up in the database, which was cross-checked as regularly as changing socks. Maybe VICAP had developed dirty feet. Why these crimes hadn't been linked in cross-check was bugging Geary and he planned to take it up with Tom, but not until he'd handed over everything he could find. No one liked to be criticized at their job, he knew that firsthand.

Bell took a bite of his salad and gave it a little more thought.

"What do you think, John? Does this man live alone?"

"I'd guess he does. All that planning. Unless he manages to hide it. But I don't think so. I think he's a loner."

"I'd tend to agree. Psychopaths who are also compulsive make awful roommates."

"And worse friends."

Bell ate his last bite of salad and the waitress appeared with his coffee.

"You?" she asked Geary.

"I thought you'd never ask."

She snorted and walked away.

"I'm glad you came to me with this case, John."

"I'm glad you kept those college babes waiting."

"Babes, Dr. Geary?"

Geary winked, then leaned forward. "Seriously, Roger. We only have three more days to nail this guy."

"Don't get your hopes too high. He's managed to elude your former colleagues for a long time."

Former colleagues. Geary still hated the sound of it.

"He got away by not being noticed," Geary said.

"Well, he's on the radar screen now. How many psychos have we put away since I started hiring you?"

Bell had been an occasional consultant to the FBI when he was hired to evaluate Geary. Once they'd met, he'd consulted on every one of Geary's cases. Bell's smile split his weathered face. "We've rarely missed, haven't we?"

"Ninety-nine out of a hundred is a damn good average."

"Be careful, John. You're not one of them anymore. They might not like you working on a case that isn't yours."

Geary shook his head. "I'm not officially working on it, Roger. Officially, I'm retired."

Bell laughed. "So I see."

"I'll finish working it up and hand it over to the Mashpee PD."

"And then you'll walk away?" Bell squinted his good eye and pressed back a smile.

"Yup." Geary nodded. "I've got a long-standing date with a golf course."

"Care for a little wager, my friend?"

"Not this time, Rog. I can't afford you."

"One dollar."

"So it's the principle of the thing." Geary sharp-eyed Bell. "You're on."

They shook on it across the table.

"I'll call you when I hear from Tom," Geary said, "later today."

Bell treated him to one more nasty-toothed smile. "Then you'll be free for golf tomorrow afternoon?"

"You bet."

Geary walked out first and could hear Bell laughing all the way to the exit.

Chapter 10

Unconsciousness blurred with sleep and waking up was a slow transformation from one darkness to another. Emily could have been floating in the sky. The sea rocked harder now than it had at first and lying still for so long without vision skewed her balance.

She had no balance.

She was inside a water-filled drum, swaying, sinking. Sometimes she forgot to breathe and her body remembered and startled like a newborn baby gripped with a sensation of falling.

She was falling.

She wished she would get there, hit the ground, go blank. Then she saw their faces and her wish evaporated.

Her children.

She would not desire death. He wanted her fear and it was hers and he couldn't have it. Her fear kept her alive and her hatred for the corn man kept her alive.

If he only knew her. She would kill him.

I am in control of myself and will not start a fight of any kind at any time.

She could see herself destroying him.

Aiki enables one to overcome himself and leads to the disappearance of the desire to fight with the enemy.

Was strength in the body or the mind? Were we defined by our intentions or our actions?

How well had she taught her children?

Untie me and give me a fair fight.

Emily ran to Maxi when she cried. No fair Sam said no fair no fair. You love me not her. Love me better love me first. I want to be best and I want to be first.

David's voice was strong when he read. David wanted a sword. I have a brown belt why can't I have a sword now? You're a child that's why. But I know the five meditations.

First is the meditation on love in which you open yourself to the desire for the wealth and well-being of everyone, and yearn for the happiness of your enemies.

Second is the meditation on pity in which your concern opens to all beings in distress, and you imagine their sadness and fear with a compassion that fills your soul.

Third is the meditation on joy in which you concern yourself only with the well-being of others and rejoice in their happiness.

Fourth is the meditation on impurity in which you consider the effects of corruption, wrongs and evils, and you contemplate the darkness of their consequences.

Fifth is the meditation on serenity in which you overcome love and hatred, desire and regret, and accept the perfection of your own imperfect life with a calmness that transcends happiness.

THESE ARE THE FIVE MEDITATIONS said the Master Buddha.

Give me a sword, Mom. I want a sword.

Aiki is love. Aiki enables one to overcome himself and leads to the disappearance of the desire to fight with the enemy. It is the way of absolute self-completion which eliminates the enemy himself.

I'm old enough. I'm ready. Give me a sword. I'll

tell you when you're ready. You may be growing up
but I'm still your mother.

Footsteps. He was in the boat. He was approaching her.

She wanted to scream but she couldn't, her mouth
was bound and the scream backfired. Inside her mind
it was loud. She heard echoes and she heard the sky
above the ocean. It was empty and light and free. She
could see it if she looked. There was not a cloud in
the sky today.

Chapter 11

Will sat on the floor of the downstairs family room, playing Monopoly with the boys on the low-slung coffee table. He had to work hard to remember which piece was his. Every now and then David would slice him a look and say, "Dad, you're the hat."

If things had gone as planned, Emily would have been back in New York by now. Their summer bags and suitcases and toys would have been strewn around the front hall and living room. If he had walked barefoot on the wood floor, he would have felt the crunch of sand. When the kids were still asleep the next morning, he and Emily would have stolen a quiet hour together and discussed their plans for the new house, obsessing about all the details ranging from their finances to the color of their new walls.

New walls.

Sam rolled the dice and cheered when he got a four. He moved his piece, the shoe, banging hard in each space. Then he turned to Will and said, "Dad! It's your turn."

Will picked up the hat but it was impossible to concentrate. He felt like a fist trapped in a rubber glove too tight to bend, but in a paroxysm of refusal couldn't stop trying.

"Play for me," he told David, and stood up from the floor.

Sam leaned back on his elbows, grinned and thrust a leg in his father's path. Will stepped over it.

"I'll be back in a little while," Will said, then stopped to look at them. "I love you guys, you know."

The boys watched as Will looked into the kids' room to check on Maxi; she was just twenty minutes into her long afternoon nap. He went into his and Emily's room, closed the door and dialed Dr. Geary's phone number. It rang and rang. He hung up and looked at his watch: it was a little after two o'clock. The promised phone call wasn't expected for an hour and a half.

He couldn't wait anymore. He needed to go outside and breathe in some air, move around. He didn't know what he needed.

He needed Emily.

Sarah was lying awake on her bed when he peeked his head into her room. "Maxi's asleep and the boys are downstairs. I'd like to step outside for a few minutes if you don't mind."

"Of course, dear."

"Are you okay?"

Her eyes looked milky. She nodded but he knew she wasn't okay. "Go ahead."

He left the house through the mudroom and walked into the garage. The door was scrolled open to the hot afternoon but inside it was coolly shadowed and damp with so much oxygen you could hardly breathe.

He thought he'd walk a little but before he made it into the sunlight he saw the bikes. They'd been parked in that very spot all summer, between Sarah's car and a path to the door. All three were old and rusted, but of the three, Jonah's chain moved quickest and his tires were the most firm. Will pinched open the helmet from where Jonah had hung it on the handlebars, shook it out, put it on his head, and fastened it under his chin. It was a good fit. He wheeled the silver bicycle out of the garage, swung himself onto the seat and started to pedal: up the circular drive, around the front garden, then back to the house. Again. And again. He was moving and it was better but it wasn't enough.

This time he headed up the road to the first driveway, then back down. There was a deep silence on the old road, except for the clicking of his gears and the buzz of insects. He circled back and returned to the house, then went back up the road, and again, and again. Finally he needed more, and went farther, this time all the way to the entrance of Gooseberry Way.

He turned back toward the house and rode steadily and hard.

Before kids, he and Emily used to bike together when they were visiting Sarah and Jonah on the Cape, and now for the first time in years he thought of one of their favorite routes. Carefree, with nothing but time, they would cross into Falmouth and segue out of town at the first detour, following Shore Street all the way to the ocean; past neat New England homes fronted by green lawns on one side, fence and beach and sun-parched one-room stilt houses pegged in sand on the other. On a summer day the heat would lift on the strong winds off the ocean. Together they would ride fast along the narrow margin between road and sand, until they came to the first entry point to the Shining Sea Bikeway. They always turned in the direction of Woods Hole, following the asphalt thread past churning sea and strips of rocky beach and blooming fields of wildflowers, pine forests and all variety of hope for a life they were just starting to piece together. He recalled his flush of happiness as he followed Emily into a canopy of shade with its flashing glimpses of houses and the seams of flowering rosa rugosa that lined the path as it nearly collided with the ocean.

The memory evaporated when Will reached the house. He turned up the drive again without slowing down. Faster. Uphill. His legs pumped and his mind raced and he rode as hard as he could but still he couldn't go fast enough.

There were many things Will didn't know, most things. But what he did know he possessed; these understandings were as dense as his own flesh. The quick oxidization of apple slices. The gradual evaporation of water. The healing power of a Band-Aid on a small child's imaginary hurt. The leaching of green from autumn leaves.

His fatherhood.

His hunger.

The particular tenor of each of his children's voices.

What he knew, he knew, and the rest were questions he asked only in the presence of potential answers. Emily once called it avoidance, but only at the beginning; later, she knew better. Will had grown up around the stalk of his parents' violent absence, comforted by layers of silence laid lovingly over him through the years by well-meaning relatives. After the funeral, his parents' deaths were not discussed, except once, with Caroline, when their grandparents had given up on her and she had been sent to join Will with their Aunt Judy and Uncle Steve and their three boys; four, including Will.

Caroline entered this branch of the Parker family with the dignity of a dethroned princess, or so Will had thought at the time; he was then twelve. Caro was seventeen and it had been eight years since they'd lived together. Will thought she was beautiful: slight and pale with very long brown hair tangling down her back. She tended not to look at anyone except Will, her little brother, her only full-blooded relative. The others she avoided as if she knew what they thought: that Caro was "on drugs and sleeping around at her age," said Aunt Judy over dinner the night before Caro's arrival, and "putting too much stress on Grandpa and Grandma," who had taken her in because at the time she was considered an easy child. "Well not anymore!" Judy had said. So Caroline was leaving their grandparents' home in upstate New York and was coming to stay with the Parkers in Westport, Connecticut, until she decided to either get a job or go to college. It was 1973.

Caro sat next to Will at the dinner table that first night while the family chattered and mostly accepted her silence, partly because it was the Parker family philosophy not to peel back someone else's layer of privacy, and partly because they didn't understand this girl who had been pried screaming from the apartment of her twenty-five-year-old boyfriend the very day of his arrest for dealing drugs. Heroin. It was bad. Caro came to the family in summertime, wearing long black sleeves. Will noticed Aunt Judy's eyes crisply record that fact and file it away behind half-lowered lids.

And so Caro came to them and stayed only briefly. Will was happy that the bedroom reshuffling had put them alone together: "They're siblings"—this was Steve—"it'll give them a chance to reacquaint." Will got ready for bed in his green summer pajamas—teeth brushed, face cleaned, hair slicked neatly behind his ears—and found her waiting for him in her black sleeves, on the edge of her borrowed cousin's bed. Will pulled back his covers and sat cross-legged on his plaid sheet and looked over at his big sister and smiled. Caro nodded, then told him something he had never known.

"They didn't die right away, Willie." She had brown eyes, a clear brown like antique light, and they reminded him of something he couldn't grasp.

"But Judy and Steve said they did."

"I know they told you that."

Will shrugged. He had not reached puberty yet and his shoulders were skinny. He felt like a baby in Caro's eyes and he wasn't sure if he wanted to know what she had to tell him. His life here had been pretty good, but hers hadn't gone as well, and maybe, he wondered, just maybe he'd be better off not knowing.

"They didn't want to tell you," Caro continued, "but you were there, so it's not like you don't already know."

She had those familiar eyes, clear and ancient as amber, and when she turned them toward the window, away from him, Will felt a thread of panic at the departure of her gaze.

"What?" he asked his sister.

"Mrs. Simon brought us to the hospital the next day, to see Mommy," Caro said softly. "Don't you remember? Daddy had died that morning in the hospital."

Will shook his head; he didn't remember.

"I went in first. You waited in the hall with a nurse. Then Mrs. Simon brought me out and you had your turn."

Caro waited and still Will couldn't recall anything other than the long-reiterated fact that both their parents had died instantly in a car crash on their way to register Caroline for summer camp, then go out to lunch. That it had all happened so fast they felt nothing, thought nothing; that the crash had worked quicker than their brains and they never had a chance to realize they were dying. "It was like turning off a light," Aunt Judy had told him quietly, thinning a tear across his cheek. "They didn't feel any pain." This simple fact had always reassured him.

"What did Mommy say to you?" Caro asked Will, her thin legs bent like jointed sticks over the edge of the other bed. Her eyes back on him.

"Nothing," Will said. "I didn't see her."

Caro's lips bunched together and he was afraid she was angry with him. Her eyes narrowed. "She told me it would be my job to take care of you because you were just a baby."

"I was four."

"Almost four. She died the day before your birthday. Did you forget that too?"

No, Will remembered that, but supposed now he had the timing wrong. It had been a store-bought cake, chocolate, with a cowboy riding a horse and a lasso bent above his hat. His present had been a small red bicycle with training wheels, a clear plastic windshield attached to the handlebars along with a metal holster for a cap gun. Everyone was there by then, it was the most family he'd ever remembered having at a birthday party, no friends. His grandma Lillian cried when she hoisted him on his new bike in the middle of the living room with all their relatives quietly surrounding him. He couldn't understand why she was crying; it was a really nice bike, and he'd wanted it badly; it was the very one he'd shown his mother at the store.

"Did Mommy tell you she loved you?" Will asked his sister.

Caro nodded.

"She died in the car," Will said, "right away, just like Daddy. She didn't feel anything. It was like turning out a light."

Caro shook her head and lay down on top of her covers, fully dressed, long sleeves and all, and was still staring at the ceiling when Will leaned over and shut off the lamp. Within the month, it was agreed that Caro would return to upstate New York, get a job, and live with Grandma and Grandpa until her eighteenth birthday that winter, at which point she would be legally independent and the choices would be hers to make.

Will pedaled fast and hard and sweat dripped off his forehead onto the backs of his hands and he kept riding. He hadn't realized he'd set his cell phone to vibrate instead of ring until now, when finally he came to rest and felt it buzzing against the front of his thigh. He was still out of breath from riding when he answered. "Yes?"

"Will dear," Sarah said. "It rang and rang. Where are you?"

"Right in front of the house."

"Someone called for you, a Dr. Geary. Will?"

He wheeled Jonah's bike into the garage, set it on its kickstand, removed the helmet. He was drenched in sweat. The screen door squealed when he opened it. Through the mudroom and into the kitchen, where he found Sarah, still talking to him on the phone.

"He said he was on his way over to the house. Will, who is he?"

"Sarah, I'm here."

Startled, she turned around, the phone still pressed to her ear. "He said he'd be here in twenty minutes," she said, and hung up the phone.

Will was downstairs changing into dry clothes when Geary arrived. Changing, decompressing, trying to compose himself. He knew Geary wasn't coming to tell him Emily had been found; he would have said so on the phone. He was coming to tell him something else, or nothing at all. Will wasn't sure what would be worse.

He was waiting with Sarah in the front hall when Geary pulled up in the dented brown car that matched his general appearance. Will pushed open the front screen door to let the old man in. Geary nodded at Will but gave Sarah his hand. She took it as if they already knew each other, pressing her hand into his.

"Afternoon," Geary greeted them.

"Tell us," Will said. "Please."

Geary's eyes slid to Sarah, and back. The distress in Sarah's face would have frightened a ghost but it didn't seem to bother Geary. He nodded and said, "Beautiful day."

Sam came bounding up the stairs. "Dad! I won the game!" David was right behind him, holding Maxi on his hip. She was groggy, pressing her hands into her eyes, newly awake. When she saw Will she reached for him, he took her, and she melted into his arms.

"Sarah, Dr. Geary and I need to talk." Will kissed the tender crook of Maxi's neck and handed her over to her grandmother.

Sam stared at Geary. "You're a *doctor*?"

"This is my costume." Geary winked. "Under my cape I'm just a regular guy."

"What cape?" Sam said.

"Boys, get your suits on," Sarah said.

"I don't want to swim." David moved closer to Will.

"Then you'll watch Maxi on the beach." Will's firm tone sent the boys downstairs. Sarah didn't bother with a bathing suit for herself or the baby; she picked up a beach bag from the floor by the wall and headed for the door. But before she left, she turned to Geary.

"If there's anything you can do to find my daughter—"

"I'll do it." Geary looked right into Sarah's eyes.

Maxi yawned and lowered her head onto Sarah's shoulder. They left and followed the boys in the direction of the lake.

Will led Geary through the living room and out onto the deck overlooking Sarah's rose garden. They could hear the distant echo of the boys' voices as they splashed into the water. The two men sat on plastic chairs under a shade awning that rolled out from the side of the house.

"How are the kids taking it?" Geary asked.

Will looked at Geary. "I've been trying to decide exactly what to tell them."

"Until we know something, you should assume your wife's coming home."

"Why?"

Geary didn't answer right away; it seemed he had something to say that wouldn't be easy.

"I have some information," Geary started. When Will leaned toward him, he pulled back. "Nothing concrete, but a lead."

"Tell me."

Geary uncrossed his legs and set his elbows on his knees. He leaned forward over steepled hands.

"Something you said this morning to Detective Snow sounded a lot like something I'd just read in an old file."

"Your research?"

"Yes."

"But aren't cold cases unsolved crimes?"

"Yes."

"I don't understand."

"It's the date," Geary said. "It's happened on the same date. I don't like to tell you this, but this would be the fifth time. Always on September third. Every seven years."

Will's lungs emptied as if an invisible hand had come from nowhere and slammed him. What Geary was telling him was worse than anything his imagination had considered since he'd gotten Sarah's first call. He'd seen Emily gone. He'd seen her hurt. But he hadn't seen her trapped by a maniac, suffering his unfathomable compulsions. Will closed his eyes and waited for the rest.

"I've been talking to my old friend Tom at the FBI. He's with VICAP—they track serial crimes."

Beneath his closed eyelids Will saw big blocks of blue and red. If he opened his eyes, he'd see the sun. He'd see nothing.

"Listen up, Will, because this isn't over yet."

Will's eyes opened to see Geary staring intently at him.

"It's a matter of the mothers."

"Mothers? The woman has to be a mother? Why?"

Again, Geary hesitated. There was more that he wasn't telling.

"His goal isn't to kill them. He holds them for five days."

"And then?"

Finally, Geary said it: "He takes the woman's child."

A deathly heat fanned out through Will's body.

He takes the woman's child.

"And then what?"

Geary sighed. "We're going to catch this asshole."

"You'll catch him now? When he hasn't been caught yet?"

"We haven't noticed him yet."

"What happens to the mothers?" Will asked.

"They're released," Geary said, "when he's finished with the child."

Will stared at the old man's face and forced himself

to ask the next question. "What does he do to the child?"

Geary didn't answer.

Will stood up. *"What does he do to the child?"*

"Keep them close" was the only answer he got. "Don't let them out of your sight."

The boys' voices rang out in the distance. They were laughing. Will fought an impulse to race off the deck and go to them.

"I don't believe this," he said to Geary.

"I know you don't. You shouldn't have to. No one should."

Emily. His children. The twist of panic Will had tried to bike away wrung at his neck. His voice scratched when he spoke. "Which one?"

Geary nodded and looked away, toward the woods. "One of the boys."

A high-pitched voice echoed over the lake, but Will couldn't tell whose it was or whether it was tinged with delight or anger. He couldn't tell.

Geary turned his eyes back to Will. "I've already been working on this with that criminologist I told you about. I promise you, Will, we're going to get a profile of this *thing* and then I'm going to get the locals behind me, and the state, and the feds, whatever it takes. I'm going to pull the string on this one, I've done it before. We have three more days. We're going to catch him."

"How do I protect them?" Will could barely hear his own voice, it was like a vapor. "What if I can't?"

From the corner of his vision, Will saw David wandering up from the lake. He stopped when he saw his father. Will tried to smile and he managed a wave, but David didn't wave back. He stopped walking and watched the two men on the porch.

David. When he was born, so small and perfect,

Emily said he was her work of art. He thrust his life into theirs with such force that he transformed them completely, taught them how to be parents, deepened their humanity, prepared them for the younger children. David had come out of nowhere and changed what mattered to them. He was their defining moment.

"Why don't you have your mother-in-law take them back to New York?" Geary asked.

"She can't make the long drive alone with the kids, especially Maxi. She cries."

"You could take them."

It was a practical idea but the thought of leaving Emily behind was impossible. Will could not leave the Cape without her.

"Dad!" David called.

"I'm coming!" Will turned to Geary. "I'll call my sister."

"Good." Geary stood up. "I'll be in touch with you. And with the police."

"Thank you, Dr. Geary."

"John."

Will nodded.

"I'll let myself out. You go do your job, Will. Take care of your boys."

Will jogged down the porch steps and joined David on the path.

"Race you!" he said to his son, and they went tearing down toward the lake.

"Dad." David stopped running when they reached the clearing just before the beach. "Why was that man here?"

Will reached out and touched David's shoulder. "It's okay. We needed to discuss something. Don't worry."

David jerked away from his father's hand. "What

do you mean, don't worry? I'm not stupid, Dad.
Where is Mom?" A cloud moved and a shaft of sun
sprang onto David's face. His pale eyes were pierced
in the center by tight black pupils.

Will faced David and opened his mouth to speak
and didn't know what he would say. How could he
tell David? How could he not tell David? He was
too smart for lies but too good for the poison of this
new truth.

"They're going to find Mommy." Will felt his stomach contract. "Dr. Geary is helping us find her."

"How?"

But before Will could try to answer, his cell phone
vibrated. He dug his hand into his pocket, pulled it
out and flipped it open. David kept his eyes on Will
as a young woman's voice asked for Mr. Parker.

"Speaking."

"Hi, this is Pam. From Stop and Shop? I got your
message? I called that other number but there's not
even an answering machine. I got your number off my
caller ID? I hope that's, like, okay. It seemed kind
of important."

"Yes." Will looked at David, lifted his chin and
pointed to the beach. "Go," he whispered. "I'll be
right there."

David did not leave.

Will hated to do it, but he turned his back on David,
took a few steps away and lowered his voice. He explained what he could to Pam, without being so ex-
plicit he'd frighten David, whose hovering presence he
could sense behind him.

"What can you tell me?" he asked Pam.

"I guess my friend told you most of it. I just wanted
to tell you that every time I see that guy? He's with
the lady that yelled at him. I think it might be, like,
his mother?"

"Why?" Will whispered.

"They just kind of remind me of that mother-son thing from New York, you know? Where they killed a rich lady to get her house? I saw it on *Most Wanted*."

Will didn't know what to make of that, coming from a teenager. It could be very true, or very false. He would mention it to Geary.

"Can you remember anything else?" Will asked. "Anything at all."

"Not really."

"Well, if you do—"

"I promise I'll call."

"Thank you."

"Sir? I hope you find her. She seemed really nice."

"Thanks for calling." Will flipped shut his cell phone and held it in his hand.

"Who was that, Dad?"

Will shook his head. He needed time to think about what to tell the children, and when, and how; he needed to find a way to help them understand the situation without terrifying them.

"Come on," Will said, "let's ask Grandma what she wants for dinner."

David followed Will to the lake. Sarah was sitting in a folding chair, next to Maxi, who was playing next to her in the sand. Sam was splashing around in the water, ten feet in front of them. Sarah's skin looked almost translucent in the sunlight. Will couldn't tell her, not yet. He would urge her to sleep tonight, take a sleeping pill and sleep as deeply as she could. He would make all the plans and in the morning he'd tell her everything.

They decided on spaghetti and meatballs, and Will went back up to the house to cook but most of all to make the call for help. He called Caroline first, and after leaving a message on her home machine remembered that she and Harry always took off the weeks just before and after Labor Day, shut down their law practice and traveled somewhere. This year it was Italy. They wouldn't be back to their apartment in New York until late on Sunday and by then it would all be over. In one way or another it would be over. Then he thought of Charlie and Val and in minutes it was all arranged: they would drive to the Cape overnight and take all three children back to New York first thing in the morning.

Chapter 12

Amy kicked aside the old take-out wrappers that crunched at her feet. She didn't like the passenger seat, especially this one. Al Snow was at the wheel of the department-issued Chrysler he'd been driving for years. He had a green pine-tree air freshener dangling from the rearview mirror and a picture of his teenage daughter taped to the dash. He kept his spare change in a nook between the two front seats.

They drove in silence through the back roads of Mashpee to Popponesset Beach. Amy had been here before, but the back-Cape roads got mazelike and she would have needed her map to find Squaws Lane. Snow didn't use a map; he knew all the turns. He brought them up Uncle Percy's Road, down Clover, and up Uncle Hank's Road, back to Kim's Path and straight onto Squaws. Amy made a mental note to check her map later; she had a gut feeling he'd driven them in circles just to prove he knew the way better than she.

According to the Department of Motor Vehicles, Mr. White number one lived at two Squaws Lane. His name was Robert R. Robertson, a dirty trick for any parent to perpetrate on his own child; it went right into the *What Were They Thinking?* file. Amy seriously hoped his middle name wasn't Robert, too.

There were only five houses on Squaws Lane, modest cabins planted close together, their tiny yards separated by rusty chain-link fences. Whoever had developed these small lots had maximized on income potential by building so close to the sea but had minimized on amenities. Like they said, location, location, location.

"Summer houses," Amy said.

Snow kept his eyes fixed on the road. "Mostly."

Number two was at the end of the short street, a gray clapboard bungalow with a small wooden deck built onto the crest of a dune. Sea grass glazed the dune as it spilled onto a wide, pristine beach facing Nantucket Sound. Far in the distance, the slate green ocean blended with a clear sky.

The silver Skylark sat in the driveway.

Snow parked the car and they got out.

"Funny," Amy said, looking at the meager house and the million-dollar location.

Snow didn't see it, or wouldn't admit that he did. "What do you mean?"

"Nothing."

They walked up a series of rotted wooden steps that ended in a concrete slab and a half-screen exterior door. The door squealed when Snow pulled it open. Amy rang the bell and they heard a single, muted *ding*. They waited. Maybe it was the sea air, but the interior door hadn't held its paint job, which flaked white amidst a mass of wood slivers. A metal trash can by the fence overflowed with corn husks and their long, golden hairs.

Finally, the door cracked open, and half a face stared out at them. The man was so white he could have been albino. Hair, skin and eyes blurred into a muted, gauzy color. He closed the door, then cracked it open again. He repeated the procedure one more time. That was three times in all, and Amy knew they had a winner.

"I'm Detective Cardoza from the Mashpee PD. This is Detective Snow. Are you Robert Robertson?"

Robertson looked from Amy to Snow, and again, and again. The final beat of his eyes rested on Snow.

"Bob?" Snow said.

The pale eyes blinked. "Bobby."

"Mind if we ask you a few questions?"

Bobby opened the door only enough to press his body out. Clearly, he didn't want them inside. In the moment before it snapped shut behind him, Amy glimpsed a neat row of shoes on a white carpet and a tall shelf of paperback books with their spines perfectly aligned.

Sweat quickly gathered on Bobby's forehead. According to his DMV records, he was fifty-two, but he looked closer to sixty.

"We're investigating a missing persons claim. Emily Parker." She showed Bobby Emily's picture. "Do you know her?"

Bobby's eyes flicked three times to the picture, then raced across the detectives' faces, and landed back on Emily's picture. He shook his head.

He was lying.

"You like corn." Amy nodded to the trash by the fence.

Bobby was silent.

"It was on sale yesterday at the Stop and Shop by the Mashpee Commons. You shop there often?"

"On Mondays," Bobby said, "they have double coupons."

"You bought an awful lot of corn yesterday. Do you live alone? Maybe you had a party?"

He didn't seem to know which question to answer first.

"Anyone live with you?" Amy repeated.

Bobby shook his head. "I don't like parties. People make me nervous."

Amy could see that. *But how nervous?* she wondered. "So you ate all that corn yourself last night?"

"Some. There's more for tonight. And the next night. I like corn. It was on sale."

Amy understood something about this man: he ate only one food, and a lot of it, and repetitively. Whatever was on sale. His unhealthy appearance confirmed that he didn't eat a balanced diet. And he did everything three times. Her guess was that he was obsessive-compulsive. She'd check the state psych records later and see if he came up, maybe find a psychiatrist or someone who could fill her in on his condition and history. He could have Emily in the house, or somewhere else; or he could be too fragile to organize an abduction. That was what Amy wanted to know. Could Bobby Robertson pull it off, would he want to, and why?

"One more question," she asked.

His eyes flicked to Amy, and he blinked—three times.

"Who was the woman you were arguing with at the store? She followed you out. Did she leave with you?"

Bobby didn't like the question. "I didn't talk to anyone at the store!" he said. "I just—like—corn!"

He bolted inside and slammed the door.

"We'll come back with a warrant," Amy told Snow as they walked back to the car.

"You need a crime to get a warrant," he said. "They don't issue them just to keep us busy on summer vacation."

"You're not on vacation, Al."

The comment sailed right over him. "I'm telling you, you need a crime."

"No, you need reasonable suspicion of a crime."

Snow shrugged. "I guess I just don't see it your way."

"A woman is missing."

"Yes, but—"

"Women don't just evaporate."

His eyebrow cocked. "Amy, spare me. You know as well as I do that wives ditch their husbands this way all the time."

Amy stopped walking. "You don't think Bobby in there is a little unusual? He was *seen* behind her on line, and he was *seen* driving off with a blond woman. Why isn't that enough for you?"

"He was also seen arguing in the store with a blond woman *not* Mrs. Parker."

Snow got into the driver's seat and pulled shut his door. Amy slid in beside him.

"The guy's a nut. I'll give you that," Snow said. "That doesn't mean he's a kidnapper. We don't even know what happened to her."

"But, Al, that's the reason we're trying to find out."

Snow backed up the car and they drove out of Squaws Lane, resuming their silence. Amy didn't know how she was going to work productively with Al Snow if they couldn't even agree on the basics. They weren't officially partners yet, and she decided that despite his seniority, she had every right to pursue this case. Not just a right, but an obligation. She for one would not let Emily Parker vanish in a mist of assumptions.

Amy dialed the station on her cell phone and told Kaminer she wanted a warrant to search Robertson's home. He didn't even question her judgment; he simply said he'd get her one. Then she told him she was thinking it might be a good idea to search the Goodman-Parker home too. Kaminer's reaction interested her.

"Good instinct, but, Amy? I'm surprised you didn't call me on that one sooner."

It had only been two hours since she'd visited Gooseberry Way. So her boss had high expectations of her; it was a good sign.

"Chief, one more thing."

"Shoot."

"I think we should put a tail on this Robertson guy at least until the warrant comes through."

"Done."

"When do you think I'll have the warrants?" she asked when he started to hang up.

"As soon as I can find out what pond the judge is fishing on."

Snow kept a steady speed, right at the limit, and didn't even glance at her as she made her calls. She looked at him after flipping shut her phone, waiting for some reaction, but his expression stayed cool. So that was how it would be. He wouldn't instigate, and he wouldn't interfere. Not the worst bargain she could hope for.

They drove north on Route 28, turning off just before the Bourne Bridge funneled them off the Cape. Tucked behind one of the many car dealerships that studded the tree-lined route was a small lot marked by an antiqued sign that read RAGNATELLI'S VINTAGE AUTOMOBILES, DRIVE AWAY IN A PIECE OF HISTORY. The license plate of the Ford driven by Mr. White #2 had been bolted on in a Ragnatelli frame.

There were about twenty cars, all classics, most of them from the forties and fifties. Amy wasn't much of a car buff but she recognized a lot of Fords and Chevys with their long, bulbous noses and curved tops. They were in pristine condition, eye benders done up in candy colors you rarely saw anymore: cherry red, swimming pool blue, cream yellow, bronze, black and white like a half-and-half cookie, cool mint green. Not to mention a nifty 1947 Ford, *salmon coral reef*. It was lined up as innocently as any other car for sale, but this one had a story to tell. Amy supposed they all did.

A one-room white-shingled office sat at the far end of the lot. Snow couldn't tear himself away from the cars, so Amy went into the office alone. She was greeted by a woman with short brown hair and lipstick that put up a good fight with the cherry red Chevy.

"Can I help you?"

Amy took out her badge. "I'd like some information about one of your cars."

"You're not buying." The woman sighed.

"Sorry."

"Which car?"

"The pinkish one out there—a 1947 Ford?"

"Yes, it's a beauty."

"Has it been driven lately?"

"Yesterday."

"By who?"

"Whom." The woman turned her head abruptly, as if to shake off the grammar. "I used to teach English, before I married Sal and got into this."

"You're the owner?"

"Wife of. Sal had the bug before I met him. I manage the office."

A framed photo on the desk showed Mr. and Mrs. Ragnatelli pressed together on a couch, smiling. The man was enormous, must have been three hundred pounds.

"Who drove the car yesterday, Mrs. Ragnatelli?"

"I don't know his name. I wasn't here yesterday afternoon. Sal said a man took the car for a test drive and brought it back later."

"Is that normal, to let people drive off with the cars?"

"Sure. You have to seduce them. People like to be alone in a car to really get a feel for it. There's a risk but we've never had one stolen. We always hold a credit card and I don't know anyone who wouldn't want to come back for their card, do you?"

"No." Through the small office window Amy could see Snow sitting in the driver's seat of a mint green Ford with a front that reminded her of a baboon's snout. "Do you keep copies of the credit cards?"

"Maybe we should, but we never have. I'll tell you what. Sal's on the road today. There's a classic car show up in Fall River. You could beep him and he'll call you back. Just tell him you spoke to Vera." She wrote her husband's beeper number on the back of a business card and handed it to Amy.

"Thanks." Amy slipped the card into her purse. "Business slow down after Labor Day?"

"Not usually, but it's been a slow summer. We're one of the first businesses to suffer when the economy starts to drift."

Snow had developed an attachment to the green 1940 Ford and it took a minute to get him out. While she waited, she stuck her head inside the pink car, looked under the hood, checked out the trunk. The car looked undisturbed. She waited a little longer while Snow went to ask Vera for a price on his green Ford. He fairly glowed all the way back to the station house.

He pulled into his usual spot in the back lot, turned off the ignition, cranked up the parking brake, and turned a grin on Amy that showed the gap between his two front teeth. For a split second, she thought he looked cute in the slightly sad way of an oversized child.

"Why don't you buy yourself that car, Al?"

"I can see myself in it." He laughed softly. "Driving

down Cape on a summer night, picnic on the beach, a glass of wine with someone special."

Amy was about to agree with him, maybe even suggest he sign up with a dating service after he got the car. But then he took his hand off the parking brake and landed it right on Amy's thigh.

"You must be joking!" She popped open the door, got out as fast as she could and stuck her head through the open window. "Al, what the hell are you thinking?"

He wouldn't look at her. "Forget it." The car revved and he pulled out almost before she had a chance to back away.

Amy went straight to her desk and tried to calm herself down. Snow's wasn't the first unwanted advance she'd ever fended off, and she knew it wouldn't be the last. She just hated when it happened at work. It didn't say much for Snow's antennae that he had picked up on signals that were nowhere in the universe. She considered telling Chief Kaminer about the incident but quickly decided against it. She was the only female detective at the Mashpee PD and thought she'd better focus on doing a good job before registering any complaints.

It was getting late in the afternoon and she forced her mind into her work. There was a message on her desk that John Geary had called her twice; she returned the call, but there was no answer. The judge was still out fishing and Kaminer was gone for the day. Amy had beeped Sal Ragnatelli seven times and he hadn't called her back. But what really made the investigation feel stalled was the forensics report on Emily Parker's car. Just hair and fibers that belonged to the family. No unusual prints on the back hatch. And last night's pounding rain had pretty well disinfected the scene.

Whoever took Emily had been careful. And Snow had waited too long.

She spent the rest of the day calling every psychiatric clinic and hospital on the Cape and off, all the way up to Boston, asking for information about a Robert R. Robertson. Mostly she left messages with receptionists. It was incredible how many psychiatrists and case workers were out to lunch at four in the afternoon. And when she did get through, she learned nothing.

Finally, Amy called in for a progress report on the team watching Bobby Robertson, but it turned out to be a day at the beach, literally. One of them had manned a towel on the sand outside the house, while the other one sat in a car at the bottom of Squaws Lane. Bobby hadn't moved, not even once.

It was almost nine o'clock when Amy got home to her place on Plum Hollow Drive. It was a pretty country house on two acres that she'd bought with her ex-husband, Peter, when they were first married, and she'd won it in hard battle in the divorce. The bottom line was that she had earned more than he had as a contractor, and paid more toward the house over the two years of their marriage. He was unable to buy her out or get a loan. She bought him out at market and would grow old paying off the mortgage and, most likely, digging up the countless vodka bottles he'd buried in the yard. But she loved it here; it was quiet and peaceful and she mostly enjoyed living alone.

She got out of her car and pinched back a few of the red roses that clustered up the cedar trellis by the kitchen door. As soon as she turned her key and stepped into her butter yellow kitchen, she could feel the hard coating of her day begin to melt off.

She picked the mail up off the floor and set it with

her purse on the table in the middle of the room. After pouring herself a tall ice water, she opened the fridge to see what there was to eat. Not much. She'd have to heat up one of those cardboardy frozen dinners again, if there were any left in the freezer. There was one: chicken and rice with a side of soggy peas and a tub of chocolate pudding. She peeled off the top and stuck it in the microwave for three minutes. When she turned around, she noticed her answering-machine light blinking on the counter next to the phone. There were two messages.

"Amy, it's Al. Sorry about that before."

Fine. Sorry. What's new?

"Detective Cardoza, this is John Geary. I don't know if you tried calling me back, I don't have one of these machines but I'm glad you do. I need to talk to you first thing in the morning. I'll meet you at the station."

DAY THREE

Chapter 13

A dream of his mother woke David at just past five in the morning. It was pitch-black and dead quiet outside the windows. But in the room where he slept with Sam and Maxi a nightlight glowed so he could see, and he could hear them breathing. Maxi was lying on her side with her back pressed against the bars of her crib. Sammie was on top of his covers with his legs in a V and his hands in fists just like Maxi did when she slept on her back. David pulled his blanket up to his chin and thought about his dream. Bits of it were already fading but he could still see the sharpest parts. His mother never came home, and no one ever mentioned it, and Maxi was grown up and she looked just like Emily but she was a stranger, and she reminded him to do his homework but it was already done. Sammie was throwing a basketball against the front door of Grandma's garage and a voice that sounded like that doctor guy who visited yesterday kept shouting *stop stop stop*. Those were the words that woke him up. *Stop stop stop.*

David didn't want to go back to sleep, in case the dream started again. It happened sometimes, like putting in the second tape of a long movie. He sat up so he wouldn't fall back to sleep. A clock next to Sammie's bed showed in red numbers that it was 5:13 A.M.

One time he had asked Grandma what time the newspaper came, and she told him about five o'clock in the morning. He remembered that now. He had overheard his dad last night telling Grandma not to let the newspaper into the house. David understood that they didn't want him or Sammie to see it, especially him, since Sammie couldn't really read a newspaper yet. They probably didn't want them to see it because their mother might be in it.

Her picture might be on the front of the newspaper. She might be dead. It could be that they didn't want them to know about it. David was tired of being told everything was all right. He knew it wasn't. He wasn't stupid and he knew his mother hadn't come home. He knew bad things happened to good people for no reason except that monsters were real and the world was not the terrific place grown-ups tried so hard to convince kids it was. He knew his parents had been making him learn aikido all these years so if he had to he could fight off the bad people. He wasn't stupid. He knew that.

He had watched his father go all around the house last night, making sure every door and window was locked, even the skylights over Grandma's loft. All locked up tight. The garage door was rolled down every night before they went to bed but this time Dad also locked the door between the garage and the mudroom. It was like going to bed in Manhattan, where everything had to be locked all the time and you couldn't sleep with your window open even in summer. You got the air conditioner or nothing, but you never got the breeze. Did bad guys only come when you were sleeping, was that the idea? Were they like bats, awake only at night? If bad guys were human, didn't they do their bad work in the day too?

David sat in his bed, listening to Sammie breathe and Maxi's plastic mattress pad crinkle when she rolled onto her stomach. And he made a decision. If Mom wasn't in her bed right now, he would go up the road and get the newspaper himself, before they had a chance to hide it from him.

He pushed back his covers and slipped quietly out of the room, leaving the bedroom door cracked open like his mother and grandma did so they could hear Maxi when she woke up. His feet crunched on some toys when he crossed the downstairs family room to the other side, where his mother and father slept. The door was shut tight. When he turned the knob, there was a loud click, and it got worse, because when he pushed the door open, it creaked. The room was very dark. He stood there a minute and waited to get yelled at. Nothing happened. When his eyes adjusted enough, he could see his dad sleeping in the bed. He'd been pretty tired the day before and David guessed he was out cold now. Out cold and alone. Mom wasn't there.

David pulled the door behind him without closing it all the way so it wouldn't click again. He crept up the stairs and to the front door. There was a loud snapping sound when he turned the lock, and another click from the doorknob, but luckily this door didn't have the creak. David paused and waited for someone to come out and tell him to go back to bed. No one did. He pushed open the screen door, which he knew squeaked pretty badly, and let it fall behind him as he ran from the house and up the road. He'd gotten this far and as long as he got the paper first he didn't care if they caught him.

It was so dark out he could hardly even see the dirt

road. His grandpa used to tell them it was an old Indian road back from the days when all the land was owned by Native Americans. They'd even tried to get the land back from the people who owned it now, but couldn't. Grandma and Grandpa still had their land and their house and their beach. At least Grandma did.

David stopped running because he was afraid he'd run right off the road. Instead, he walked fast up the old Indian road, past the turnoffs for the two other houses that sat by the lake. You couldn't see your neighbors out here unless you passed them in your car, and then they always pulled up next to each other and talked. It embarrassed David whenever Grandma did that, pulling to the edge of the road and rolling down her window so she could chat with strangers she said were her old friends but whom she only saw if she ran into them in passing. It wasn't like in Manhattan where you lived in a big building with hundreds of people you saw all the time and made a big point of never talking to. It was different here, really dark, not too many people, but when they turned up you had to act like you knew them.

When he got close to the main road it was a little lighter and he could see the mailboxes, three for mail and two for newspapers. He started to run again and reached the mailboxes just in time for the sun to break into the sky. Just like that, it went from night to day. He wasn't sure which newspaper box was theirs so he just took one and ran back down the road with it.

When he got far enough from the main road so he couldn't be seen, he stopped. He pulled off the white plastic sleeve and unfolded the newspaper. He held the big paper in front of him and looked over the whole front page. He didn't see his mother's picture anywhere.

He opened to the next page, and there she was.

In the picture, she looked happy, and that confused him. Then he realized that of course they would have used a picture from before. She was smiling in one direction and looking in another. That was his mom, always doing two things at once. Smiling and looking. He threw the paper down and stamped it into the old dirt road and sat on top of it and started to cry.

After a few minutes, he got off the paper and shook it out. He sat back down on the dusty road because it didn't matter—his pajamas were already dirty. He read the words under his mother's smiling-looking picture. The headline said MISSING SINCE MONDAY and the short article said her name, that she came from New York, that she was visiting her mother on the Cape, that she was a mother of three, that she always wore the same bracelet, and that she hadn't been seen since she went grocery shopping two days before. There was nothing David didn't already know. He kept reading.

The article said that Mrs. Parker's husband was un-cooperative and had hung up the phone. David remembered that, but it hadn't seemed like a big deal when it happened. People were always calling up asking questions you didn't want to answer; his parents called them telephone solicitors and said you didn't have to talk to them. If they called during dinnertime, they either got a nice sorry-but-no-and-a-hang-up or a mean leave-us-alone-and-take-us-off-your-list-and-a-hang-up. Yesterday's call was a little different because his dad had said something about his mom, David remembered that. But he got frustrated the same way and hung up the same way and it seemed like just another call he didn't think he deserved. It must have been someone from this newspaper, so he stuck it in the article, how Dad had gotten mad. Dad got mad sometimes, so did everyone, so did Mom, so did

David. But reading it here made it seem evil, like Dad hung up the phone because he knew where Mom was and didn't want to say so. David knew his father wanted to find his mother. He knew that. He kept reading.

In a little box next to the article was the number of people in the country who were missing so far that year and still hadn't come home: 515,109. Underneath, it said that people who went missing were hardly ever found. It said that people who kidnapped other people hurt them right away, then killed them. It said that if the kidnapper wanted money, they asked for it right away. It said the police were too busy and without any clues they didn't know where to look, so they moved on to other things. Maybe that was why Dad was talking to that man yesterday. Maybe he had hired his own private detective, like they did sometimes on TV. Maybe they would have to find her all by themselves.

David bunched up the newspaper and stuck it under his arm so he could run as fast as he could back to the house. He flung open the screen door and the inside door and raced down to his father's room. He kicked open the bedroom door and turned on the light. His dad sat up right away and stared at David like he was a ghost.

"What happened?" His dad sounded confused. "What happened? What's wrong?"

"I know." David marched over to the bed with the dusty, crumpled newspaper. He flattened it out and turned to page two. Mom's face smiled and looked.

His father grabbed the newspaper and lifted it up so he could read it. Then he calmly laid it back down on the bed. "Come here." He moved over to make room.

David stood where he was.

"Come *here*."

David didn't move. "You lied to me, Dad. You told me Mom was okay and she'd be back."

"She probably is okay and she probably will be back."

"Did they call and ask for money?" David asked.

"Did who call? Sweetie—"

"The kidnapper. Was that who called you on your cell phone yesterday? Because if he called and asked for money, she might still be alive."

His dad couldn't think of what to say. He sat frozen like Sammie did when he thought there was a monster under his bed. Sam wouldn't get up to go to the bathroom and ended up wetting his bed, and when Mom found out he cried like a baby. Dad just sat there and took a big breath. But there was no monster under this bed and his father knew it. He was quiet because he thought something bad had happened to Mom.

"They didn't ask for money," David said, "did they?"

His father shook his head. "David, I'm sorry, but we can't give up hope."

"What is hope, Daddy? Is it like Santa Claus? Because you know I know he isn't real, but I still take the presents because I want them."

"Take the presents, David. Don't give up because if we all give up we'll lose her."

"But how do you *know*?" David had his hands in fists. He wanted to hit something so he hit the bed and the newspaper jumped.

His father leaned closer to David and looked at him in the way that said he'd better listen. "This is really important and I need your help. I don't want you running up the road, or going down to the beach alone, even though you're eleven and you're the oldest. I need your help with this. Sam will follow your lead. Promise?"

David nodded.

"Second, I don't want Sammie scared, so don't tell him about this." He pointed to the newspaper. "You know how his imagination runs wild. Promise me you won't tell your brother."

David thought it over. He'd promise, for now. Like Santa Claus. He'd pretend, he'd take the presents, and then he would decide.

Sammie flew into the room in his airplane pajamas and landed next to Dad in the bed. "What's that?"

"It's a newspaper, butthead."

David jumped Sammie and dragged him off the bed and tried to tickle him into a ball. Sam laughed and tried to tickle David back but he was too fast; quick as a wink he was under the covers next to Dad.

Sammie stood up and caught his breath. "Maxi's awake."

"I don't hear her crying," Dad said.

"She's got her eyes open. She's all red. She looks pretty weird."

Dad jumped up and ran out of the room and the door smashed against the wall and he kept running.

Chapter 14

Maxi's eyes were wide open, her dilated pupils darting at an invisible spot on the ceiling. An aura of heat appeared to quiver over her bright red skin. Will lay the palm of his hand on her forehead. She was on fire.

He scooped up her limp body and shouted, "David, get Grandma!"

Footsteps thundered up the stairs, others ran in his direction.

"Sammie," Will ordered, "get dressed *now*."

Maxi felt like a sack of burning coals in his arms. Her head flopped over like a newborn with no neck control and he instinctively raised a crooked elbow to catch it. Wisps of her hair were glued with sweat to her forehead. She breathed in deep, raspy spasms. Will took the stairs two at a time and headed through the mudroom toward the garage. Sarah appeared, groggy but already dressed.

"Get the boys into the car," Will said. "We're taking Maxi to the hospital."

"You go," Sarah said. "I'll stay here with the boys."

There was no time to explain. "Sarah, *please* get them into the car."

He pressed the button to open the garage door and it scrolled up while he unlocked the back doors of

Sarah's car, so the boys could jump right in. Sammie raced in first and buckled himself up. When David ran into the garage, Will stopped him.

"Go to the fridge and grab Maxi's medicine."

David darted into the house and was back in a split second with the small plastic bottle of amoxicillin.

Sarah sat in the backseat, between the boys, holding Maxi. Will reversed the car out of the garage and in the rearview mirror saw a moment of three faces suspended in panic: David's forehead rutted with worry; tears pooled in the rims of Sarah's eyes; Sammie's gaze fixed down, toward his sister. Will raced the car as fast as the old dirt road would let him. The deadly quiet was broken only by the crunching of the wheels over raw earth and the coarse wheezing of Maxi's struggle for breath.

The drive to Falmouth Hospital was only seven minutes but it felt like an hour. Will pulled up in front of the emergency room, grabbed Maxi from Sarah's arms and ran toward the entrance. Sarah stayed behind to park the car. The boys followed Will through the automatic double doors that slid open when they sensed him coming.

The emergency room was in chaos and he ran into the fray with his children, looking for help. Nurses and doctors seemed to rush in every direction. Will hated the sickening antiseptic smell and fought the inner cascade of blunted sensations, of echoes stirring like agitated ghosts. He had suffered hospitals for the birth of each child, and he would have run through fire for their survival, but every time he entered these cold halls, he became porous, absorbing every possible loss.

There had just been a head-on collision on Route 28 and a badly injured family was being wheeled in on stretchers. David and Sammie watched as one by one, four bloody children strapped onto gurneys were rushed through the admitting area and into the next room. The swinging doors slapped against each other as attendants kicked them open for the next stretcher. The mother wasn't moving and they had a tube down her throat. Two EMS attendants worked on her as they hustled her into the room with her children.

Will tried to shoo David and Sammie out of the way but it was too late, they had seen it all. He looked at his sons and saw them spiraling away from safety and didn't know how to stop it. Maxi was wilted against his shoulder and no one was coming out of that room to help her. He reached out his free hand and pointed Sam and David toward the admitting desk.

The male nurse behind the high counter was busy on the phone.

"Excuse me," Will interrupted. "My baby is sick. I need someone to help her."

The nurse looked at Maxi and squeezed a drop of compassion into his smile. "I can see that. We just got a car crash in and everyone's on that now, but I'll call up to Pediatrics and get them to send someone down." The nurse put his call on hold, pressed a red button on his phone, and his unruffled voice amplified over the loudspeakers in a general call for a pediatric M.D. to come to Emergency.

Will sat the boys next to each other in molded orange seats that were bolted to a strip along the waiting room wall. Their eyes stayed on their father as he paced with Maxi, rocking her and whispering a lullaby in her ear. David was holding tight to the bottle of antibiotics.

Will realized that he hadn't given Maxi any medicine since he'd arrived on the Cape, and now he wondered whether Sarah had actually remembered to do it as she'd said she had.

"Let me see that bottle."

David handed it over.

Will carefully read the label. It was dated September first, the Saturday Emily had joined him in the city and taken Maxi to her doctor. She had started her medicine that day. Monday would have been her third day, the day Emily vanished in the afternoon. Had Maxi gotten any of her antibiotics since then? It was Wednesday now. It was a ten-day prescription. This should have been Maxi's fifth day, and yet the bottle was more than three-quarters full. Will's stomach somersaulted. He himself had been there since yesterday morning. He should have taken charge of it; he shouldn't have left it to Sarah, knowing how she overlooked things under normal circumstances. It was his fault this had happened. His own fault.

And then he remembered something else. The morning of his parents' accident, he had pestered his father to help mow the lawn. His father's patience had snapped. "It's too dangerous," he'd said. "When you're older you'll help me." He took the time to settle Will on the front steps, where he watched his father for the last time. Sleeves rolled up, sinewy arms, a sweat gathered on his neck. If his father had not lost time on Will's five-minute distraction, would they have left that much earlier? Would they have passed the danger zone on the highway minutes before anything happened?

Will looked over at his sons and knew that as a father it would be impossible to hold them responsible for such a fateful mistake. He welcomed all their distractions, and had already forgiven them, in advance, for any of their life's errors. He tried to recall his father's face when the mowing was done and he prepared to go inside, but it vanished as if erased by the efforts of his memory. If he could just remember, if he could see it, he would be forgiven.

"Dad," David said, "your phone's ringing."

Will heard the crescendo of his cell phone and wondered how long it had been ringing. He shifted Maxi so he could get the phone out of his pocket.

"It's Charlie." He sounded rushed.

"Are you at the house?" Will asked. "I had to run out—"

"I wanted to tell you we got a late start. Val wasn't feeling well last night. She was worried about the baby. The obstetrician told her to sleep before we got going, but we're on our way now."

"Is she okay now?" More hours of waiting split open in front of Will. Had he made a mistake relying on them, given Val's pregnancy? But she'd been healthy and the baby wasn't due for nearly three months. "Maybe she should stay home and rest, Charlie. You could come alone."

"We're already in the car," Charlie said. "We should be there by noon."

A woman in a white coat hurried toward Will. She wore a badge reading MARY LAO, M.D, PEDIATRICS.

"All right," Will said. "We'll see you then."

Before he could flip shut his phone, Dr. Lao reached for Maxi, who had fallen asleep on Will's shoulder. "Come with me," she said, and they followed her through the swinging doors that had swallowed up the injured family. The bloodied mother was being frantically worked on by a team of doctors under a bank of lights. Will turned away from her and kept moving.

Dr. Lao hurried past them until she found a free examining table. She placed Maxi gently down, snapped on a pair of rubber gloves, pressed open Maxi's right eye and shone a penlight directly into it. The pupil rapidly contracted. Dr. Lao repeated the procedure with the left eye. She took Maxi's pulse with her finger. When the doctor slid the tip of an electronic thermometer into Maxi's ear, she screamed.

It was one of the most beautiful sounds Will had ever heard, as good as a baby's first cry after birth. She was conscious enough to respond to pain; it had to be a good thing. He ground his jaw and choked back tears. The boys watched him, bewildered.

Dr. Lao nodded her head. "How long has she had an ear infection?"

"My wife took her to the doctor on Saturday." Will handed Dr. Lao the bottle of antibiotics. She looked at the label and quickly reached the same conclusion as had Will, moments earlier.

"She hasn't been getting her medicine," Dr. Lao said. "The infection's spread through her sinuses, hopefully no farther. She has a fever of 106. That's too high. I'll have to admit her and get her on intravenous meds right away. She should be fine, but when she goes home she'll have to continue on her antibiotics for the full course. Will that be a problem?"

"No," he said. "I can explain what happened."

"Not now. We have to get her admitted." Dr. Lao saw a nurse and snagged her with an order. "Get this baby upstairs to three. I'll be right up."

Sarah found them just at the moment Maxi was whisked away by the nurse and Dr. Lao turned to look at Will. She seemed to notice David and Sammie for the first time. "Are these your children too?"

"Yes."

"Sometimes the younger ones get lost in the shuffle, don't they?" Dr. Lao didn't smile. "Make sure your baby gets every single dose of her meds after she's released. This could have been very serious."

"It's my fault," Sarah said.

"No." Will gently squeezed Sarah's arm. "I take full responsibility. She's my child."

"Where's the mother?" Dr. Lao asked. "I'd like to talk to her too."

Standing there in the hospital with his damaged family and not a clue to the answer to Dr. Lao's question, Will felt an onslaught of warped proportions. He was four years old again, standing in the Jack Sprat Funhouse with his three cousins careening around him. Laughing. Testing their transformations in the multitude of bent mirrors. He stood fixed in one spot. There was a rounded mirror on the ceiling and he looked up into it and saw himself, all alone, squashed flat. His tears, when he cried, seemed to fall backward for miles.

Chapter 15

"Dr. Geary, this is not your jurisdiction. Please let us handle it." The girl detective gave him a patronizing smile and started typing on the computer. Why did they always do that when they wanted you to go away?

"Sweetheart, I'm retired. I have no jurisdiction, which means I can do anything I want."

Her fingers froze, the screen stopped flashing and she skewered him with her dark eyes. "Don't call me sweetheart."

The flat of Geary's hand flew up in a gesture of peace. "Didn't mean it—just wanted your attention." He winked, then regretted it.

Amy Cardoza sighed deeply and swiveled her body around to face him. She crossed her legs, then she crossed her arms. Her eyes flicked at the wall clock. "Five minutes, flat. Pull up a chair."

Geary moved fast, scraping a chair across the floor.

Just then Snow walked in, holding a yellow smiley-face card with the bright red legend *Have You Seen My Nose?* "Need you to sign this for Suellen," he said. "Don't forget, we've got the birthday cake to-morrow at five."

Amy signed the card without looking at Snow, and handed it back. "You might as well stay for this, Al."

Geary couldn't help taking a little satisfaction when Snow sat down next to Amy and she inched her chair away. Geary sat opposite them at a small rectangular table half covered by mailboxes, in-boxes, and a shiny striped bag with the head of a stuffed bear sticking out of the top. Snow leaned over to slide the birthday card into the bag.

Amy looked at the clock again. It was 9:07 A.M. "Go."

Geary balanced his brown accordion file on his knees, and one by one pulled out each of his manila file folders.

Snow shot Amy a skeptical glance but she ignored it.

"That was one minute," she said.

Geary opened one of his files and laid each of the five newspaper article printouts on the table in chronological order. Then he opened another file, and on top of each of the articles he placed a printout with a heading that read *Federal Bureau of Investigation: VICAP* in blue across the top. From a third file he took a sheaf of loose yellow pages torn from a legal pad and covered with his own handwriting, or "scrawl" as Ruth had called it. He sorted out the yellow sheets between the five piles.

"Two minutes," Amy said.

Geary sat back down and watched their faces as they tried not to look too interested in his piles. He let another thirty seconds go by. He knew the headlines and printout headers would start his argument for him. When they were ready to pay attention, he spoke.

"September third, 1973, Roz Gregory disappears in

L.A., outside a restaurant where she just had lunch with her boyfriend. He stays behind to pay the bill. She goes out to the car. Two minutes later he comes out and she's gone. Seventeen days later, a decomposed head is found in the Santa Monica dunes. The head belongs to her son, Evan, age eight, who disappeared five days after his mother on September seventh. Roz Gregory doesn't return and a body is never found. Case never solved."

"California?" Snow said. By the white dust on his collar, Geary figured he was eager for a reunion with the second half of his doughnut. But Geary had more to say, and if he pitched his case right, Snow wouldn't feel like eating.

Amy glanced at the clock. "Go on."

"September third, 1980, Louisiana. Terry McDaniel disappears from a softball game where her seven-year-old son, James, is pitching for the Baton Rouge Bombers. When his team comes into the dugout, she whispers to him she's going across the street for a cup of coffee. Takeout. She never comes back to the game or anywhere. Five days later, James disappears from his house while his dad is mowing the lawn. Five days after that, his right arm surfaces in a swamp twenty miles away. The rest of his body is never found, but his mother's is, perfectly intact, no apparent cause of death. An autopsy turns up traces of pancuronium but it can't be determined that this drug alone could cause death. The dad buries the arm in the casket with Terry's body and the newspaper has a field day. The police vet him as their number-one suspect but he clears. Case never solved."

The wall clock read nine fifteen. Snow's foot was tapping the air but Amy ignored him. Her eyes stayed fixed on Geary and she nodded soberly. He felt that rush he used to get in the bureau's conference room when he briefed special agents on a new case for the first time. He always knew when he had their attention; their eyes froze as he brought to life a killer they now knew would undermine their lives until they found him.

"September third, 1987, Fleetwood, New York. Marjorie Lipnor leaves her two kids alone in her apartment for five minutes so she can go three flights down to the laundry room in the basement of her building. The wet clothes never make it into the dryer. Five days later, the torso of Daniel Lipnor, age six, is found in a toddler swing in a playground two towns away. Dead three hours at most. Chest covered in fresh pinpricks. The next day, Mrs. Lipnor is found wandering around Bronxville Village, naked, disoriented. She can't remember anything that happened and never recovers her memory. Fingers point at the ex-husband but he clears. Two years later, she hangs herself while her older son is at school. Case never solved."

Snow looked only mildly interested, but Geary could see the freeze in Amy's eyes.

"I'm into this twelve minutes now, Detective Cardoza," Geary said.

"Continue."

Geary picked up the fourth pile and leaned slightly forward.

"September third, 1994, Cape Cod, Massachusetts. Janice Winfrey disappears from Race Point Beach where she's spending the day with her husband and son, Chance, age seven. She goes to the ladies' room and doesn't come back. Five days later, Chance vanishes while his father's back is turned so he can use a urinal in the men's room at Bradlees at the Falmouth

Mall. Winfrey alerts store security, the store shuts down in forty seconds flat, and the boy is never found."

"I remember that." Snow leaned forward. "Every station on the Cape worked it."

"You worked on it?" Amy asked him.

Snow nodded.

"On September twelfth," Geary continued, "Chance's left arm turns up under a wharf in Woods Hole. Janice Winfrey turns up—"

"Naked," Snow said, "on a bench at the aquarium. I'll never forget it."

"Alive," Amy said.

"Sort of." Snow shook his head.

Geary put back the fourth pile, and picked up the fifth.

"September third, 2001," he said.

Amy closed her eyes. "Emily Parker disappears from the parking lot in front of Stop and Shop." She opened her eyes and looked at Geary. "This is the third day."

"That's right. She's got three children, Detective. The boys are seven and eleven."

Amy pressed the heels of her hands against her forehead. Then she looked back over at Geary. She kept her voice nice and cool. "What's on that pad of paper you're holding?"

Geary's hand flattened a crease out of the top page. "Thank you for asking, Detective Cardoza." It was the snapshot he'd formulated after his lunch with Bell and his conversations with Tom at VICAP. He'd stayed up most of the night working on it. He'd hand over the case as complete as possible, and meet Roger Bell for that game of golf later in the afternoon; he'd win that dollar bet and have the last laugh for once.

"Please, Dr. Geary, read me the profile."

Geary cleared his throat and read from the scrawl on his yellow pages. "Male, aged middle-fifties, white, educated, keeps his mind sharp with games and books, lives alone, works alone or in a field where he can call his own shots, no family or estranged from family, a psychopath with psychotic tendencies but not a full-blown psychosis. That means he can function in the world. Anal-compulsive, plans and schedules everything, keeps his appointments, probably complicates his life with more scheduling than he needs. In fact this man can't breathe if his life doesn't work like clockwork. Some kind of mother fixation, probably based on childhood abuse, probably at the hands of his mother. Why every seven years? I'm going to guess that the abuse either started or seriously escalated when he was seven years old. I'm going to guess that he committed his first crime when he was twenty-eight years old. Psychosis in white males usually blossoms into violent behavior, if it's going to at all, when they're in their late twenties. And seven factors right into twenty-eight, so I button his starting age right there. Jump up seven years, four more times, to this week, and we have a man who is now fifty-six years old. That's about the age of our Mr. White from the grocery store on Monday—"

"Bobby Robertson," Amy interrupted.

Geary's eyes riveted to her face. "You found him?"

She nodded slowly. "Go on."

"Good work, Detective."

She sloughed off the compliment. "Please continue."

Geary looked at his notes. "Why always on September third? That's hard to say. My guess is that something happened to him when he was seven years old, on the third of September. So every seven years on that date he begins the cycle of his crime. This man is trying very hard to work something out with his mother. Maybe she didn't love him enough, but he loves her. He doesn't want to kill her. He killed the first two by mistake, but he's working on perfecting the pattern, and every time he gets better at it. That's why the last two mothers survived, at least he didn't kill them himself. One killed herself, and the other one was committed to Taunton State pretty soon after they found her."

Amy nodded and made a note.

"His goal is to keep the mothers alive, but to leave them destroyed. He always kills the children by dismembering them and presenting one of their body parts for discovery. He's taunting us, giving us a puzzle in the form of a body, one section at a time. He has two more crimes planned. He's doing the first of those two right now, but he wants us to stop him. He recognizes what he's doing is barbaric, but he can't stop himself."

"But he waits seven years between each one," Amy said. "How does he live with himself if he has any real consciousness of what he's doing?"

"That's the trick," Geary said. "We call it restitution, psychic erasure."

"He actually forgets what he's done? That's hard to believe."

"Sure is. But so are his actions. The minds of these people swing to wild extremes, Detective. They find a path inside themselves to act on aberrant impulses, and when they're finished, they shut down that path. For them it's like taking a vacation to an exotic place, but as soon as they're home, the experience fades away. During the in-between times, they save up subconsciously for their next trip."

Snow, who had been listening quietly, sucked in some air like he'd just remembered to breathe.

"His personality is organized," Geary continued, "his life is organized, and his crimes are highly organized. He's the most organized repeater I've ever seen. This man abducts people from common places in broad daylight, and he does not leave a single clue. Except once, in Woods Hole, a footprint. But there must be a hundred thousand brand-new size-twelve Nikes out there. Only if we catch him—"

"When we catch him," Amy said firmly.

"When we catch him, we'll have the footprint to link him to at least one crime. He's also repeating his fifth crime in the same state as the last, which breaks his pattern. It puts the two most recent incidents in the same jurisdiction, which makes it easier for us to link them, and once we do that, we can tie up all five, because the pattern fits perfectly."

"Bobby Robertson." Amy shook her head.

"Do you have a tail on him?" Geary asked.

"Oh yes." She turned to Snow. "Al, get Chief Kaminer."

Snow took the order and left the room.

"I see the Sarge partnered you up with the department hotshot." Geary winked.

"I can handle it."

"Yup. I can see that too."

"We need to get the state and the feds in on this," Amy said in that stiff tone of hers that was starting to sound like good training to Geary's ears. "We only have two more days."

"Maybe," Geary said.

"What do you mean?"

"I have a feeling the newspaper might scare him, one way or another, but it'll have some kind of effect, whether it pushes him down or pulls him out. That means he might not act at all, or he might act sooner."

"Dr. Geary, you know as well as I do that once the

feds get here, the media's going to be all over this. We'll use it to our advantage." She nodded decisively. "More witnesses, more leads."

"Yes and no, Detective. If it drives him underground, he might not try for the kid, but I'll wager he'll kill Mrs. Parker."

"It's a gamble, then," Amy said. "There isn't much choice."

Snow returned to the room with Kaminer, a small, tight man with curly blond hair that didn't look fully real. But despite the nonsense on his head, Geary could tell by the way Kaminer looked at him head-on that he meant business.

"I hear you've done some homework, Dr. Geary," Kaminer said.

Geary laid it out for Kaminer, who sopped it up like a dry sponge, nodding every few seconds. Meanwhile, Amy worked the phone, checking up on her leads and typing fast into the computer as she talked. When the front desk transferred in a call for Amy, she was on the other line, and Snow took it for her.

Amy slammed down the phone and spun around. "Robertson stayed home all night but he left the house five minutes ago. He's driving south on 28. They're right behind him."

"Update me," Kaminer said.

She filled him in on Bobby Robertson, aka. Mr. White number one. "I got an interesting call back this morning from the State Psychiatric Outpatient Clinic up Cape. They have a Robert R. Robertson who's been coming in for outpatient services twice a week for three years, mandated by the courts. They caught him shoplifting from a kids' clothing store and found out he had a record but no convictions. He's kept all his appointments at the clinic. I've got the name of his caseworker, Sally Harmon. I already put a call in to her."

"Find her."

"Yes, sir."

Kaminer turned to look at Snow, who shifted in his chair to demonstrate that he had the phone pressed to his ear. He appeared to be on hold. Still, Kaminer pulled back a smirk, like he'd caught Snow doing nothing. Either someone came back on Snow's line just at the magic moment, or he acted like it, because he started nodding and uh-huhing and then he snapped, "Hold on." He shouldered the receiver and spoke to Amy. "What was the name of that car dealer?"

"Sal Ragnatelli."

Snow's face seemed to gather in the middle like someone had pulled a string inside his head.

"When?" he asked the caller. Then he hung up the phone. "Well, Amy, you got your call back from Ragnatelli's beeper."

"That was him?" She looked annoyed.

"That was Detective Martino up in Fall River, returning all the calls on Ragnatelli's beeper. He's dead."

"What?" Amy stood up. "When?"

"Sometime yesterday. They found him in front of a textile factory off Main Street, propped up like he was sitting. People saw him the night before but they thought he was homeless."

"Cause of death?" Kaminer asked.

"Stabbed in the back numerous times. He was sitting in a lot of blood, but no one saw it until the morning."

Kaminer looked at Amy. "Does this tie in to your missing persons?"

"Yes, sir, it might. Ragnatelli was a vintage car dealer, one of his vehicles was seen driving out of the Stop and Shop parking lot at the time Mrs. Parker disappeared. It was reported to be driven by an older gentleman with white hair, and it was reported that there was a female passenger with blond hair."

"Mrs. Parker's a blonde?" Kaminer asked.

"Yes, sir. Another car was seen leaving the parking lot at about the same time, also with a white-haired driver, also with a blond female passenger. This second car belongs to Robertson, sir. But he's been home. Caruso and Miles have been watching him."

"So he couldn't have gotten to Fall River," Kaminer said.

"No, sir."

"What about your other Mr. White, number two?"

"We haven't found him, Chief. If he killed Ragnatelli, my question is why? It would break his pattern, and if you believe Dr. Geary's profile, this man wouldn't do that."

"Unless something scared him," Kaminer said.

"He doesn't sound like someone who could get scared," Snow put in.

Geary shook his head. "Everyone's scared of something."

"By the way, Detective Cardoza, your warrants just came in, both of them."

"Excellent, sir. Thank you."

"I'll give you backup for Robertson's house. You going to exercise that second warrant for Gooseberry Way?"

Geary's ears perked up. "The Parker home?"

Amy said, "I want to take a closer look, just routine. Well, more than that. There was a rolled-up rug I want a look at. So—"

"Detective," Geary interrupted, "you'll be wasting your time."

Amy looked a little sorry when she said to him, "Will Parker hired you, Doctor. I don't think you're in a position to defend him."

"You're working for him?" Kaminer's eyebrows squeezed together into a minus sign.

Geary shook his head. "He's not paying me. I offered my services gratis."

"Why?" Kaminer asked.

"My book on cold cases, Chief. That's all I was interested in when I started this."

"But not now," Amy said.

Geary felt a pinch of disappointment that she doubted him. He was surprised at himself; maybe Bell was right, and he cared more than he had realized. Cared in the compulsive way that used to keep him late at work; that drove him to refine his search for human potential on both sides of the coin; drove him to the top of his field until age mandated that he stop. So maybe Bell was right and he couldn't stop; maybe he was out of the job but still in the work.

"I like this family," Geary said, and knew at that moment he'd lost the bet. "I want to find Emily Parker before our latest flavor psycho finds her son."

"I'll hire you as a consultant and put you on this case," Kaminer told Geary like it was a reprimand. "You can't work for Parker and for us, pay or no pay. Are your papers in order?"

"Should be on file at headquarters in D.C. I was a top-ranking special agent, Chief."

Kaminer eyed him keenly. "I know your history, Dr. Geary. Here you'll rank as detective with the Mashpee Police. Nothing fancier than that."

Geary swallowed his own crow. "Thank you, *sir*.

Now that I work here, can I make a recommendation?"

"Fast."

"Let me bring Will Parker in here for an interview, I'm convinced the family's not involved, and if we clear him quickly we'll save time. I can get Dr. Roger Bell in to corroborate. He'll be on the Cape a few more days."

"*The* Roger Bell?" Kaminer looked mildly impressed at the name of the famous criminologist.

"Known him for years. He consulted for the Behavioral Science Unit. Full disclosure: I already ran this case by him. He's already familiar with it."

"And he helped peg our repeater?"

"We worked up the seeds of my profile together."

"I hope he doesn't expect to get paid by us," Kaminer snapped. "We don't have a budget like the FBI."

"No, sir. He's in it out of habit, like me."

"Fine, do it. I'll sit in." Kaminer turned to Amy and Snow. "Amy, you take the warrant and some backup to Robertson's. Check it out."

"One more thing, sir."

Kaminer snapped his fingers and rotated his hand to get Amy talking faster. That was a move Geary had never seen before.

"I'd like to interview the surviving mother, Janice Winfrey."

"*After* you sit in on the interview with the husband and *after* you talk to the Harmon woman." Kaminer looked over and Geary thought the little man's eyes twinkled, though with humor or challenge, he wasn't sure. A fissure of a smile cracked his face. "Take Geary with you to meet Janice Winfrey—see what our new resident FBI shrink can make of it. Matter of fact, take him on the Robertson warrant too. You can use Snow's car."

"My car?" Snow asked.

"You're going to Fall River. Hook up with the detective running the case—Martino? I'll call ahead. Use the patrol car out front. I want frequent reports, so take notes."

Geary burped down a little chuckle. He hadn't meant to replace Snow, but it sure felt satisfying. He smiled at Amy and reached for the phone on the desk behind him.

"Got a golf appointment to cancel for this afternoon."

Chapter 16

Amy Cardoza turned onto Squaws Lane and parked two houses down from the beach. They would wait here until the backup arrived. She picked at the tape that held the photo of Snow's teenage daughter to the dashboard, trying to peel it off, and trying not to. It wasn't officially her car yet.

"Nice neighborhood." Geary sat beside her in the passenger seat. He flicked the tree-shaped deodorizer hanging from the rearview mirror and it swung hard in Amy's direction, emitting a puff of pine fragrance. "Funny, though."

So he saw it too: the modest house in the fancy location. She was starting to like him.

"Real estate." She shook her head.

"What I don't get is how the ocean can belong to anyone."

"I think it's just the beach," she said, "and the view." She looked through the windshield at the blue sky and wind-frothed ocean. This was what she loved about the Cape, these pockets of tranquility she fell into when she wasn't looking.

Geary's body swiveled quickly in her direction, startling her. "You have that phone of yours?"

"My cell phone? Of course." She pulled it out of her purse and handed it to him. He knew to flip it open, but that was all. "You're kidding. Don't you . . . ? Never mind, here, dial your number with the area code but not the one. Then push send."

She watched as he read a handwritten phone number off the back of Will Parker's business card; his thick forefinger carefully pressed one button at a time before referring back to the card. When he was through, he flashed her a smile and winked.

"Will!"

Amy watched unease spread through Geary's expression as he listened. "Why the hospital?" He paused. "We wanted to see you today—" Another pause, but this time the spirit sprung back into his face. "The cops *we,* that's who. They're hiring me, son of a gun, so now I'm working for you on the taxpayer's buck!"

He laughed quietly to himself as he flipped shut the phone, though Amy knew his amusement was mostly for her benefit.

"What's going on?"

Geary turned to her and spoke seriously for a change. "His baby girl's in the hospital."

"Why?"

"Just an ear infection that got out of hand. It's not about this."

"How do you know that?" She heard her tone sharpen, and registered Geary's dissatisfaction as he sat hard into the bucket seat.

"You're making a mistake," he said. "Will Parker isn't involved in his wife's disappearance. You've met him. He's a nice guy. He's got family coming to take his kids off the island. No way is he going to hurt them."

She looked at Geary, his rumpled face, wild white

hair, unclean clothes. "Don't try to tell me you haven't seen worse than that."

He smiled and a band of silver shone on the left side of his lower gum. "You got me there, missy." He seemed to catch himself, and his smile dropped away. "Looking at the history of these crimes, it just doesn't jibe. Never has. Won't this time, either. You'll be wasting your time in their house. You'll be wasting Emily Parker's time."

"I've got the warrant," Amy said, "and I don't see why I shouldn't use it, just to make sure. I don't think taking shortcuts and working on assumptions is the way to go."

"You learn to take shortcuts."

"I haven't."

"You will."

The breezy quiet evaporated in the crush of three squad cars pulling into Squaws Lane, wheeling past them and stopping in front of number two. Amy put their car in gear, drove up behind them, parked and got out.

Sand was blowing everywhere. Amy raised a hand to shield her eyes and evaluated. She had six uniformed men. Kaminer had given her Petersen, Shechter, Partow, Sagredo, Graves and Landberg—the most seasoned patrol officers he had. And he had given her Geary, who regardless of anything else had more experience in crime investigation than all of them put together. Counting herself that was eight cops with a collective spectrum of skills that ran from hot to cold, she being the coldest yet the one who would give the orders. Kaminer must have been having himself quite a field day. If Robertson came home and things got out of control, the big question would be whether she would run the show or the show would run her. Or maybe her cadre of veteran cops would just run circles around her, giving Kaminer a good yarn to spin until he segued into retirement.

Or maybe Kaminer actually believed in her.

She gave the officers a quick rundown of what they were looking for and sent Graves and Landberg to watch the back of the house. Then she walked up to the front door and rang the bell. Waited. Opened the screen door and knocked, hard. Waited again. She opened her purse, took out her wallet, and removed a credit card. Geary issued one of his chuckles, which Amy was learning had the effect of a sibling poking you in your weak spot, begging for reaction. She kept her cool and bent down to see the lock.

"Fast learner," he said.

"I don't see any reason to damage his door."

"That's not what I meant, Detective."

She slid the card expertly past the lock mechanism and it popped. The door opened and she stepped inside. Sagredo stepped in next to her, gun drawn, and shouted, "Police!"

The other officers fanned out through the living room. Partow and Sagredo scuttled down a hall, and Petersen and Shechter moved toward what appeared to be the kitchen. The house was quiet except for the swish of the waves out on the beach and the soft thudding footsteps of the officers.

"I have a warrant!" Amy held it in her hand. "We're coming in!"

"Who are you talking to?" Geary asked her. "There's no one here but us."

"You're cute," she said.

He winked. "Just following procedure?"

"You bet."

The room was as white as the man. Walls, furniture, bookcases, carpet—all white and pristine. Bobby Robertson must have spent all his time cleaning, whatever

time he had left over from his other pursuits. The
bookcase Amy had noticed yesterday extended along
the wall and was neatly lined with a collection of
books on one side and small boxes on the other. A
small, old television set and a new VCR sat on a white
metal filing cabinet across from a futon couch covered
in . . . white. The furniture was all either cheap or old
or both. There was no clutter. A putty-colored computer sat on a white metal cart by the kitchen door.

"In here!" Partow's voice ricocheted from down
the hall.

Amy and Geary followed the voice to Bobby Robertson's bedroom.

A single bed was pushed up against the wall. Next
to it was a small bedside table with a lamp on it,
Across the room was a dresser. It was almost like the
room of a child, simple and unpretentious, except
there was nothing on the walls and every surface was
bare. A dozen white oxford shirts hung equidistantly
in a closet without a door.

Partow was kneeling next to the bed, holding up
the white bedspread like he was pulling the hem of a
skirt out of a mud puddle. His expression looked as
disgusted as if he'd just stepped in the mud, or worse,
with bare feet. In front of him was an open plastic
box, designed flat to slide under a bed.

Amy stood over the box and saw it right away. Hundreds of photographs of children. Dressed in play
clothes, dressed in costumes, half undressed, naked.
Every child in every picture looked terrified. Crying.
Faces stiff and cracking into fear. Eyes squeezed shut.
Eyes frozen open. Bodies straight as soldiers, holding
their breath. Bodies contorted, in the hot middle of pain.

"All somebody's baby," she whispered. "Every
one."

Geary stood next to her, looking down. He shook his head and said nothing.

There was commotion from the living room.

"Tag it," she told Partow as they turned toward the noise. "We're bringing it in."

Officer Petersen was taking the small boxes down off the bookshelf, opening them, setting aside the ones filled with videotapes. And there were many. Officer Shechter was standing in front of the TV, his back turned to the horrifying image on the screen. It was a snuff film, starring the saddest little boy Amy had ever seen in her life. Shechter's eyes were wet, his mouth taut against more reaction than his dignity could contain.

"Oh my God." Amy stopped walking. "Are there more?"

Petersen nodded slowly.

"We're taking them all. We're watching every inch of those, and the minute we find him, he's a dead man."

She braced herself against the steep climb of rage she felt toward this animal who could entertain himself with the destruction of children. She looked at Geary, who stood beside her. He'd gone ashen.

Amy took her cell phone out of her purse and speed-dialed dispatch. "Buzz Caruso and Miles, tell them he's our man, but to keep following him. Tell them to keep a tight circle on him, and if they think he's leading them to Mrs. Parker, call for support." She hung up but held her phone in her hand as the tape played a close-up of the child screaming, the lens tightening.

"Turn it off," Geary said.

Amy felt her blood racing through muscle, skin tightening against the surge, a swelling behind her eyes. It was as if her body was refusing the offerings of her mind. "Tag it all," she said, "and keep looking."

"You're doing good work." Geary hunched his shoulders and stepped toward her, a little paternally she thought, but it had the calming effect of a protective gesture.

"If this is good work—" She was stopped by the bleating of her cell phone.

"Detective Cardoza?" The woman's voice was sonorous and warm. "I'm returning your call. This is Sally Harmon."

"Yes, Ms. Harmon."

Geary's eyebrows twitched. Amy raised her chin to the door, and he winked; he would stay inside to supervise so she could take the call outside.

Walking out into the sun and the air and the sand-encrusted wind was a relief from the darkness of all that white. Her long hair slapped against her face and she angled herself away from the ocean.

"The message says you're calling me in connection with Bobby Robertson?"

"Your client's in serious trouble, Ms. Harmon."

There was a pause.

"For what?"

It sounded a little rhetorical to Amy.

"You're his caseworker?" she asked Harmon.

"I've been his caseworker for three years. He's been rehabilitating well."

"I'm at his house," Amy said, "and I wouldn't agree."

Fifteen minutes later, as the officers continued their search of the house, attic and basement, and carried archives of child pornography to their trunks, Sally Harmon's powder blue Hyundai ground to a stop in front of 2 Squaws Lane. The door opened and out stepped a woman with bleached blond hair teased around her face. She wore pink lipstick, blue eye shadow and false lashes. Her brown penciled eyebrows were drawn in an ironic arch. She looked worried, but when she saw Amy she managed what appeared to be a smile.

"Sally Harmon." She shook Amy's hand and a gold charm bracelet jangled on her wrist.

"Detective Amy Cardoza," she introduced herself. "This is Dr. John Geary, my partner."

Geary's glance was half surprise, half smile, half thank-you. She hoped her decision to trust him added up better than had her first impression, which had been less than a hundred percent.

Sally turned to look at the beach. "Bobby has a gorgeous view." She shook her head. "He was doing so well."

Amy described the trove of material they'd found in his house. "Does that sound like rehabilitation?" she asked.

Sally considered the question. "I know it sounds horrible, but it's not as off target as it looks to you. We know we can't change the core of these people. We just aim to change their behavior. Has Bobby committed a crime?" Her face seemed to darken as she waited for the answer.

"If he's trafficking on the Internet, yes," Amy said. "We've seized his computer but there's more. A woman is missing. It fits into a larger picture, going back years."

Sally's expression lightened. "A woman? He's terrified of women. He wouldn't touch one if his life depended on it. That's partly what we work on in our sessions."

"He wouldn't necessarily tell you everything," Geary said, "would he?" He looked at Sally critically, as if trying to see under the makeup and the hair.

"I suppose I can't really know," Sally said. "But I've been seeing him twice a week for three years. I doubt he's capable of overpowering an adult."

"Just a child?" Amy said sharply.

Sally Harmon's face pinched around the mouth.

"Do you always shop with Bobby?" Geary asked.

Sally nodded her head. "Sometimes. It's part of the therapy."

"You were seen arguing with him at the store," Amy said.

Sally thought back. "That's the woman? Ash-blond hair, lovely smile?"

"You remember her," Geary said. "Did you see him with her?"

"They were picking through the corn bin at the same time. Her bracelet fell in and I returned it to her." She shook her wrist to rattle her charm bracelet. "Hers was silver."

"Bobby was behind her at the checkout. What were you arguing about, Ms. Harmon?" Amy noticed that Sally Harmon's teased hair barely flinched in the wind.

"I told him he'd bought too much corn, just because it was on sale. We've been working on his flexibility."

"That's it?" Amy asked.

"Pretty boring, huh?"

"No," Geary said, "I wouldn't say that."

A wave snarled onto the shore so fiercely it captivated Sally's attention. After a second she looked back at Geary and narrowed her eyes. "He's a sick man, I grant you, but he isn't capable of taking a grown woman against her will. I was with him that day. We drove back to the clinic together and he dropped me off. So you see?"

"Did he stay, or did he leave immediately?" Amy asked.

"He left."

"How far is your office from the grocery store, Ms. Harmon?"

Sally Harmon looked at Amy a moment before answering. "Three or four minutes."

"That's plenty of time for Emily to load her trunk, John, don't you think?"

Chapter 17

Bobby Robertson fit the profile but Geary knew it was rarely that easy.

"We've got no evidence," he told Amy as she drove them back to the station.

"We've got the pictures, we've got the tapes. When they check out his hard drive we'll probably have more."

"Circumstantial. It's not enough."

"We'll get him. If we could get his car into forensics, we'd have him cold. But he'll lead us to Emily Parker before we have his car, so it'll be homework by then, dotting the i's—"

"Crossing the t's, yeah yeah yeah."

She cast him one of her razor-sharp glances and he toned it down.

"If he leads us to Emily, and if we find her alive, then it's easy. But what if he doesn't?"

She pulled into a parking spot by the back entrance. "He will."

"Maybe. There's something bothering me, though." Geary liberated himself from his seat belt and got out of the car. Amy slammed shut her door and faced him over the hood.

"What?"

"I don't know," he said. "Something."

One of Bell's comments over lunch kept ringing: "Professional, certainly. He has the facility to hide his victims and control when and where he presents them. That takes not only ingenuity, but means."

Geary agreed with this assessment. But as far as he could see, Bobby Robertson was a professional basket case and whatever means he had probably came from the state. The man was a crazy salad of nerve and nervousness that did not sit well in Geary's stomach.

"You're right," she said. "We should keep our options open."

She opened her door, leaned in and jabbed a button on the console to radio dispatch, even though they were right behind her through that brick wall. A voice answered, scratching the air with codes followed by a plain vanilla hello.

"Buzz Landberg and Graves," Amy told the voice. "Tell them to head over to eighteen Gooseberry Way. Tell forensics to meet them. If no one's home, tell them to get into the garage and tag a rolled-up rug in the left corner by the automatic door. If someone's home, tell them to wait, and I'll come right over with the warrant. I've got it with me."

She ended the call and shut her car door in one swift action. "Happy now?"

"*Happy*'s not the word. Neither is *impressed*. You've got the right idea but it's the wrong option."

"So where else do we look then?"

Geary shook his head. There was nothing worse than pitching a tent on wet sand. No foundations and no support.

"I'm reporting in to the boss," she said. "Coming?"

On the way down the hall, Amy poked her head into the dispatch office. "You reach them?"

They must have said yes, because her dark features

clouded over with that determined look he was getting
to know so well. She snaked through the hall and
turned into the front lobby to collect her phone messages. Funny, Geary thought, that they were all rigged
up with cell phones and beepers on top of all the high-
tech gear in the patrol cruisers, but they still used
those pink message slips instead of voice mail. It was
a damn good thing, too, because he would have drawn
the line right there and told Kaminer to keep his name
off the payroll; he would have kept on cowboying the
case instead. Voice mail. Like traveling blind through
a maze, turning and turning and never reaching the
destination of a human voice.

Amy reached her hand through the slot opening in
the Plexiglas divider, then lifted her eyes to Suellen
at the front desk and froze on something. Geary came
up behind her and saw what. Sitting at either side of
Suellen, like assistant receptionists, were the two Parker boys. They were wearing police hats on their
heads and badges on their T-shirts. They were playing cards.

"Hello?" Amy's breath fogged the Plexiglas. "What's
this?"

Geary winked at the boys. The little one waved and
the big one just stared. He wondered why they were
still here; where was that sister of Parker's?

"They're sitting with me while their dad's meeting
with the chief." Suellen looked like a grandma in her
element. She made Geary think of Ruth again; she
would have made a fine grandma, but for that you
needed kids of your own. He pushed that old disappointment back down.

"Where?" Amy asked.

"His office."

Geary followed Amy as she turned back into the
hallway, left then right then left again, and came to a

door at the end with the seal of the State of Massachusetts like a target dead in the center. She knocked
briskly.

The door swung open at Kaminer's hand. Roger
Bell and Will Parker sat next to each other on two of
the visitors' chairs facing Kaminer's big wooden desk.
They pivoted toward the door at the same time. Bell
nodded at Geary. Green short-sleeved shirt, green eye
patch. Classic Bell.

Geary looked at Will, who lifted his chin in greeting.
"Saw your boys out front."

"My sister's out of the country. I've got friends on
their way up." Will turned to Kaminer. "I'm trying to
get the boys off the island."

"Good idea," Kaminer said.

"How's the baby?" Geary asked.

"Doctor says she'll be fine. I'll have to keep her
with me."

"That shouldn't be a problem," Bell said. "He's
only really interested in the boys."

Will's eyes rested a moment on Bell, as if he were
unable, or unwilling, to process that simple statement.

"Well, boss, time's wasting." Geary slapped Kaminer on the shoulder, went straight over to Bell and
Parker and sat in the one free chair.

Kaminer stood there, shaking his head so his fluffy
blond hair bounced. "I'm not your boss *yet*." He
turned to Amy. "Update, please." He marched around
his desk and sat down in his high-backed executive
chair.

She was the only one standing. Will Parker stood
up and offered her his seat. Geary noticed the way
she rebuffed the offer: stoically, with one quick shake
of her head. But he also noticed that her eyes settled
on Will just long enough to get a good look at the
only man in the room tired enough to deserve a seat

and civilized enough to give it away. Parker stayed on his feet and the chair stayed empty.

Amy glanced at Parker, then at Kaminer. "Sir?"

"He can stay," Kaminer said.

"But—"

His eyes flashed at her. So he'd made up his mind to wield his signature double-edged sword: he'd simultaneously trust Parker and encourage Amy to investigate him. Kaminer's strange sense of irony was starting to grate, but he was the boss.

Amy launched into an account of their search of Bobby Robertson's house. Kaminer, Bell and Parker listened carefully.

"What about the Harmon woman?" Kaminer asked.

"I told her to leave Robertson alone. I told her if she did anything to scare him off leading us to Mrs. Parker, we'd book her for hampering an investigation."

"They're following him now?" A flicker of reprieve passed over Will's exhausted face. Geary could see Will's mind working the possibilities around his hopes: Robertson leading the police directly and neatly to Emily.

"Right now," Amy answered.

Geary shook his head. Bell was watching him, waiting. Geary could feel his old friend's agreement before he even spoke.

"It's not sitting with me," Geary said. "I don't think we should shut down because Robertson's a pervert and he's got the right color hair. I'm not convinced he fits the profile enough."

Kaminer's head tilted back. "Speak."

That momentarily stalled Geary, because he *was* speaking.

Bell jumped into the bubble. "Your Mr. Robertson is a suspect to be taken seriously, yes. But I must say,

I share Dr. Geary's feeling. It's often a mistake to accept the first answer. Foregone conclusions often mislead. Would you agree, Mr. Parker?"

Will looked surprised to be addressed by Bell. "I suppose so."

Bell took the opportunity to rest his gaze on Will in a way that would have seemed inappropriate without having engaged him first. Smart move. Bell didn't really care about Will's answer. Geary wondered how long they'd been sitting there before he and Amy showed up; he wondered what that conversation had been. He'd seen Bell in action a hundred times, and his gut told him Will had already passed the test.

Kaminer leaned forward and his elbows dug into a mess of papers on his desk. "Here's the plan. I've got the state and the feds on their way. We're going to work with them, no turf battles, there's too much at stake. And I'm posting someone at the top of Gooseberry Way. We want to know who goes in and out. And I'm relieving Caruso and Miles, they need some sleep. I'm putting Petersen and Shechter on Robertson's tail."

Good, Geary thought; they'd seen Robertson's collected works of pedophilia and would watch him like starving hawks.

"You two"—Kaminer fixed his eyes on Amy, and Geary assumed he was the other part of the pair—"get up to Taunton, talk to the mother who survived."

"Excellent choice." Bell pursed his lips under his tightly trimmed goatee. "The question will be how much her mind is capable of remembering."

Taunton State Hospital sat like a derelict castle on a massive green lawn at the end of a long private drive. As they drove slowly toward the parking lot, Geary noticed a sallow-skinned young man tilted at the curb, watching them like their Chevy was an alien ship that had just entered his territory. The young man waited for the spaceship to float past him, like the good boy he had probably been, learning all his traffic rules by rote, before the monster entered his mind and transported him elsewhere. Geary and Amy didn't mention it; they parked the car in silence and walked onto the lawn. Geary could see that Amy was avoiding eye contact with the patients, like the one sitting cross-legged on the grass, rocking like an anchorless boat, vacant eyes suspended on an approaching storm or maybe a departing pirate. Geary wondered if his partner had learned that trick of avoidance in cop school: don't look them in the eyes or they might get spooked and attack. It was the opposite in his clinical psych studies: if you didn't make eye contact, you would lose them.

The inside of the building was all cold, hard surfaces: stone and concrete, metal and glass. Some doors were manacled, others not. The only sign was the single word VISITORS, with an arrow pointing to the left. They followed it through a swinging door into a long hallway.

"What now?" Amy didn't look too thrilled to be there.

"Follow the yellow brick road, I guess."

Gritty sunlight pooled on the worn stone floor. They passed door after unmarked door, until finally they saw it again: VISITORS.

"Makes you feel really welcome, doesn't it?" Amy said as she pushed open the door.

The room was empty except for a gray metal desk on which sat a computer. There it was again, VISITORS, blinking in the middle of the screen. There was no mouse or keyboard. They approached the computer, glanced at each other, and simultaneously reached out their fingers to touch the word. A screen appeared with a touch keyboard, and instructions to spell the name of the person they wished to see. Amy took the honors, touching W-I-N-F-R-E-Y, J-A-N-I-C-E. ENTER. Another screen flashed on, reading *Janice Winfrey, 5th floor, See Nurses Desk.*

"Okay then!" Geary clapped his hands, once, and an echo coiled into the unnatural quiet.

"Shh!" Amy hissed. She looked like Alice on her way through the looking-glass, wondering if it was just a dream or she had accidentally joined the ranks of the hospital's lawn people.

Geary put his arm through hers. "Come, dear, we'll take you right to admitting. Don't be afraid. The rabbit *is* real, but he's friendly."

Amy jerked her arm out of his and tried to scowl, but a grin arched the corners of her mouth instead.

They found the elevator and traveled up to the fifth floor. When the doors scrolled open, they were met with an odd tableau of faces framed in a window in the top half of a door. About ten people were pressed together, apparently waiting to be let into the tiny foyer separating the elevator from the ward. They were obviously patients, so heavily medicated a few didn't respond to the sight of visitors coming out of the elevator. Others did, and Geary saw curiosity and apprehension spark in some faces. One of the patients looked more present than the rest, with healthy skin tone and lucid eyes, and for a split second Geary had the feeling he'd seen that face before on someone, anyone, everyone, a face waiting for an elevator at work at the end of another day, except that he clutched a Bible so hard his knuckles were white.

A tall nurse in an ordinary white uniform walked briskly to the door with a set of keys in her hand. She said something that evoked eager nodding, then turned and unlocked the door. Geary and Amy pressed themselves against the wall to make room as the patients flooded into the foyer.

"Can I help you?" the nurse asked so brightly it seemed out of context.

"We're visitors," Geary said.

The smile didn't flinch. "And who are you visiting?"

"Janice Winfrey."

The smile dropped and her eyebrows lifted. "Oh? She hasn't had a visitor in years. And you are?"

The patients had packed themselves into the elevator. The nurse's foot was wedged against the door, keeping it open.

"Friends," Amy said.

"Oh?" She obviously didn't believe them. "Well, why not? Maybe *you* can get through to poor Janice. Down the hall to the right. Tell Nancy at the desk you saw me." Her hard red fingernail tapped the name tag below her left shoulder: MARGARET NELSON. "I'll be back in twenty minutes. We're going out on a grounds pass." She smiled at her crew in the elevator, and they nodded and twitched in anticipation of their excursion.

Nancy at the desk barely looked up at them. When she heard that Margaret Nelson had okayed their visit on her way to the outside world, she shrugged her shoulders, took a key off a peg board marked only by numbers, and muttered, "Follow me."

They were led to room 513. Nancy unlocked the door, pushed it all the way open and walked away.

Seated in a shabby green chair in a corner of a room with two single beds but only one dresser was the woman who had once been Janice Winfrey. She faced the window, but her expression was blank, not absorbing the summer afternoon, or the other patients milling on the lawn, or the cadre of her fifth-floor neighbors lucky enough to be out on the grounds with Margaret Nelson as their tour guide. Whatever Janice Winfrey saw, it was not outside her eyes, and it was not inside this moment.

She was a small, fine-boned woman with light brown skin. Her hair was cut in a quarter-inch bowl around her skull, nearly shaved, with just enough left to stop her from looking like an inmate. She wore a bright orange flowered housedress you could have bought at the five-and-dime, a far cry from what she must have worn in better days: a tailored dress, Geary decided, pale blue, a string of pearls on her fragile neck.

Amy approached her first. "Mrs. Winfrey?"

Janice didn't react.

"Mrs. Winfrey, I'm Amy Cardoza. This is Dr. Geary."

"John," he said. "Is it all right if we come in?"

She could have been a wax statue.

Geary had seen people like this, in a kind of living coma that locked them outside their minds but inside their pain. It was like the opposite of amnesia, where instead of forgetting they'd get lost in a flood of memory; a hatch got stuck open, and they endlessly drowned in their trauma but never died. Crippling, but not killing. It must have been a living hell; he could only begin to imagine it.

It was a long shot, but he decided to try to connect with her. He approached her slowly, kneeling in front of her so their faces were level. He looked into her eyes; they were like marbles, empty jewels. Up close he could see that her skin was covered with the creased fissures that would eventually deepen into age. She was only in her thirties, but she seemed a thousand years old. Amy stood back a good five feet, watching. When Geary reached out, he could see Amy at the edge of his vision, shaking her head. He did it anyway, touching Janice's hand as gently as he could.

Janice's eyes·blinked, only once, but it was a sign of reaction.

Amy took a step closer.

Geary breathed deeply and watched the eyes. "We were hoping to talk to you," he said, "about Chance."

Janice's eyes slammed shut. Her lips tensed.

"Back off," Amy whispered. "You're scaring her."

Geary pulled his hand away, but stayed close, still kneeling in front of her.

"There's another woman," Geary whispered, "a mother, like you. She disappeared. She has children."

Janice had refrozen. There was not a flicker of anything, anywhere on her.

Geary felt Amy's hand clamp down on his shoulder. Her eyes were brown, he now noticed, like Janice Winfrey's, but alive. Amy gripped his shoulder and her eyes begged him to stop. There was a tenderness in her face that upset him, and he didn't know why. She shook her head.

"She wants to," Geary said, "but she can't."

Margaret Nelson appeared in the doorway, smiling. "You see?" she said. "Nothing. She's been here almost seven years, and she's never spoken, not once."

The patients they saw on the way out, the ones with grounds passes that gave them the chance to sway and rock and talk to figments of their imaginations in the fresh outside air, seemed lucky compared to Janice Winfrey.

They didn't say a word until they were back in the car. Amy put her hands on the steering wheel and her forehead on her hands. "What does he do to them?"

"That's the question." Geary rolled down his window and waved at a young woman whose head bobbed in rhythm with her feet as she walked. She synchronized her hand to wave back in tempo.

Amy steered the car away from the hospital grounds

and to the road that fed them onto the highway. The air-conditioning was on but Geary kept his window open so he could feel the rush of air and hear the whiz of traffic. Amy didn't object. She must have felt it too: relief, just to be out of there.

They were over the bridge and back onto the Cape when her phone started to ring. She reached into the space between their bucket seats and dug her hand into her brown leather purse. He wondered what was in there; it always took her a full twenty seconds to find that phone. And here she was, driving.

She answered, and listened. Her eyes stayed on the road but Geary didn't like it. He didn't like being the passenger in a car when the driver was doing more than driving, and he didn't like the look of surprise on her face.

"When?" she said, then listened again. "Is that a confirmation?"

She tossed the phone back into her purse without looking.

"Emily Parker's hair," Amy said. "Forensics matched a sample found in the car to a sample from her hairbrush."

Geary didn't get it; how did they find hair in Robertson's car if he hadn't been picked up? "I thought we were going to wait, see if he led us to her."

Amy sped up as they approached their exit from Route 28 onto 151.

"You're over the speed limit." Geary chuckled, but she didn't slow down.

"It wasn't his car," she said. "It was the 'forty-seven Ford."

The one they'd had impounded from Ragnatelli's Vintage Automobiles, after Ragnatelli turned up dead.

"So it wasn't Robertson—"

"There's more."

Amy veered onto their exit. Geary held on to the dash so he wouldn't spill into her lap.

"CLIS turned up something in its database."

The Criminalistics Laboratory Information System, the FBI's scientific reference. Geary had used it often.

"Traces of pancuronium were found in Marjorie Lipnor's blood."

"It had to be a fresh sample," Geary said. "It doesn't last long in the bloodstream. It would have been gone by the time she killed herself."

"There were traces noted from the initial samples, from right after they found her. CLIS crossed it with everything else found in the other cases, what little there was. Terry McDaniel's blood showed traces of pancuronium too."

"But she was found dead, and pancuronium doesn't kill you." Then Geary understood something. "It's a muscle inhibitor. It freezes the body temporarily, but not the mind."

Amy squeezed her eyes nearly shut, as if trying to block the image but not the road.

Chapter 18

Emily felt nothing but the subtle rocking of liquid suspension, bent past hunger, engulfed by thirst, floating in water but not of it. Naked, with no body, just a head that was an echo chamber of distorted sounds. A grinding motor. The halting of a motor, its puttering out. The scream of gulls congregating. The swish of ocean air and a reedy scrape against the boat's hull like a blade etching its way into her brain.

The sounds and the smells.

She stank. The boat stank. But she could not smell the corn man, he was so clean. He observed her and she could feel him with her hearing and her smell. She was his baby in a jar, something to be considered, then turned from in disgust. She was a thing on his floor. He considered her.

"Ignore him," Sarah said of the boy at school who hit Emily when she tried to kiss him. "He'll come around."

She was six years old, unable to ignore anyone.

She had three smooth-edged nickels in her pocket to remind herself she was better than him. She was fifteen cents richer than he was and would keep her kiss for someone who wanted it.

Three coins in the palm of her mind:

David was her work of art.

She guided Sam.

Maxi would walk any day now.

"Don't hover," Sarah said. "Let him learn for himself."

At seven Sam let her tie his sneakers, wanted her to. David tied his own at five.

"Don't hold her so much. She'll never learn to walk."

Maxi pulled herself up a chair leg, found her wobbly balance, stretched her arms and said, "Up, up, up." Emily lifted Maxi until their eyes were level. They kissed.

Footsteps, metal twisting on metal, he was hooking up his hose again.

"Never forget that I love you," Sarah said.

Footsteps and the drag of hose on the floor and the assault of ice-cold water. Emily's muscles chilled and hardened. Her blindfold soaked through. He hosed her head to toe like a dirty sidewalk.

He never spoke.

Footsteps away from her and the water stopped. He did something at what must have been a sink. Then he did something with the hose. She could see the corn man in his white jacket coiling the hose. The open and shut of a cabinet door. He had put the hose away.

Footsteps.

He dropped something soft onto the floor next to her and she could feel him lowering down, the darkness and weight of his body reducing itself to her level. He was sitting next to her on the floor. Sitting on something. A towel? Protecting his white pants? Bastard. She tried to twist her body away from him but his thick, clammy hand fell onto her waist and stopped her.

Sarah kept a studio downtown so she could paint, so she could leave Emily alone while Daddy was at the firm building his partnership and maintaining it so she could eat and have clothes and toys and so they could afford a babysitter.

"Justine will give you dinner, Emily. Don't complain."

"I *hate* Justine. I want you to stay home with me."

"I'm going to my studio. I'll be back later. Never forget that I love you."

"If you loved me, you wouldn't leave me."

"Nonsense. I love you more than anything."

Sarah's hands cupped Emily's face, soft lips planted a kiss on her forehead. Emily believed her.

His hand moved slowly across her abdomen. He put a finger into her belly button and swished it around. He flattened his hand and ran it down to her crotch, skimming the hair.

The painting showed a little girl running naked in a field of buttercups. You only saw her back. Running. In front of her, you sensed laughter.

The air in Emily's lungs turned wet and congealed. The fingers bent, but failed to probe. The hand moved down her legs.

The little girl turned around. Wrong. Not laughter.

The fingers grazed her kneecap then continued down her shin, along her instep, to her toes. He took the baby toe in two fingers and squeezed hard. Moved to the next toe, and the next, until he had systematically squeezed every one. She waited for him to repeat the bizarre exercise on her other foot but he didn't. His hand moved back up her leg, hovered over her pubic hair, then traveled up along her ribs.

"Daddy will be home in time to read to you tonight, Em, honey."

"Get into bed, Sammie, and David will read to you. I have to bathe Maxi. I'll be in to kiss you in a little while."

The palms of his hands circled her breasts like helicopters observing a forest fire. When they landed, two fingers twisted her nipple.

"Ignore him, and he won't bother you anymore."

"But it isn't fair, Mommy!"

"No, it isn't fair."

He moved on to her other nipple, pinching and twisting hard.

The recipe had been in their family for years, it wasn't written down. Heat some oil and sauté diced onions until they're clear. Cook the curry powder with the onions. Put in a chicken and dump a whole quart of plain yogurt on top. A splash of vinegar. Crush the shells of ten cardamom seeds and put the seeds into the pot. Throw in some sliced carrots and if you want, potatoes. Later add frozen peas and raisins. It was very easy. Once you learned it you could alter it over time to suit your taste.

Chapter 19

"Daddy, I want to be a police officer when I grow up!"

Sammie was still wearing the police hat, but not the badge, when they left the station house and headed down the front path toward the parking lot. David had returned his hat to Suellen, embarrassed, Will thought, at having worn it at all. He was at that age of slippage, still tugged by the delights of childhood, yet peering around the bend at his preadolescence. He still liked to play, but didn't like to admit it.

Will checked his watch: it was just past noon. They would have time to check in on Maxi at the hospital, then get back to the house to meet Charlie and Val.

"Excuse me!"

Will stopped short at the sudden voice, yanking Sam back from crossing the parking lot alone. David, two steps ahead, stopped walking and turned around to look at the man who seemed to have come out of nowhere, jogging quickly in their direction. He was in his thirties, with wavy blond hair and pale, freckled skin. He wore white pants, creased sharply down the fronts, and a tangerine Lacrosse shirt with the collar up in a style that went out with the eighties. A camera hung from a strap around his neck and he clutched a half-size spiral notebook with a pen trapped in the coil.

"Mr. Parker!"

The voice sounded familiar to Will. "Who are you?"

A smile bloomed on the pallid face as the man stopped right in front of them. "Eric Smith, *Cape Cod Times*." He presented his hand in greeting, but Will remembered the phone call too well and declined the handshake.

"Come on, boys." Will pulled Sam forward, and with David next to them started across the parking lot.

"Mr. Parker!"

Smith trotted up behind them. A car entered the parking lot and Will instinctively pulled the boys back onto the walk.

"Any news about your wife?"

Will ground his teeth and waited for the car to pass. He was about to try crossing the parking lot again when it occurred to him that the first time he rebuffed Eric Smith, on the phone, he'd paid for it in print. And he understood that if he paid, his children paid; Emily paid.

"No news," Will said.

"I understand there's a special agent from the FBI on the case."

Will hesitated. "Not really," he said. "He's retired and I've hired him privately." A small bit of misinformation, since Geary was now officially with the police, but Will wasn't sure how much it was safe to tell.

"Can you give me his name?"

Could he? Will didn't know. "That's it for now. Sorry."

"I understand, Mr. Parker. Just one more question if you don't mind."

Will did mind but clearly it didn't matter. He nodded.

"I understand that Dr. Roger Bell's been brought onto the case. Why would a celebrated criminologist be talking to the Mashpee police if this were just a missing persons?"

"It's my wife. She's not just some *missing person*—" Will stopped himself. "Listen, he's a friend of the retired agent. He summers here, I think."

"Summer people?" Smith jotted something down before he got an answer.

"I'm sorry?"

"Dr. Bell and the agent, they come here for the summer?"

"No," Will said. "I don't know. Maybe."

The front door of the police station swung open and out came Roger Bell, with a big smile on his face as if he'd just finished joking around with someone inside. When he saw Will and the boys and Eric Smith, Dr. Bell didn't miss a beat in his step or lose an inch of his smile. He just kept walking in their direction. When he got close, his hand came out like an anchor.

He greeted Smith with a laugh. "Based on your appearance, you would be the local news, I assume."

"And you are?"

Dr. Bell stepped between Will and David and draped an arm over both their shoulders. "Cheese!"

Smith didn't wait to get a name before he snapped the picture. He was a creative reporter, Will guessed, the kind who filled in the blanks later and let the editors print corrections the next day if necessary.

"Thank you." Dr. Bell pumped Smith's hand. "Now I'm afraid my friends have an appointment. If you don't mind." Bell turned around, and with an expansive gesture of both arms took David, Will and Sam with him. They crossed the parking lot together, leaving Eric Smith alone on the curb.

"Which one's your car?" Bell asked.

Will lifted his chin toward the SUV. "It's rented."

"Of course."

They came up next to the driver's side, and Dr. Bell turned to the boys. He put his hands on his thighs and leaned slightly forward. "You must be Sam. First grade or second?"

Sam grinned. "Pirates wear black eye patches, not green."

"Then perhaps I'm not a pirate."

"Take it off."

"Sammie!" Will said. "Please excuse him, Dr. Bell."

Dr. Bell eked out a smile that seemed distinctly practiced. Will assumed the man had probably endured endless comments about his eye patch, yet the bright color, that green, begged for attention.

Dr. Bell shifted his good eye to David and winked. "And that makes you David, fifteen, no?"

David tried to repress a smile.

Dr. Bell squinted his good eye. "Twenty-three?"

"Eleven," David told him.

"Ah, eleven, an interesting, transitional age."

Will found the man a little strange. He opened the back door to let Sam and David climb in, then slammed it shut.

"They're charming boys, your sons," Dr. Bell said.

"We think so."

Dr. Bell's eye narrowed as he seemed to measure Will's state of mind. "Do you trust the police to find your wife?"

"I don't have much choice, do I?"

"No." Dr. Bell shook his head. "I suppose you have not been given much choice in any of this."

"You think they're wasting their time on Robertson, don't you?"

Dr. Bell cocked his head, pursed his lips. "My old

friend Dr. Geary has a point, I'm afraid, when he says that Mr. Robertson doesn't fit the profile perfectly."

"I take it you've worked with him before."

Dr. Bell nodded. "Many, many times."

"How often have you been right?"

Will thought he heard someone crunching along the gravel and turned, expecting to see Eric Smith lurking behind them, notebook poised, but it was just a police car driving toward the back parking lot.

"Nearly always," Dr. Bell answered.

"So we could be no closer than we were yesterday."

"Possibly not." Bell's eye slid toward the SUV. "They seem to be coping."

"I don't think they're taking this too well, actually," Will said. "How could they? She's their mother."

"If things don't . . . improve . . . it will get worse." Dr. Bell paused to consider Will for a moment before saying, "The children may need counseling."

Will nodded, but he knew that in the worst-case scenario no amount of counseling would help his children.

"I'll see if I can come up with some names for you on the Cape," Dr. Bell said. "And in New York."

"Fine. Thank you." Will squeezed the trigger of the driver's door and it popped open. He wasn't ready to make plans for *after*. There was no after. There was only now and before.

Dr. Bell smiled. "I'll need a way to reach you."

"Of course." Will slipped a business card out of his wallet. He wrote down his cell number, and Sarah's number. "You can call on either one." He got into the SUV, rolled down his window and cranked the engine. He wanted out of the parking lot, away from the police station with all its people who were schooled in expecting the worst, away from the buzz-

ing residue of Eric Smith. Away. Back to Juniper
Pond, where soon Charlie and Val would be arriving
to take the boys off the island to the relative safety
of home.

Dr. Bell waved. "I'll look into it today."

The boys buckled themselves up in the backseat as
Will reversed out of the parking spot.

"What exactly is going on, Dad?" David asked.

Will glanced into the rearview mirror and saw both
his sons riveted to it, waiting for their father's answer.
The boys still didn't know he was sending them away,
and wouldn't until the last minute. He didn't want any
arguments or bright ideas.

Keep it simple.

"The police are going to find Mom."

Sammie's face opened in a smile. He relaxed into
his seat and looked out the window. But not David.
He remained tensed forward, watching Will's re-
flected eyes.

"How do you know?"

Will pulled over to the side of the road just before
it turned onto Route 151 and twisted around to face
Sam and David. "They think Mom was taken by
someone—"

"Kidnapped," David said.

Will nodded.

"Why?" The relief vanished from Sammie's face.

"I don't know why," Will said. "We'll find out eventually, but right now the thing is just to find her,
right, guys?"

Both boys nodded, a little dazed.

"They think they know who took her, and they're
following him."

"And if they follow him," David said, "they'll find
her?"

Will nodded. "They're going to call the state police

and they'll also get help from other agencies if they need to."

"Like the FBI?" David asked.

"Like on TV?" Sam.

Will nodded. "Probably the FBI. They're like the brains of the whole country. They try to know everything that's going on, good and bad."

"But they can't, right, Dad?" David said. "Know everything?"

"They know a lot more than most of us," Will said, understanding that in their gaps of knowledge, Emily could be lost.

He turned around and started to drive. For a second he felt himself rise on a current of fear; the peppery swell in his muscles, the collapse in his lungs, the craving for oxygen. He and Emily had prided themselves on sheltering their children as much as they could living in the heart of the city; giving them the richest childhood possible, building their confidence so when the time came to face the world they'd have an inner buffer. Out of thin air they'd invented love, created a family, and in the warmth of their home deciphered meaning from the code of a cynical society. They had succeeded better than anyone had a right to hope for. Until now.

"Where are we going?" Sammie asked.

Will felt her hand reach behind his neck, the gentle warmth of her fingertips calming him as he drove. Their voices contained her; she resonated everywhere. She was gone but not gone, living inside his skin.

"To the hospital." Will kept driving, kept breathing. "To see Maxi."

Sarah was in the waiting area on the pediatric floor, reading a magazine. She looked wretched, Will thought; whatever sleep she'd managed the night before had clearly not provided much relief. Her face seemed to sag with compounded worry. When she heard the slapping approach of their feet on the buffed linoleum floor, and slanted her eyes off the page to see them, he felt a twist of guilt, as if she were his own child and he had abandoned her and returned too late.

Will leaned down and kissed Sarah's cheek. "How's Maxi?"

"She's sleeping. The IV's already working. The doctor said she'll be fine." Sarah's eyes teared and she tried to blink them dry. "Look at that police hat!"

Sammie lunged into what he must have considered to be an official pose: legs hinged open, fists ready under his chin.

"My goodness." Sarah smiled, then looked at David and held out her hand. He slipped his into hers and she held tight.

"Can we see her?" Will asked.

"Yes," Sarah said. "I'll show you."

Will, David and Sam followed Sarah down the hall to the room Maxi was sharing with two other babies. The walls were painted yellow, decorated with posters of Sesame Street characters: Elmo, Zoe, Big Bird, Cookie Monster. Mylar helium balloons were tied to the railings of all three cribs, and night tables were crowded with colorful stuffed animals. Even Maxi's small table boasted a few gifts—a yellow fabric doll, a fluffy white kitten, and an orange velour hand puppet shaped like a crab. Grandma had visited the gift shop while she waited. Maxi's balloons, one green and one pink, read *I Love You* and *Get Well Soon*.

Maxi was fast asleep, curled into the upper corner of her institutional metal crib, with its sheet hopping with lambs. A tiny needle was taped to her lower arm and a long, flexible tube reached through the slats of the crib over to a tall IV stand where a bag slowly emptied. Will put his hand on her forehead, and on her cheek and on the back of her neck; everywhere he touched her she felt dry and soft and warm, but not hot. Her fever had broken. The color in her face was pinkish, but not red. Her eyelids peacefully domed over her eyes. She looked like a healthy baby sleeping. Will carefully and quietly lowered the railing and leaned in to kiss her cheek. She drew in a long breath, and sighed.

"I should speak with Dr. Lao," Will whispered to Sarah. "Stay here with the boys?"

"Of course."

He clicked the side of the crib back into place, left them, and waited at the nurses' desk for the doctor to answer her page. Dr. Lao came hurrying down the hall, her short black hair swinging at her jaw.

"Mr. Parker," she said as soon as she was within his range. "Your baby's doing well. She responded to the antibiotics right away. Her fever's way down. Have you seen her?"

"She looks great. Dr. Lao, I'm very grateful. Thank you."

She touched his arm. "Sarah told me what's going on. I want to apologize for my reaction when I saw you in the emergency room. I jumped to a conclusion. It was wrong."

"No, it was right, but for the wrong reasons. Maxi never should have gotten that sick. I was distracted."

"You're human, aren't you?" She smiled. "Memory breaks down under stress. In case you need to talk to someone . . ." She leaned on the nurses' counter to jot a name and number on her prescription pad, tore off the top slip and handed it to Will. "She's a psychologist here at the hospital but she also has a private practice. She's very good with traumatic stress disorder. Call her."

Will folded the paper and put it in his pocket.

"She can also refer you to someone who works with children."

"Thank you, Doctor. You're actually the second person this morning who's offered references." Will didn't want references; he wanted his family and he wanted this to be over; he wanted to regain his hard-won belief that happy endings were even possible.

"Give yourself some room to react to all this," Dr. Lao said. "Now as far as Maxi's concerned, you and Sarah should make a system so her meds won't get forgotten. Put up notes, do whatever it takes. Okay?"

"Okay."

Her beeper went off and she glanced down at it.

"I want to keep Maxi here tonight, but unless something changes, you can pick her up in the morning. I informed security and they're going to post someone outside her door, just to be sure. She's safe here, Mr. Parker. She'll just sleep." Dr. Lao started to walk away, then looked back. "Don't hang around here too long. Do something with your older kids to try to relax if you can."

As she disappeared around the corner, her words resonated: *try to relax if you can.* How? It was hard enough after a hard day at work, or a few hours with the kids when they were fighting. But how do you relax when someone you love, someone whose existence spills meaning into every corner of yours, someone cleaved to your identity, has vanished? And now you're told she's being held by a maniac; and then you find out this maniac wants to carve up your babies. But he'll return your wife! Yes. He'll return her a shell. And you know your life is over. It's over. Everything you've shared, and planned, is gone.

Except the children. He still had his children.

Chief Kaminer had promised him that the "game"

now was about waiting out time, finishing the five days of slow torture, psyching out the psycho. Waiting for the monster to either lead them to his hiding place or try to steal one of his sons. It didn't feel like much of a game, this business of their lives shattering. So they had until Friday. Then?

Will realized he was standing in the middle of the hall, in a shaft of his own silence, with his eyes squeezed shut and his fists tight in his pockets. He looked around as the blue walls of the pediatric ward drained into the brittle gray of his thoughts. When he remembered that his three children were yards away from him, the anxiety that had become his lifeblood triggered awareness like a morning jolt of caffeine. They needed him. They would need him more than ever from now on.

Just as Dr. Lao had promised, a security guard was now posted outside Maxi's room, and she was still fast asleep. Sarah and the boys were standing by the window, looking out. There was such a quietness to them that it seemed as if they were listening to something, or to nothing, or maybe just taking in the reprieve offered by a moment of simple silence.

Will kissed Maxi on her forehead and whispered in her ear: "I love you, sweetie. See you later."

Sarah, David and Sam stopped by the crib and blew her kisses. Then, without speaking, they filed past the guard and out of the hospital. The boys drove back to the house with Will, who followed Sarah in her own car.

Charlie and Val were not at the house when they got back. As soon as they were parked and out of the car, Will pulled out his cell phone. He had to find out what was going on. Sarah and the boys meanwhile stopped by the front garden and she began what they had all heard before; it was what Emily called her mother's "tour," when she recited both the Latin and common names of each plant. It was a nervous twitch of Sarah's and for the first time Will appreciated it; anything to rivet the boys to something small and usual, away from the larger picture. The trees, not the forest, today just one tree.

Will took the opportunity to go into the house alone. He tried to speed-dial Charlie and immediately discovered his cell phone battery was dead. Only now did it occur to him that he hadn't charged it in days. He shoved it in his pocket and hurried to the bedroom he shared with Emily. Her address book was on the dresser, on top of the novel she was in the middle of reading.

As soon as he opened the red leather cover, he smelled her: lilacs. He hadn't seen her for three days and knew he may never see her again. The address book was filled with her writing, different colors, pen and pencil, and he brought it to his face and breathed in her scent. Then he put it down on the bed and with shaking fingers found the phone number.

Charlie's voice mail answered his cell phone, and so did Val's. At their home, the answering machine picked up. Will left messages everywhere, then hung up the bedroom phone and went upstairs; maybe they had left a message here.

The answering machine's red light was blinking the number one. He pressed PLAY and listened to Charlie's voice, clipped, urgent.

"Listen, Will, we had to turn back. The doctor thinks Val's in labor. He wants her in the hospital. If she's in labor, he needs to stop it if he can. It's too soon, Will. It's two and a half months early. I'm sorry. I'm *sorry*. She's been incredibly upset since you called.

I'm going now. If Val's okay she says I should come back alone. I will. I'll call you—"

The machine cut him off.

Will's stomach cascaded. He went back down to the bedroom, got Emily's address book and started flipping through the pages. The names of their friends and family started to blur as he searched for the right person to come save his children. But finally he understood that there was only one person, that Geary's first suggestion had been right.

In the morning, Will would get Maxi from the hospital and drive Sarah and the children back to New York. He would tell Sarah tonight.

He lifted Emily's address book to his nose and closed his eyes and drifted into her scent. If there was a pinprick of hope left in the universe, he had to find it. He would find it. He would.

"Stop! *Stop!*"

He heard the second shout first.

"Stop!"

Will bolted up the stairs and out the front door. The boys were racing around the cul-de-sac, their sneakers skidding clouds of dust into a fog. Sarah stood at the edge of her cactus bed, her neck straining with each *"Stop!"* Laughing, Sam chased David, reaching to grab his shirt and almost getting it before the distance between them expanded. David was taut as an arrow, accelerating with determination, going fast, faster— faster than his brother could possibly run. Proving he could not be beat. Sam's backside was white with dust; his knees were scraped and bloodied. Will could see he had fallen, which must have been when Sarah's nerves had snapped.

"That's enough!" Will called. "Boys, come back to the house!"

David glanced back over his shoulder. A grin shadowed his face so quickly Will wasn't sure. Then, at the top of the circle, David turned onto the old Indian road. Sam pivoted forward to catch his breath, then resumed the race, following David into the flickering afternoon shade.

Will sprinted past Sarah and gained on Sam.

"Come on, Dad. Let's catch him!"

Will kept running. He could hear Sammie shuffling to a stop behind him, watching the chase unfold as if he had passed the baton in a relay. But it wasn't a race, it wasn't a game, and Will understood his sons couldn't know this. He felt like the linchpin of a seesaw, moderating his sons' rivalry with no hope of neutralizing their fierce imbalance or of convincing them of the simple fact that they were on the same team. Will knew that the race was a yearning, a distortion of something they couldn't say. The most primal impulse in their small bodies was to find their mother, as fast as they could.

"Stop!" he called to David. *"Stop!"*

Sunlight carved a gap in the shade, and just as David passed through it, brightening his gleam of sweat, Will caught up with him. Will was close enough to hear the heaving efforts of David's breath and the crunch of each foot as it barreled over the raw earth. He could feel the strife of David's pumping limbs. He sensed that David felt him close, and was proud of the determination that kept his son running. Proud and terrified.

"Stop!"

David twisted to the left and bounded over a log into the woods. For a split second he looked back to see if Will had made it. Will was right behind him. He reached out and caught David's arm as it paused in an effort to propel himself ever forward.

Will loved David. Had loved him first. Loved him more stubbornly than he had known was possible.

A quick glance at the ground reassured Will that the fall wouldn't be too hard.

One tug on David's wrist stopped him. A pull reeled him backward. But what Will hadn't expected was David's agility in response. David swung his body under Will's arm and reversed the force. Will toppled into the air with a stunned pride only a father could feel for a child whose accomplishments were greater than he had imagined. The body that hit the ground was not David's. And the fall was sharper than Will had guessed.

But even so, Will had won.

David stopped.

Chapter 20

By the time Geary and Amy got back to the station, it was late in the afternoon and the sun was low in a pale yellow sky.

Amy drove into the back parking lot and slowed to a stop. The lot was filled to capacity by state police cars, an unmarked van Geary recognized as from the Crime Lab—big, no windows, nice and clean—and the tidy sedans favored by the feds.

"And so the fun begins," Geary said.

Amy drove around the other side to get to the public lot out front. This time she stopped short.

"Didn't take long, did it," she said.

Four television vans were parked off to the side, just out of view of the front entrance. The *Cape Cod Times*'s very own Eric Smith was holding court with a group of reporters, having his day in the national spotlight. Geary wondered how long it would take before Smith found his seat across from Larry King for his proverbial fifteen minutes.

"They're going to ruin the grass," Geary said.

Amy shook her head. "They don't even see the grass."

She drove past the reporters and they all stopped talking to take a good, long look.

"You want to go first, or should I?" Geary asked.

"I'll take the honors."

Amy pulled into a parking spot, unlatched her seat belt, paused a moment to collect herself and opened her door. They sprinted over in a pack, pads and microphones out, red lights flashing on their industrial-strength video cameras.

Smith squeezed himself past NBC and CNN, who Geary could have sworn shot her loafer out just a moment too late to trip the local reporter. Too bad.

"Are you Retired Special Agent Dr. John Geary formerly of the FBI?" Smith rattled.

"Don't you think the *retired* and the *formerly* cancel each other out?" Geary winked.

"I'll take that as a yes." Smith scribbled on his pad.

"Would you mind spelling your name for us, Detective Cardoza?" the tall CNN gal asked with a dazzling smile.

"C-A-R-D-O-Z-A."

"Detective Cardoza"—CBS; needed a shave—"will you make a statement about the status of the Emily Parker case?"

"She's missing," Amy said. "That's all."

"Dr. Geary"—CNN; that smile—"we know Dr. Roger Bell has been consulted on this case. Why would two of the country's top behavioralists be here if it were just a missing persons?"

Geary smiled back. "Haven't you heard of retirement?"

"But, Dr. Geary—"

"No further comments right now, folks." Geary turned around and started walking, relying on Amy's good sense to follow.

They made it through the front doors with the usual relief, but Geary knew there would be no slowing down; at this point in the game, it was out of one fire and into another.

Suellen nodded at them from behind the reception glass. "Boss said to send you right to the conference room when you got here."

They walked quickly down the hall, made the turn, and opened the door to what had just this morning been a sleepy room. Not anymore. State and federal agents had turned the long windowless conference room into a living brain, with specialized teams running each lobe. They'd even brought their own computers, and now the ordinary space designed for sitting and talking and dusting off your doughnuts was a beeping, whizzing, clicking, ringing nerve center. You barely noticed the framed seascapes hanging on the walls.

It was going to be a long night. They would sleep in shifts, if they did at all.

Kaminer orchestrated a volley of introductions that left Geary with the basics he'd been able to eyeball the minute he'd entered the room. First of all, the FBI guy with the short silver hair was in charge: Reed Sorensen. He was the oldest, maybe a whopping fifty, a special agent from the Child Abduction and Serial Murder Investigative Resources Center. Geary recognized him, but not so long ago his hair had been brown; he must have worked on some nasty cases on his way up the ranks. Sorensen had brought along a new trainee from Quantico, Janet, a woman young enough to be his daughter except no decent man would expose his own blood to something this grotesque. The CASMIRC duo had the head of the table staked out with their laptops, phones and file folders, which was the other way Geary knew Sorensen had the reins.

Down the line and around the table they met an agent from the bureau's Critical Incident Response Group. There was a three-agent team from the state's Crime Scene Service Section; that had been their white van in the parking lot, loaded with the latest in mobile forensics. Then there was the pair of state criminalists who looked like Barbie and Ken and talked like parolees on the mend. The state had also sent in its own ViCAP agent, a young guy with a pockmarked face, introduced as a member of the original team, which didn't mean much, since the state hadn't gotten on track with its own Violent Criminal Apprehension Program until six years ago. Better late than never. Half the agents at the table were new resources, since their divisions had come into being toward the end of Geary's career. In the early days, they toughed it out with brain juice and elbow grease and pounded the pavement like there was no tomorrow. Today it was all high-tech connections, and he had to admit, it got the job done a whole lot faster. Time made the difference between life and death, and the deaths were never pretty.

Right there next to the state ViCAP guy was Tom Delay from VICAP, the FBI's master program, the umbrella operation staked on a capital I that Geary had had his hand in starting back in 1985. Tom was one of VICAP's know-it-alls who usually had to keep his chair warm and work the phone. Geary was surprised to see him out of his cage.

"Out for good behavior?" Geary came around the table and shook Tom's hand. Tom laughed and his stomach bounced mightily.

"They heard you were on the case and no one else was willing to come," Tom said.

"Yeah, sure." Geary grinned.

Kaminer saved the BSU special agents for last, either because they were at the other end of the table or to make them suffer before getting introduced to the great John Geary, who had founded the unit that trained them. The Behavioral Science Unit was his baby and everyone at the bureau knew it. The other thing everyone knew was his history with a certain female agent at Quantico. So they'd sent him two girls fresh from training; one last test to see if he could live up to the defense that saved his career.

Geary marched right up to them with his hand out like a soldier's. "Special Agents," he said, and shook their hands briskly.

"Dr. Geary," the small blond one said. "Tamara Jones. I'm honored to be working with you."

"Ava Ingram," said the tall brunette, pumping his hand like he might spout water.

Geary liked being a living legend and he wasn't going to screw this up. There was an empty chair at the foot of the table, next to where Jones and Ingram were parked. As soon as Geary glanced at it, both girls jumped to pull it out for him. He squelched the chuckle that was bubbling up his throat, nodded once in appreciation, and sat down.

"Thank you, Special Agents Ingram and Jones." His tone sounded so professional even he was impressed with himself. Amy cut him her sharpest look. He slumped an inch in his chair at the foot of the table. It was like in a family; regardless of your rank, once they knew you, you lost half your credibility.

Kaminer stalked behind Geary, who turned around to watch the local boss fight for the scepter. The blond curls bounced with each step. It would never work. Sorensen, with his silver helmet and mean eyes, would clip Kaminer down in one stroke.

"Update!" Kaminer said, nodding his chin at Amy.

Amy stepped forward and began, but before she got into her second sentence, Sorensen was on his feet.

"Thank you, Detective, but we're up to date on all the details. We're all copied on your report, so unless you have something new to add—"

"It's all in the report, sir," Amy said.

Kaminer glowered.

Sorensen's face was hard but his smooth voice was a smile that got everyone else looking in his direction. Nice.

"We've found that the most efficient way to work is to keep the information flow fluid in every direction"—he glanced around the table, receiving nods from the team—"and to avoid repetition. Minutes add up to hours, and that's probably all we've got left to catch the man we'll call Mr. White, for the sake of expediency, before he apprehends one of the children."

"Bobby Robertson," Kaminer said.

Sorensen's eyes slid in his direction; his face didn't change. It was hard like an arrow and pointed at Kaminer's curls. "Unless he was in Fall River at the same time he was observed to be locked inside his house on Cape Cod, that would be doubtful."

Kaminer forced a dismal smile. "No, I meant Robertson was Mr. White. We don't know who the second guy is."

"We use a code name to avoid discussions just like this one. They waste our time." Sorensen glanced at his watch. "That was forty-five seconds, gone."

"Jesus, Sorensen—" Kaminer blushed and did his monobrow, not a winning combination.

Sorensen's eyes slid around the room, stopping on every face except Kaminer's.

Geary had seen this before: the locals getting excited to have a high-profile case draw the state and feds into their arms, thinking it was going to be their chance to prove their mettle, then the top fed squashes them like a troop of busy ants clogging the path. Listen and learn, that was the way; but Geary wasn't about to point that out to his new boss. Amy, on the other hand, looked like she already got the message. She stood behind Kaminer with her hands folded behind her back, her keen eyes taking it all in. She was a smart detective, and Geary had a feeling she saw her chance to catapult her inexperience. Twenty-four hours with this task force would be like two years on the job.

"Why did Mr. White drive such a showy car," Sorensen asked the room, "when in the past the abductions were discreet?"

Brad, the state's ViCAP agent with the cratered face, leaned forward. "He wanted to be stopped."

"Or," Sorensen's trainee Janet said, "he wanted to be *seen*."

"Bingo," Geary said. "The car's a broad gesture. Mr. White's as deliberate as they come. He's upping the ante this time, increasing the challenge."

"My question is why?" Sorensen asked.

"He's tired," Ingram said.

Not bad, Geary thought. "Could be."

"He wants to stop," said Jones, "but he can't. He feels driven to complete the full cycle of his plan."

"But it's exhausting"—Ingram—"to carry out such an ambitious plan over so many years."

"His subconscious is having trouble carrying the load." Jones.

Ingram: "The seven-year pauses between incidents require a substantial amount of restitution. Very few minds are complex enough to handle it."

"I've seen it before," Sorensen said.

Geary leaned back, nodding at his BSU team. Clever girls. Kids. Women. No . . . agents. He shook his head to squeeze forward what Bell would have called "better thinking." The man claimed you could control your thoughts, and that was supposed to have been Geary's way out of the sexual harassment charge; he was supposed to convince himself he hadn't propositioned the woman, so when he testified, he'd be telling the truth. The New Truth, Bell had called it.

"You disagree, Detective Geary?" Sorensen's eyes landed on him.

Detective Geary. It was the first time he'd heard it said. Strange. He'd been Special Agent Dr. Geary half his life. Detective. Maybe *better thinking* would get him used to it, or maybe not.

"Bug flew in my ear," Geary said, shaking his head again for effect. "Special Agents Ingram and Jones are on the right track." He nodded at Ingram and Jones, who beamed at him. He felt a bolt of pride to know he was still teaching new behavioralists even though he'd retired.

Amy stepped forward. "The witness who called in seeing the second Mr. White refused to give his name."

There was a hush, just the whiz of the computers, until Geary heard his own voice: "The asshole called it in himself."

"Which means the physical description, another fiftyish man with white hair, could be wrong," Sorensen said.

Janet: "He might not be a Mr. White at all—"

Ingram: "But he used the same description. That would indicate he saw Robertson talking to Emily Parker. He saw Robertson behind her on line. He saw her discomfort with him—"

Tom leaned over his belly and joined the conversation. "He was watching her in the store."

"All we can assume now is that he's a man," Sorensen said. "He could be anyone, any age, any
description."

"Mr. Anyone," Brad said.

"No." Geary shook his head. "Mr. White still fits
the profile. Male, mid-fifties, educated, mother
issues—"

"Obviously," Kaminer muttered.

Geary ignored that one. "I don't know what color
his hair is, but the rest of the profile stands. He likes
head games." Geary thought about Janice Winfrey,
whose mind had been so fully scrambled and cooked
in one small week. "In the past, he drew his lines
closer. He stayed inside the crime. But this time is
different. This time he's not just reaching into the
mother's head, he's trying to reach into ours."

Bell, Geary thought; he'd consult the Great Mind
for a reality check on their psycho's new-and-
improved end game.

"Sir?" Amy leaned forward, toward Sorensen.
Kaminer leaned forward too, as if he could intercept
her question. "How do we handle the press?"

Sorensen nodded. "We're holding a press conference in about twenty minutes, our statement's being
drafted right now."

"We'll need to hold something back," Geary said.

"Eric Smith's already written up the basics about
the mother's disappearance," Amy said. "And he's
been talking to the national media."

Sorensen planted his elbows on the table and
clasped his hands. "We're going to tell them we're
dealing with a serial crime, but we won't talk about
the children. The children are the watermark. Only
Mr. White will know."

DAY FOUR

Chapter 21

David could hear the TV upstairs; Sam must have been watching the Cartoon Network. It was quiet without Maxi. She was coming home today and David was glad; he didn't like the hospital, didn't want to have to go there again. It was creepy with all the sick and hurt people.

He got out of bed and stood there in his pajamas a minute pretending his mother was home. She'd be in the kitchen, making pancakes and eggs, pouring them their juice. He knew that in the winter she snuck drops of echinacea into their juice because they wouldn't take it straight. He knew that and pretended not to know, and drank the juice, and made her happy without her knowing. Or maybe she knew he knew about the drops. Maybe they were both pretending. Maybe she was pretending now and this was a big fake-out. Maybe she was upstairs making pancakes. Maybe it was Tuesday morning and not Thursday morning and she had come back late and it had all been a nightmare and was over now.

It could be over now.

He bypassed the bathroom and went upstairs to the kitchen.

A bowl with soggy Gorilla Munch sat next to a puddle of milk on the counter. Sam's breakfast. The cartoons were on too loud.

Dad sat at the dining room table, which was a worse mess than ever. He had a pad of paper and a pencil, and he was dialing the phone.

"Morning, David." Dad hung up the phone. He looked pretty bad. David thought he might have stayed up all night; maybe when the last movie ended he watched the next one, and the next one after that. David didn't know what his father did in the middle of the night but it probably wasn't sleep anymore.

"What time is it?" He didn't know why he asked because he could see the kitchen clock. It was after nine. They never slept that late.

"I called school already," his father said, "so don't worry about that. They said nothing much happens on the first day."

"Who did you talk to?"

"Mrs. Someone." His father tried to smile but it came out crooked, wrong.

"Don't know her."

David took down a bowl from the cupboard and poured himself some Gorilla Munch. His mom was big on the health food cereals and they were pretty good once you got used to them. He finished the box and threw it out. He wondered if Dad and Grandma would keep buying it or go back to the regular brands. He poured in some milk and got a spoon and sat at the counter with his back to his dad and wanted to listen, wanted to find out what was going on. But his dad had stopped dialing and now the only sounds were David's own chewing and some tinny laughter from the TV. After a couple of minutes Dad spoke. "David." That was all he said.

David put down his spoon and twisted around.

Dad flattened his hands on the table. "We're going

home today. You'll stay with Grandma and I'll come
back here and wait for Mom."

"What about Maxi?"

"We'll get her from the hospital. Then we'll go."

"I don't want to go."

"You're going. We're all going."

"You told us yesterday they were going to find
Mom. We should wait for her. We shouldn't leave."

"We're going. Finish your breakfast and get
dressed, honey." Dad stood up. He was wearing the
same wrinkled shorts as yesterday and the worn-out
black T-shirt with the big red foot stepping far out in
front of a little man and the bubble words KEEP ON
TRUCKIN' underneath. David always felt embarrassed
when Dad wore that old shirt, but they said it was the
first present Mom ever gave him when they were dating because Dad liked the Grateful Dead. Mom even
played some of their songs on her cello just to make
Dad happy. David always left the room when she did
that. Old people were boring but right now he
wouldn't say anything to his dad about the sorry old
shirt and he wished he could hear Mom's cello playing
anything, anything at all.

"No."

"David, I need your cooperation. We have to go to
the hospital and get Maxi."

"I don't want to go there."

"We have to. It'll just take a few minutes."

"Please, Dad. I'll stay here with Grandma."

His father looked at him for a minute; he was thinking something over. "You're coming with me."

Sam came into the kitchen. "What?"

"I'm staying here," David said.

"Sam," Dad said, "get dressed. You and David are
coming with me to get Maxi."

"But we hate the hospital." Sam glanced at David.

"Just get Maxi and bring her back. We'll wait here with Grandma."

"Grandma's sleeping. Now get dressed."

"I'm awake." Grandma came into the kitchen in her bathrobe, all groggy but smiling. "Let them stay with me, Will dear. You'll be gone an hour at most. We'll be ready to go when you get back."

Dad looked at Grandma and kept thinking. David knew that look, when Dad didn't believe something but for some reason thought he shouldn't argue. He was the boss at work and was used to telling people what to do, but at the same time he knew if he bossed you too much the whole show would backfire. Half the time he covered it over with a big joke. Sometimes Mom told them that Dad was under a lot of pressure. Well what about the pressure of being a kid? What about the pressure they were under now? Their mother was gone. Their *mother*.

"I'm staying here with Grandma," David said again. He did not want to go back to New York without his mother. If no one else could find her, maybe he could.

"Me too." Sam stepped up next to David.

After a minute Dad took a deep breath and let out twice as much air. "All right. But no one leaves this house."

"Where would we go?" Grandma picked up her kettle and walked to the kitchen sink.

Dad slapped his pocket to make sure he had his wallet and keys. Then he walked over to David and Sam and gave them both a kiss on the forehead.

"I'll be right back."

"See you later, Dad," David said.

He watched his father go into the mudroom and a minute later heard the rental car rev up and drive away.

As soon as he was gone, David went downstairs to

get dressed and Sam followed. They got on their shorts and T-shirts and socks and sneakers. Then David went into their parents' room. There were bills and coins on the dresser. David scooped some up and filled his pocket.

"What are you doing?" Sam asked him.

"I'll tell you later."

"You're stealing Dad's money."

"I said I'd tell you later! And I'm not stealing it. I'm borrowing it."

"Grandma!" Sammie called out.

David stuck out his foot and tripped Sam but he didn't fall too hard. "Don't, or I won't take you with me."

"Where?"

"Keep quiet, or I won't tell you."

Sam looked confused and mad and curious.

"Shh, okay?" David pressed his finger to his lips.

"Okay, I guess."

They went upstairs to look for their grandmother, but she wasn't in the kitchen. On the way through the front hall to check her bedroom, David saw that the front door was open and Grandma was standing outside in her robe, talking to some man. It was that man from yesterday—the doctor they met outside the police station. Dr. Bell. David opened the screen door and Sam followed him out. Cool. He had a red sports car.

As soon as he saw David and Sam, the doctor said, "Hello there, boys," and winked his one eye.

"Hi, Dr. Bell," David said.

"I met your grandsons just yesterday," he told Grandma, "with their father, at the police station."

David and Sam milled around the car while the grown-ups talked. Something about a name the doctor checked out for Dad. He heard Grandma say, "You could have just called." Then the doctor say, "It gave me an excuse to drive the car."

"That *is* rather a magnificent car you're driving," Sarah said. "My late husband loved old cars. I spent quite a few Sunday afternoons roaming around those classic car shows. Let me guess. That one's a Corvette?"

Bell smiled and waited for Grandma to keep guessing.

"From the late fifties. I'll guess 'fifty-six, 'fifty-seven, 'fifty-eight?"

"It's a 1957 Corvette model 283." Bell nodded decisively. "I just bought it this week, as a matter of fact. There was a convention over the bridge in Fall River. The dealer drove a hard bargain, but I drove away with the car." His laugh was sudden and hard, like a handful of coins dropped on a tile floor.

"Do you collect?"

"I'm considering it. I'll be retiring soon and I'll need something to occupy my spare time."

"Why not," she said, "if you can afford it? Jonah certainly enjoyed the cars, though I only let him buy one at a time. He'd hold on to it for a year, then sell it for another car. I think he enjoyed trading more than owning."

The doctor looked over at David and Sam and they stepped back, away from the car. Then he smiled and stepped toward them.

"Would you boys like to get in?"

David shrugged but Sam jumped on the offer. He slid right into the driver's side, leaving copilot for David. It wasn't fair—he was older, but he'd hesitated. They sat in the car and pretended they were racing together in the Grand Prix.

"Boys." Grandma's voice snapped them out of it.

"I'm showing Dr. Bell to the bathroom. I'll be right back."

The grown-ups went inside and David saw his chance.

"Come on." He got out of the car. "Don't slam the door. Be quiet."

"Why?"

"Are you coming?"

Sam got out and eased shut his door.

David walked up the drive, past his grandma's gardens, toward the old Indian road.

"I don't think they want us to leave the house," Sam said, trailing behind his big brother.

"It doesn't matter," David said. "We have no choice."

As soon as the house passed from view, David broke into a run. The dirt road was long and narrow and crowded with trees on either side, nearly blanking out the sky. Sunlight glinted through the web of leaves. The whole family loved this magic road, and when his mother drove, she slowed down so they could float in the cool green light.

Chapter 22

Amy Cardoza sat alone at a computer in the report-writing room, *updating*. She sipped her cold coffee. It tasted like bitter sludge but she drank the rest of it. She hadn't slept all night and she needed the caffeine.

She typed a paragraph about yesterday's press conference, editing out her own point of view, which skewed it in her memory like a bad dream: standing stony-faced with Sorensen, Kaminer and Geary in front of the police station; tired eyes dazed by the television lights; the shallow sensation of a shortness of breath; working to keep all expression off her face as Chief Kaminer delivered the agreed-upon statement into a bouquet of microphones:

"Emily Parker disappeared from the parking lot in front of a grocery store in Mashpee on the afternoon of Monday, September third. The timing and manner of her disappearance suggest we may be looking for a serial abductor."

"What makes you think it's a repeater?" Amy recognized the crime reporter from the *Boston Globe*: wiry with big glasses. She had seen him interviewed on TV.

"We can't comment on that right now."

"Do you have any leads?" asked a young man from a Rhode Island local station.

"We're considering every possibility. There are several suspects we're looking at right now but that's all we can say at this time."

"In the past, have the victims been found alive?" It was a woman's voice; Amy couldn't see her behind the more aggressive front row.

Kaminer glanced at Sorensen, whose eyes slid away.

"I'm afraid I can't comment on that right now, either."

"What are the odds Mrs. Parker is still alive?" The reporter from CNN leaned forward.

"We'll hold another press conference tomorrow," Kaminer said, "but at the moment there's no reason to think she isn't. We're very hopeful we'll find her alive." He looked right into the camera, eyes narrowing, and seemed to address Mr. White directly: "We'll search every square inch of the Cape. We'll search the state. We'll search the whole country. There will be no place left for you to hide."

There were a few moments of eerie silence, broken by Sorensen's assistant, Janet, who passed out copies of Emily Parker's photograph. Emily was an attractive woman, and in this picture, she looked relaxed, and she was smiling. Why were they always smiling?

"One more question, Chief."

"That's it for now. Thank you." The team turned around and walked back into the station. The reporters chased them all the way to the door.

Amy hoped the cruiser Kaminer had ordered to sit at the entrance of Gooseberry Way had succeeded in keeping the vultures away from the family. It was all they needed now, to be hounded by the press.

She scrolled down the computer screen and began

her summary of the next item: the forensics report just back on the rug from the Goodman-Parker garage: nothing but typical household dirt and fibers, sand, soil, and pizza sauce. Chalk one up for the old man. Geary had a powerful instinct, she had to admit it. How had he known with such certainty she'd be wasting their time on the rug? She typed a brief paragraph, for the record, and left it at that.

She ran a finger down the seam of the empty paper cup, where the white silhouettes of two Parthenons came together unaligned. She closed her eyes and recalled the soft comfort of her empty bed, the well-worn sheets, the give of her pillow as she turned her head. And in the waking dream of her thirst for sleep, she saw Emily Parker. Saw her, somewhere in the dark, bound and gagged, slowly drowning in a capsule filled with liquid terror. Hovering in front of death while it mocked the value of her life, knowing it would be over soon, deepening into the consciousness of that knowledge. Then it never happened, and as in a nightmare, time melted in the heat of fear. Amy saw Emily Parker, face distorted against the hard inner surface of a glass jar. Trapped. She saw Janice Winfrey. Saw them experiencing something worse than their own deaths.

Enfolded in the shadows of her plastic sleep, Amy saw a mother witnessing her child's terror, his helplessness, his pain. A mother witnessing the brutal death of her beloved child, then left alive to relive it.

Amy's stomach lurched and she swallowed an upsurge of bile.

So that was it.

She opened her eyes to cold fluorescent light. Her fingers closed around the paper cup, crushed it, and aimed it across the room at the garbage.

"Score!" It was Geary's voice.

Amy spun around, her adrenaline working harder than the coffee. There he was, standing in the doorway, grinning.

"That was cute," she said.

"Doesn't take much, does it?"

"It takes a lot more than you to scare me." She pressed her fingertips to her temples and squeezed shut her eyes. "The caffeine's starting to get to me."

"Why don't you go home for a few hours, catch some z's?" His nod punctuated the suggestion, as if the decision had been made. "No one can stay awake that long."

"What about you?" She looked at Geary, whose appearance never seemed to change from its state of overwrought, rumpled antagonism. "You've been up all night too."

"I'll sleep when I'm dead."

"That's a good line. Mind if I borrow it sometime?"

"Be my guest."

She jabbed the PRINT button and her updated report began to spew out of the printer.

"Got something to cheer you up." Geary's watery eyes had that twinkle. "Snow's back."

"Finally!"

"Nice and refreshed after a good night's sleep."

"What are you telling me?"

"Guess he got back from Fall River past his bedtime."

"So he *went home*?"

They hurried down the hall toward the conference room. Geary pushed open the door and Amy stepped into the buzz. Every laptop was on; every face wore a sheen of fatigue. Some of the agents were out in the field and had left behind the ghosts of their blinking computers. Half the Cape was on the case now and the entire East Coast was on alert. The hiding places were dwindling, but not fast enough; with all their resources, they still hadn't figured out where to look.

Snow, sitting with Sorensen and Janet, looked buffed and rested. When Amy got close, she smelled his sweet cologne intermingled with the locker-room odor of sweat and bad breath.

"Al!" She patted his shoulder and forced a smile. Sorensen watched her, grimly amused. "Have a nice vacation?"

"What vacation? What is this?" Snow ran a hand along the crease of his pants. "I stopped at home for a shower and a shave. I had no idea what was happening here."

"Didn't turn on the TV? Didn't listen to the radio? This investigation is all over the news," Amy said.

"Actually, no." Snow lifted his shoulders in a sheepish shrug. "But I wish I had. I would've come straight over."

"And put in a little overtime?"

"Okay, Amy, I get it." He shook his head and glanced at his knees, then faced her with his most patient expression, as if his tolerance would discharge her anger. She imagined Snow's wife must have decided to leave him at just such a moment, her resolution bursting recklessly against his blank slate. "Do you want to hear my report or not?"

She pulled up a chair and squatted onto it, leaning forward so abruptly Snow tilted back to make room. "You're lucky the chief isn't here right now. I'd fill him in on *everything*."

"Go for it, Amy." He smiled—he actually smiled. And she understood that if she ever did tell Kaminer about Snow's advance, he would offer that same blank expression and simply deny it.

She wanted to scream.

"You should have filed your report first," she

snapped, "then gone home to visit your teddy bear. I don't care what you found, we needed it *yesterday*. We're working against the clock. We have *no* time."

Geary's hand on her shoulder, his quick squeeze, calmed her enough to start her lungs pumping again.

Sorensen kept on watching her and she wondered what he was thinking and tried not to care. She tucked her hair behind her ears, sat back and crossed her arms over her chest. "We're listening."

Snow ran his tongue along his upper teeth before he started. "Sal Ragnatelli bought a booth at this convention every year for ten years. He was there rain or shine. People who knew him liked him. He was easygoing and joked around a lot. But this year"—Snow looked fleetingly at Sorensen, then landed his eyes on Amy—"something happened. He was upset about something, so upset he closed his booth in the middle of the day on Tuesday. His buddies say he never did that before—those booths, they cost a bundle, and midday foot traffic's the busiest."

"So he closed down in the middle of the afternoon," Amy said.

Snow nodded. "Came back a couple hours later, upset. Opened his booth, stayed open till closing time. All he'd say about it to the guy in the booth next to his was that someone was messing with his head."

Amy leaned forward. "Did he describe the person?"

"Not really. A customer, male, wanted to buy a top-of-the-line vintage Corvette, but when it came to the money"—Snow shrugged—"apparently the customer wasn't into friendly bargaining, wanted to press a low-ball price on Ragnatelli, kept pushing it. He'd set a meeting, then mess with Ragnatelli's head for a while."

Sorensen paid close attention as Janet typed into her laptop. Some of the task force agents had stopped working and started listening in. A few got up and gathered around Snow.

"Ragnatelli said"—Snow removed a tiny notebook from his shirt pocket—"'If he wants to steal a car, why doesn't he do it like every other thief, just take it when no one's looking? This nut's trying to get me to *agree* to practically give it to him.' That was verbatim, word for word."

"And then?" Amy asked.

"He worked his booth, shut down on time and went back to his motel. The girl at the front desk saw him come in a little after eight, then go out again just before nine. I checked every store and restaurant in the area and found out he ate a burger at the Truck Stop diner, called his wife from a pay phone, then drove to an all-night drugstore and bought himself some aspirin, generic. The pharmacist remembered him comparing prices." Snow paused and seemed to notice how many people were listening. He sat up a little straighter. "The pharmacist was the last person who saw Ragnatelli alive. He mentioned Ragnatelli looked at his watch a few times, like he had to be somewhere, but he didn't seem to be rushing to make his appointment."

"Then?"

"That's it. He was found dead the next morning. The local cops put his death at ten thirty p.m."

"So Ragnatelli didn't give enough customer service." Tom shook his head. "Gotta provide the customer service."

"Or maybe he gave a little too much," Geary said. "Maybe his mistake was talking to this customer in the first place. This was someone who didn't like hearing no for an answer."

"The Corvette?" Sorensen asked Snow.

"Gone."

"Plates?"

"Dealer plates, found next to Ragnatelli's body."

"Beautiful." Ingram nodded at Jones.

"He made it clear he got his way," Jones said.

"Seized control and gloated over it." Ingram.

"Okay," Amy said. "So whoever killed Ragnatelli drove off in the Corvette. And whoever abducted Emily Parker had her in one of Ragnatelli's other cars, then returned it."

"Ragnatelli was the only person who could have identified him," Brad said, hovering close.

"He didn't really want the car," Geary said.

"No." Amy closed her eyes, then opened them. "He wanted to erase a witness."

"He knew Mrs. Parker had been connected to the Ford," Sorensen said calmly. "How?" His bloodshot eyes scanned the room. "Did the media report that?"

"No," Brad said. "I've been checking as many outlets as I can. They don't have anything new, except that we're here. That went out nationally last night."

Sorensen nodded heavily, once. "So he knows we're piecing his puzzle together"—his eyes sliced at Amy— "and he knows we linked her to the Ford." His cool evaporated as he pitched forward and slammed the table so hard Janet's laptop shook. *How did he find out we traced her to the Ford?*

Silence. All these experts, and no one knew.

"He's going to escalate his deadline." Geary looked at Sorensen. "He's setting his calendar back, to today."

"I'll alert Fall River that Mrs. Parker could be in their jurisdiction," Amy said. "I'll send out an APB on the Corvette."

"How hard could it be to trace a car like that?" Snow asked.

"Not hard," Amy snapped at him like a rubber band, "if it's still on the road."

Chapter 23

Dr. Bell took just a minute in the bathroom, then came out with that wry smile of his. His goatee bothered Sarah; it forced you to notice his dark lips and yellow teeth.

"Thank you. My morning coffee travels faster than my car." He laughed.

"I'll give Will your message," Sarah said. "He'll be back soon with the baby. I'm sure he'll be interested in speaking with the psychologist."

"I'm happy to help."

He offered a hand, and she leaned forward to shake it. It was still wet.

Sarah opened the screen door, glancing around for the boys. They weren't in the car. She couldn't see them anywhere. She wondered if they had gone down to the lake.

Dr. Bell curved his long body down into the sports car and pulled shut the door with a loud crack.

"If you see the boys up the road, would you mind asking them to come home?" Sarah shielded her eyes from the harsh sun so she could see the doctor's face.

"Certainly." He started the engine, then looked up at Sarah. "I'm terribly sorry about your daughter, Mrs. Goodman. I'm sure she'll turn up."

Sarah nodded and waved as the bloodred Corvette sped up the drive.

Turn up, like a lost shoe. His insensitivity made her angry. Coming over when he could have called, just to give him something to do with his morning. The arrogance of doctors. She wondered just what kind of a doctor he was.

Sarah walked down the grass slope next to the house, around to the back gardens.

"David! Sam!" Her voice echoed vaguely. "Boys!"

She didn't like them disappearing like this. They had all promised Will they'd stay in the house until he got back.

She hurried down the path, into the clearing, then through the clot of trees that hid the house from the lake. All was tranquil: the hammocks were still; toys lay just where they'd been dropped by the children. In the distance she saw a fisherman with his line hovering in the water. She saw the old reaching tree. But no David and Sam.

"Boys!" She walked as quickly as she could back up to the house. "Boys!"

The bottom door was locked, so she went up around the other side of the house, through the garage entrance. The mudroom door was also locked. Will had sealed the house up tightly the night before. Sarah had lain awake in bed all night, thinking of everything, trying not to think, tormenting herself with questions that had no answers. Wondering if Emily had her key and, if not, how she would get into the house with all the doors locked. When she came home.

For Sarah, it was the unbearable sorrow that pulled her down from any possibility of hope. For Will, it seemed to be a fear of lurking danger—locking all the doors and windows, not letting the boys out of his sight, insisting they leave for New York today. In the middle of the night, her uncontrollable thoughts had wondered if he knew more about Emily's disappearance than he'd shared with her. It was as if he expected more disaster.

Sarah went into the house through the front door, weaving in and out of rooms.

"David! Sam!"

The house was empty.

She went back outside and jogged up the drive, past her fragrant summer gardens, and into the cool shade of Gooseberry Way. If that Dr. Bell had come upon the boys and offered them a ride in his Corvette just to give himself something more to do, she'd really tell him off. That had to be it—she was sure.

She walked slowly back down the road, calling the boys' names every now and then, knowing they weren't there. She wondered if there was any way to reach Dr. Bell before Will got back. She could call the police station and ask for John Geary. She remembered Will saying they worked together.

She went into the house and straight to the kitchen phone. She took out the local phone book from the counter drawer, looked up the number and dialed. When she asked to speak with Dr. Geary, she was put on hold.

"Detective Geary?" he answered, as if he wasn't quite sure it was his own name.

"Dr. Geary, this is Sarah Goodman."

"John to you, my dear."

"Your friend Roger Bell stopped by this morning with some information for Will."

"Roger Bell doesn't skimp on service," John said. "Never has."

"Anyway, he had his fancy car. I think he may have taken the boys for a ride. I can't find them anywhere. I was hoping you'd know how to reach him. Will went to get Maxi and I promised him I'd keep the boys home."

"Bell drives a Nissan. I wouldn't call it fancy."

"Oh no," Sarah said, "this is a beautiful red Corvette, a classic. The boys were really interested in it. That's why I think he may have taken them for a drive."

Chapter 24

John Geary stood in the conference room with his back pressed against the wall, listening as Sarah described the events of that morning. Will sat next to her, holding his baby girl in his lap a little too tightly. His face was a study in the abandonment of confidence, with black-and-blue swaths under his eyes like he'd been punched in the face.

"He's a doctor," Sarah said, and looked right at Geary. "He's your friend. I naturally trusted him."

Geary was listening but he couldn't believe it. Roger Bell driving a *Corvette*? Killing car dealers? Stealing kids? He had known the man nearly thirty years, and like most criminal psychiatrists he was nuts but he wasn't a psycho.

Tears drowned Sarah's pale eyes and she broke into a sob. "I looked everywhere for David and Sam, *everywhere*."

"I shouldn't have left my boys." Will's voice was a hoarse whisper. "I should have made them come with me."

No one responded, because it was true: he should have, but now it was too late.

"It's not your fault, Will," Sarah said. "It's mine."

Poor old woman, it was a different world from the

one they'd grown up in. Locked doors, daughters missing, grandchildren stolen, good friends turned inside out into freaks.

Sarah repeated every detail of the morning, again and again, staring at her hands clasped in her lap. Geary listened to the clink of every coin of fact as it dropped into his brain, but there was no resonance; his mind fought back with disbelief that his old friend could be a serial killer. Geary just didn't buy it; he had known and trusted Bell half his life.

Yet Geary knew that if he wanted to, his old friend could have gotten past the cop who had been on guard at Gooseberry Way that morning; Bell was on the case, after all, and his credentials were beyond question.

Geary knew that at this moment Sarah's house and grounds were swarming with police, and if the media hadn't wormed their way in by now it would be a miracle.

He knew that all the roads radiating twenty miles from Gooseberry Way were blocked.

He knew that if the Corvette was still on the road, it would be an easy target.

He knew that if Roger Bell was behind the wheel, he was as good as dead.

He also knew they had a good chance now of saving the boys. And a good chance of finding Emily Parker, possibly even alive.

What he had trouble *knowing* was that Roger Bell was Mr. White.

Geary heard a voice vibrating outside his head. Talking to him.

"How long have you known this?"

It was Sorensen, his laser eyes digging a path into Geary's brain.

"Bell never collected cars," Geary answered.

"How long have you known?"

"I still don't know."

"Your Dr. Bell may be Mr. White." Sorensen's words spread into every corner of the room. "You must have suspected."

Geary focused his eyes on Sorensen, the sharp face, tight silver hair, eyes filled with all the horrors he'd seen. Here was a man who could believe anything.

"Never."

What was it they said? The closer something was to your face, the harder it was to recognize. Could Geary possibly have been that nearsighted? That totally blind?

Bell nearly fit the profile—nearly. He wasn't compulsive about his schedule, which had been a key point, and his mother had died when he was a toddler. He'd been raised an only child by an adoring father and loving stepmother. Other than the early loss of his mother, there just wasn't any significant emotional conflict in Bell's life that Geary knew of. He just couldn't peg it; it didn't make sense.

Yet he had seen it before: a seemingly untroubled mind exploding with venom.

The ideas to retire to the Cape, write a book on cold cases, define Mr. White as a criminal mastermind, even coauthor the book—all had come from Roger. Had it all been planned to lead Geary right to this point? Was it possible that all their years of friendship could evaporate in a labyrinth of betrayal?

Geary stepped forward, away from the wall, and shook his head. "No way. It isn't Roger."

Sorensen turned away in disgust.

"Listen to me, Reed," Geary said. "I've known Roger too long to just snap my fingers and fall into line here. I'm listening to my gut. It isn't him."

Sorensen turned back slowly, deliberately using too

much of all their valuable time, and stared hard at Geary. Geary didn't like it. He stepped forward and said it again:

"No way."

"John." Amy's tone was firm. "Everything points to him now. Try to look at it like any other case."

But this isn't any other case anymore.

Geary pulled his eyes away from Amy's. "I'll be back," he said, and walked out of the room.

He knew they were trailing him while he drove back to Cotuit Bay Shores—knew and didn't care. He kept the speed limit as he curved along the lanes and drives, past the neat lawns and gray clapboard houses seasoned by years of Cape air. He came to his own house and kept driving. Two dead ends along, he turned into Forsythe Court. Roger's house was the first saltbox on the right. The rooster weathervane on his roof spun in a breeze.

Roger kept his lawn pristine, mowing it himself once a week, but his house had always looked unique on this circular road with five nearly identical homes— and now Geary realized why. All the houses boasted neat flower beds spilling with pansies, petunias, snap-dragons, daisies, potted geraniums, trellised roses. Neighbors had individualized their homes through flora, but not Roger. His house was notable on this court as the only one without a single flower in the yards or windows. He just had his weathervane, rusty and crowing year-round. It was also the only house with three police cars parked haphazardly out front, the driver's door to one of them left gaping.

Geary pulled into the driveway and got out of his car. The garage door was down and he took a look through one of the two grimy windows. There, in the garage, sat Roger's blue Nissan. Geary turned and walked up the fieldstone path to the front door. He rang the bell and just for good measure banged the brass door knocker a couple of times. The door swung open and there was a cop he'd never seen before.

"Detective Geary, Mashpee PD," he introduced himself.

The cop was young. He looked Geary up and down, and kept his thoughts to himself. Good thing too— Geary wasn't in the mood for bullshit.

"What can I do for you, sir?"

"I take it the suspect isn't here."

"That's correct."

Other cops were picking through the house. Geary didn't like it. He turned and walked back down the path. The unmarked car that had followed him drove into the court and once around; he saw now that his chaperons were Officers Sagredo and Graves. Geary waved. Sagredo waved back, Graves said something to him and they drove out of the court, stopping just at its entry.

So Roger was out, even though his car was in. No one walked anywhere around here, except maybe to the docks, though that was unlikely with the gear needed for a typical outing on a boat. Still, Roger moored his SeaRay Sundancer just down Old Post Road at Point Isabella on North Bay, and it was possible he'd decided to go for a quick, unencumbered run at the sea.

Geary got back in his car and drove out of Forsythe Court, slowing down to let Sagredo and Graves keep a close tail.

He saw it as soon as he turned onto Point Isabella Road, parked in the four-car lot near the docks: the Corvette. Sleek and tomato red, it was long and low to the ground with a little bubble of a hood and a chrome grate shining on the front like bared teeth.

Geary pulled into an empty spot. Sagredo and Graves pulled in right next to him. They all got out of their cars together; they'd all seen it; there was no point pretending. The Corvette was here. But only Geary was able to see that Bell's boat was gone.

Bell had always kept a boat here. It was what had lured him to the Cape years ago. Geary now remembered one of their many outings together, motoring past the horizon line, Ruth back at the house preparing their dinner. He remembered the swell of their friendship, the ease of that afternoon. Hot, windy, eerily bright. He remembered noticing the rash on Bell's chest, barely visible under the curls of graying chest hair. But in this sun he saw them distinctly: a web of scar tissue spanning his chest, connected by individual points.

"Someone play dot to dot on your chest, Roger?"

The laugh, coolly humored. Steering the boat into the wind.

"A dermatological outbreak as a child," Bell had answered. "I barely notice it anymore."

The memory made Geary feel sick. He walked out onto the dock, into the wind, and stopped at Bell's empty mooring. He thought of Daniel Lipnor's torso still warm in the baby swing, dripping blood, fresh pinpricks covering his small chest. He was six years old, big for his age, looked seven.

Seven years old. Every seven years, to the day.

What had happened to Roger when he was seven, on the third of September?

What had happened to his chest?

What was he hiding under that eye patch?

A cold sweat gathered on Geary's skin and nausea rose in a wave. He fell to his knees and braced the palms of his hands on the edge of the dock. He could hear the footsteps of Sagredo and Graves as they walked toward him, then stopped. They were watching him, that was all—doing their job. He leaned over the dark water and vomited into its chill.

"Roger has a boat," Geary said softly.

"What kind of boat?" Amy crossed the room to stand in front of him. She took his face in her hands and steered it in her direction. "Where does he keep it?"

"Never Land."

Amy blinked. "What?"

"He named it *Never Land*. Peter Pan. The motherless boy who couldn't grow up."

"John, we're losing time."

"It's a SeaRay Sundancer, small, interior cabin, functional galley, latrine. Nothing fancy. Moors it at Point Isabella on North Bay, but it isn't there now. He must have taken it out. He parked the Corvette at the dock."

Kaminer and Sorensen were on their phones like wild animals on a fresh kill. In minutes, they were told that Bell's boat had been at his mooring only intermittently for a week.

"Every marina!" Kaminer barked into the phone. "All up and down the coast, down Connecticut, up to Maine. Every dock on the East Coast, do you hear me? Every little podunk dock in every backyard!"

"Sir," Amy said, "what do we do about Robertson? He's still under surveillance."

"Bring him in," Kaminer said. "We'll get what we need to book him on trafficking child pornography. I'm not letting that sicko loose in my town. I've got grandkids."

Geary forced himself to stand up. He felt a little dizzy, shook his head to dislodge the demon, wanted some coffee, needed to wake up. Had to face this new, bitter truth, but didn't want to, still couldn't fully believe it.

Will Parker got up and walked over to Geary. Parker, who had met the worst luck of his life, yet at the same time was luckier than Geary had ever been. Life should never get that paradoxical, Geary thought. He had seen it so many times, the pitiless hand extending unforeseen from the side of the road, destroying futures. He had seen people shocked out of a complacent trust in the safety of their world's perimeters. Other people. Never himself.

Will stood in front of Geary and held out an arm to steady on. Geary took it.

Chapter 25

"Down here?"

The hatch opened and Sammie's voice drifted in on a cloud of fresh air that found Emily's nose like a magnet. The quick slap of sneakers down the steps, someone just behind him, the corn man, *the corn man, no.* Did Sam see her? She could feel him moving around the boat like he was on a school trip, discovering something new. She felt the movement of his looking around, the pause of his recognition. She could almost see his ecstatic face for a split second before it fell into despair. She grunted through the tape, grunted and shook her naked body.

"Mommy!"

A voice thinned by fear. How she must have looked to him. An impostor. Was everything she had taught him to believe wrong? Hadn't she taught him not to talk to strangers? Hadn't he learned how to defend himself? All those words and all those lessons, had she failed so badly? Was Sarah wondering the same thing? Was it Emily's own fault she was here? She should have worn a bra, she should have taught her children better, she should have stayed home every single minute, she should never have desired those hours alone to work or even just for shopping.

The sharp, squealing noise. The pounding on the floor.

A thud of struggle and Sammie's sharp cry, the blotting of his voice, panic electrifying her and she couldn't move. She listened to him thrash on the floor so close she should have been able to touch him.

The corn man grabbed her arm and gave her another shot and her body died again and her brain burned.

Her brain became a thing in itself. A floating muscle. Alive without instruction, like a severed limb. Rebellious. Kicked with hatred for her circumstances. Her brain combusted and left her body, throwing fire into the air until there was no oxygen left to breathe.

Something was wrong with her baby boy and she couldn't help him. Her soul urged toward him and she couldn't flicker a muscle to help. She was stone. Burning stone.

And there was no more air, her burned-up brain had sucked it all away.

Chapter 26

Will drove and drove and everywhere he turned there was access to water: water trapped in interior ponds, water breaking against the ubiquitous shores. And as he drove he saw boats everywhere: boats for sale, boats dragged behind cars, boats docked at crowded marinas, boats launched into ponds from public beaches, boats anchored half a mile into the ocean, white sails drifting on acres of blue. He drove and he looked and sometimes he saw them, the police, driving ahead of him or passing next to him and he wondered, *Have they found her? Have they found my children?* and he kept driving because he knew they had not. They were driving everywhere and nowhere, just like him.

Sarah sat in the backseat entertaining Maxi, who blissfully knew only enough to miss her mommy. She held her pink velour bear against her face like a pillow. *When you were only one, Mommy got sick and died. You were only a baby and you can't remember her. I don't know who those other shadows were you think you remember. We all imagine things.* He would raise Maxi alone.

No one will ever hurt you. You are loved.

David had never admitted to being afraid of the

dark, but Sammie had. Emily sitting on the side of Sam's bed, tucking his blanket under his chin, smoothing her hand down along his soft cheek. "Monsters are pretend." Bending to kiss his forehead, and again. "There's no reason to be afraid of the dark." David listening from his own bed, catching Will's eye as he stood in the doorway watching his sons collect up their mother's love. David's eyes breaking from his to follow a shadow as it shifted across the ceiling. "You have nothing to worry about." Emily standing, smiling at Sam. "Mommy and Daddy are here."

They had trained their children to trust the world.

They had trained them to forgive their enemies and, at the same time, recognize the moment when it was necessary to fight.

Had they heard the snap of their own innocence breaking when they understood they had never really been safe and their enemies did not deserve forgiveness?

Will's foot pressed the accelerator and he passed the speed limit. Images of the bright day flashed by, skimming the sides of the car like light grazing a bullet. But in this nightmare, the bullet never arrived anywhere. It continued forward, gathering momentum until its speed blinded you and you couldn't see it but you knew it had passed through your life because when it vanished it left behind a devastated future.

He remembered this moment. He was only four. The cowboy, the chocolate cake, the red bike he'd wanted.

Mrs. Simon running from her house.

His body remembered the freefall, landing in a deep cushion of forgetting.

He was falling now, peeling away from the core of his life.

Driving. Falling.

He blinked his eyes to stay focused on the road.

Then Sarah's hand slipped from behind onto his shoulder, and the gentle press of her fingers into his muscles brought him into the moment, like a pause from rewind.

"Will," Sarah whispered, "Maxi's asleep."

He glanced in the rearview mirror and saw Sarah looking away, trying not to embarrass him. How long had he been crying?

"We can't keep driving around forever."

Chapter 27

Amy Cardoza stood bleary-eyed in front of the enormous map of Cape Cod that had covered the conference room wall since she first joined the Mashpee Police Department. It was dated 1995, and up until today had been adequate for their purposes. At this moment, it looked more decorative than informative, with its hand-drawn lines, pastel colors and glaring omissions. To get his *update,* Kaminer had mobilized every local police station to every town hall in search of permits for docks built in the last six years.

Cops and agents were out on foot, walking beaches, searching for an elusive SeaRay Sundancer called *Never Land.* Amy felt the inching dread of suffocation in this airless room with its nonstop electronic fizz. She was still a little in shock from the news about Dr. Roger Bell stealing the Corvette, and by inference killing Ragnatelli, and by inference having driven off with Emily Parker in Ragnatelli's '47 Ford. And she was disturbed by the obvious conclusion that had they known about Al Snow's visit to Fall River twelve, even eight, hours earlier—before he went home for his beauty rest—they would have had a better chance of saving Emily Parker's life. And her sons would be on their way home instead of lost . . . missing.

Amy squeezed shut her eyes and pushed out the haunting thought that it was too late. If Mr. White— Roger Bell—was working on schedule, Emily would still be alive and possibly even conscious; and the boys, or at least one of them, had at least until tomorrow.

It was impossible to keep still. As Amy's mind raced, she walked the floor in front of the map, thinking, projecting shapes onto the island's contours that weren't there, aching to clarify the picture.

Even Will and Sarah had left with the baby, saying they had to look, couldn't just wait. Amy could picture them, driving the routes, following any sign for a boating launch. Spinning wheels of desperation.

There were hundreds of miles of shoreline surrounding Cape Cod, along with a complex system of bays, estuaries, rivers, inlets and creeks fed by Cape Cod Bay, the Atlantic Ocean and Nantucket Sound. There were dozens of registered private marinas and public docks, and hundreds of private docks not including those built without permits, hidden in the brush of people's backyard waterways. And then there were the neighboring islands of Nantucket and Martha's Vineyard. Both islands' police forces were on high alert and additional VICAP agents were flown in to help direct the effort to find Emily, David and Sam Parker.

Geary hunched over the table with Special Agents Ingram and Jones, as well as Sorensen, Kaminer and Tom Delay, forcing himself to work the problem through his supple mind as if he alone was responsible for finding the Parkers. Amy knew that Geary and Bell had a long history, that they had woven themselves together over the years, but began to suspect there were underlying knots and that was partly what Geary was searching for. That he thought he could unravel the dilemma of this long friendship by solving two crimes at once: catching a serial killer, and unearthing the real man inside the one masquerading as his friend. Amy felt for him, and hoped he got his answers.

"He wants to get caught," Geary said, "which is why he dropped so many crumbs. Once we recognized the trail, he knew it would lead to him."

"Easy," Ingram said, shaking her head.

"Too easy." Sorensen tapped his pen in sharp staccato against the edge of the table.

"Exactly," Geary said. "If he stuck to his precedent, five days, we'd have an extra day and we'd find him."

"But he acted today," Jones said, "one day early, like he can't help himself."

Ingram nodded. "Like he feels he has no choice but to try and win this game."

"We need to understand his motive for acceleration." Amy left the map and joined the group. "Why? To win? Or to satisfy something deeper in himself? And why did he need to accelerate so badly that he took two boys instead of one, as usual?"

"Was it incidental," Tom asked, "that he took two kids this time?"

"Opportunity?" Kaminer said. "The boys were both there, and he saw his chance."

"Maybe," Amy said, "or maybe not. Isn't Roger Bell smart enough to figure out how to get one kid into the car instead of two?"

"Please," Geary said, "we don't know for sure it's Roger."

Amy nodded in agreement to disagree; there was no point arguing details now. "If Mr. White used the ploy of offering them a ride up the road in the Corvette, he could have had them go one at a time. He didn't need to take both."

"How did he get past the cop at the head of the road?" Tom asked. "Even if he could have gotten both kids into the trunk of the car, it would have been noisy. The cop would have noticed something."

"How did he get Emily Parker into his car in the middle of the afternoon, in a crowded parking lot?" Geary scanned the room like a teacher waiting for the right answer, as if he already knew what it was.

"They were drugged," Ingram said, and heads all around the room nodded.

"How?"

"Aspiration," Jones said, "or injection. This way he could have easily subdued both boys and hidden them in the car, then driven right past the officer."

"Or could he have disposed of one of them, the older one, since he goes for boys who are six, seven years old?" Sorensen shook his head at the possibility of his own suggestion.

"Could be," Kaminer said.

"Mr. White showed he was willing to kill extraneously to pursue his goal," Amy said, "when he stabbed Ragnatelli."

"Which means one boy could be in the boat, the other one in the trunk of the Corvette," Sorensen said.

"Or on the side of the road," Tom said.

"Gooseberry Way's been checked up and down, every square foot," Kaminer said. "He'd have had to take the time to dig a grave."

"No," Sorensen said, "he didn't spare a minute. He has one goal, and if he killed David, then that boy will be in the car."

Amy pictured David curled in a trunk. She'd found a man like that once. He'd looked like a frightened baby, stillborn, vomit on his shoes. And the smell. She forced the image out of her mind.

"So let's assume that's what happened," she said,

"and that Mr. White has Sam with him, and they're on the boat. How long will he wait before he begins the dissection?"

There was a pause, in which no one seemed prepared to speak. Then, finally, it was Geary. "That depends which is stronger, his need to hurt the child or terrorize the mother."

"The boys weren't always killed on the fifth day," Tom said. "Only Daniel Lipnor. The others were done gradually. A day or two."

"What goes on during that day or two?" Amy asked.

"Does he sexualize his victims?" Sorensen asked. "The mother? The kids?"

Geary answered, "There's been no direct evidence of a sexual component."

"But Dr. Geary?" Ingram asked. "Can't the sexual component be subverted into the violence?"

Geary nodded. "What's the behavior you'd expect that *doesn't* happen? We need to look at that."

"If he's torturing the mother's mind by torturing the child's body, wouldn't rape be one of the obvious torments?" Jones glanced at Geary and Ingram.

"You'd think so," Geary said.

"Meaning?" Sorensen asked.

"His sexuality could be so deeply repressed it can't express itself sexually. There is sexual titillation from other sources."

"Like violence," Amy said.

"It's almost a cliché." Sorensen shook his head.

"It's not rape," said Jones, "and it's not pedophilia."

"It's vicarious torture," Ingram said. "Destroying one person through the destruction of another."

"And not just anyone," Tom said.

"No," Amy said, "the woman's own child."

"Efficient asshole." Sorensen smirked.

Tom shook his head. "What about his targets? Most serial criminals work close to home, or in a pattern that fits their professional movements. Or they're drifters. But not Mr. White. He has a set job with a set routine, but this guy strikes all over the map. So he seems to choose his victims randomly, according to access."

"He's looking for someone who fits the profile and who's available. He's not after a specific individual." Geary leaned forward, gnarly hands folded in front of him. "Criminals who hurt someone they know usually cover their victim's face so they can't see the reaction, because believe it or not they care what that person thinks of them. Or they mutilate or rape postmortem so the victim will never know their attacker's true nature. Did Mr. White know his victims?"

"No," Ingram said.

"Definitely not," Jones agreed.

"Probably not," Geary said. "We can't be sure until we get the chance to talk to him, but the indication is no. He forces his primary victim, the mother, to witness cruelty worse than most of us can imagine. . . ." Geary's voice trailed off in an apparent loss of energy.

"But the mother-son relationship, the age of the son—how does he know?" Tom asked.

"Research," Geary said. "He keeps his eyes open, and researches until he's sure he's got the right match."

"So he stalks them first," Sorensen said.

Kaminer took in a sharp breath and checked his watch. "We need to nail his time frame for today."

Kaminer's impatience usually riled Amy, but their lack of time was starting to suck the air out of the room. It was getting hard to breathe, knowing what was happening, or about to happen, somewhere on the shores of Cape Cod.

"How much time we have depends on Mr. White's anxiety level," Geary said.

"He took two boys, one day early," Sorensen said.

Amy nodded. "He's anxious."

"I'd say it was already building seven years ago," Ingram said.

"Daniel's torso was delivered fresh," Geary said, "to a place it would be found immediately. The other children had body parts buried or sunk. Those had to surface with nature."

"That's right," Amy said. "A head in the dunes, an arm in a swamp, another arm buried under a wharf."

"Why the torso in a swing?" Sorensen asked. "Why the departure from gradual detection?"

"He was getting anxious seven years ago," Amy said. "The pattern started to change back then."

"Up until then," Jones said, "he needed time—"

"To facilitate his restitution," Ingram said. "He hid in the gradual alterations of nature."

Jones glanced at her. "Nice."

"Surfacing with dune erosion," Ingram went on, "rising in water as gasses trapped in the flesh lightened its weight, tangled up in seaweed and dragged onto shore—"

"Cut the poetry," Kaminer snapped.

Amy had an idea. "Has anyone checked the tides?"

Tom shot up and jogged around the table to his computer. He struck at the keyboard with his quick, heavy fingers until he found the Web page he wanted. "Looks like tides vary up and down the coast. They're all over the place. Depends on what body of water you're in." His eyes darted around the screen. "It looks more complicated when you're into the bays and estuaries. There's a whole network of tidal variations, heights and currents, flood currents, ebb currents, slack water periods." He looked across the room to Geary. "It's Sanskrit to me."

Amy stood up and walked across the room, back to the map with all its possibilities. It was starting to come to her now.

"He didn't go very far. He's hiding her somewhere off the Cape, but close by, because he has to get the boy onto the boat. He'll only dock as long as he needs to. Then he'll go back to his hiding place. Somewhere tucked into the folds of the shoreline—a cove or a river or a bay. Somewhere you'd get beached if you were there at low tide. Somewhere undeveloped, remote, no houses."

The room was quiet; they were all listening.

"My guess is he acts during the low tides," Amy continued, "possibly in the middle of the night, when the noise is less likely to be heard by other boaters. He drops one signature body part into the water just before the first morning tide goes out." The image, as she said it, sickened her. "I'm wondering . . . if we could understand how the tides fluctuate around the coasts, we might be able to focus our search. He'd avoid the places the currents are roughest. He wants cooperation, predictability, not interference."

She turned around and faced the map. The lines she'd been studying earlier transformed into a lucid image, as when a scribble congeals into a recognizable landscape. Where before she saw outlines of land bulging into ocean, she now saw its inversion: notches pulled inward to create secret places. It was like a gift from the echoing depths of her exhausted mind.

"Interesting," Geary said, and Amy felt the rush of validation. It was better than coffee or even sleep.

Sorensen stood up and looked at the map and she knew he saw it too.

Amy turned to Kaminer, who was nodding, pleased. She knew he spent some of his spare time on the water. "How many times a day do the tides change?"

"I've been fishing the Cape my whole life," Snow said. He was standing in the doorway, holding a take-out tray from Dunkin' Donuts with a dozen coffees and a box of doughnuts balanced on top. "You can average the tides at two in and two out, every day, give or take."

The sight of Snow standing there, nice and rested, with his precious offering *that he wasted more precious time to go and get* ignited Amy like dry air on a flame. She hadn't realized how far gone she was until she heard the snap of her own voice. "What the hell is that, Al?"

Snow ignored her and walked to the long table, where he set the coffee and doughnuts down at the end. The room was hot with Amy's anger and no one made a move toward the tray.

She felt her teeth grinding, felt herself making possibly the biggest mistake of her career. Losing her temper in front of Kaminer, Sorensen, Geary . . . just when she was on the cusp of *seeing* Mr. White scuttling across the map. They were all watching her and she imagined what they were thinking: she couldn't handle it, or maybe she'd had her period. Well, she could and she didn't—that wasn't the point. Snow had sabotaged this investigation from the very beginning, and he was still doing it. They needed everyone 24/7 at this point, everyone, even the weakest links.

Coffee. Doughnuts.

She walked over to the cardboard tray and box, and in one quick gesture swept them onto the floor.

"That's enough, Detective!" Kaminer stood up. Then he actually chuckled. "I could have used that doughnut."

Nervous laughter rippled through the room.

She felt it coming: booted off the case, suspension or, worse, demotion back to the squad car. She should have talked to Kaminer about Snow two days ago before she let herself get this twisted up. Should have, could have, would have. It was too late now.

"We're all a little delirious," Kaminer said. "I slept two hours at home before and I'm sharper now." He glanced over at Sorensen, who was right up close to the map, staring into it.

Sorensen turned to face the room. "Alert the Coast Guard." He turned to Amy and she felt herself sinking like a deflated buoy. "Detective, go home and get some rest."

She couldn't believe it—that was all? No reprimand? Just a time-out to catch a little sleep in her own bed? She didn't want to leave, but knew better than to argue.

"Thank you, sir."

"I don't want you driving, Detective," Kaminer said.

"I'll be fine, sir."

"Snow, drive her home. On your way back"—he winked—"pick up some more of those doughnuts."

Amy felt a swell of resentment, but kept her eyes down as she walked across the room and out the door with Al Snow right behind her.

Chapter 28

As they glided into Shoestring Bay, Marian was surprised to see another boat tied at the dock. It was a small white cabin cruiser with a scripted blue name so chipped it was impossible to read. She had never seen anyone else here before but surely this dock belonged to someone; this just confirmed her feeling that they were trespassing.

"Maybe it's time to find a paying berth, Henry," Marian said.

Henry steered them forward. "Let's make this quick." He docked just long enough for Ted to carry their suitcase off the boat and Marian to help Daisy onto solid ground.

Daisy windmilled her arms in the moist summer air in a swashbuckling good-bye to her uncle Henry, the now-repaired and shortened charm bracelet dinging like noon bells on her fragile wrist. Henry saluted and ahoyed as *Everlasting Love* drifted off.

Marian hated to see her reverie on Martha's Vineyard end, but such was life. It was time to step back into civilization.

"Come on, ladies." Ted picked up their suitcase and started up the hill. Marian pulled Daisy along, behind Ted, to the path that cut through bramble at the foot of Simons Narrow Road. At the first hint of pavement, Ted set down the suitcase so he could pull it on its wheels.

"It was a good visit," he said. "Relaxing."

"I surely could have used another day, though."

"Why did we have to leave?" Daisy pulled away from her mother's hand and turned back toward the bramble. "I want to stay forever."

"Well, we'll see you then." Marian joined Ted at his side and kept walking. They chuckled as they heard Daisy's feet pattering up behind them.

"What time's the bus?" Ted asked.

"Four o'clock. We'll have lunch at the Mute Swan like always."

"Yay!" Daisy now ran on ahead. "I'll have fish 'n' chips! Yahoo!"

The roadside restaurant was just a few hundred feet up the road. It was a ramshackle place, perfect with a noisy kid like Daisy. Marian thought she'd ask the waitress if there was some kind of lost and found where she could leave Daisy's bracelet. No, someone else's bracelet. That was the whole point. Even though Daisy had tried to goad her into keeping it, it was a matter of principle to return it.

The Mute Swan had a healthy lunch crowd for a Thursday, but there were a few empty tables at the back of the restaurant. Luckily they wouldn't have to wait for a table at the front counter, with its glass display of scrimshaw knickknacks, Beanie Babies and homemade fudge—Daisy magnets. They'd avoided the trappings of the civilized world on Martha's Vineyard for a blissful three days and Marian was not ready to start shopping for stuff they didn't need.

Daisy's white shorts were already cloudy at the bottom, and Marian winced to see her daughter skip through the restaurant to their table in the far corner.

The purple halter top needed to be retied at the neck before it slipped down the girl's reedy body. It was a beautiful sight, this child who loved every inch of herself. Marian wondered if she could keep that fire burning all through Daisy's teens. She swallowed that every-mother's-dread of seeing her child's innocence lost to the wiles of time, and sat down at the table, facing a window with a glimpse of the bay. Ted sat next to her.

"Daisy!" His firm voice pushed her down into a chair. But not for long; she bounced back up like a rubber ball.

"I'm going to look at those Beanie Babies up front."

"Oh, you are?" Marian cocked her head at her daughter.

Daisy planted her hands on her hips and sugared her voice. "Please oh please. I just want to look."

Ted couldn't curb his smile, and then it drew out Marian's, and they were lost to their daughter's considerable charm.

"Two minutes," Marian said. "And don't leave that counter. If you can't see us, we can't see you."

Daisy skipped away before her mother finished talking.

Someone had left a copy of the *Cape Cod Times* folded on the chair next to Marian. She picked it up, fanned it open and handed a section to Ted.

"We probably haven't missed much," she said, and began to read.

Chapter 29

The corn man gave Emily another shot in her arm
and just like the other times her body went instantly
numb. Then for the first time he came behind her and
tugged at the blindfold. It slipped off. Total darkness.
She could not open her eyes. Then she heard a sound.
Her baby's first cry at birth, an echo that resonated
with everything she knew, a sound edged in certainty.
The corn man's fingertips pressed her eyelids open
like sliding doors.

Darkness was cut with diamond-bright flecks of
light. She couldn't close her eyes against the shock;
they stayed open, and she felt the sharp pins of light.
And then as her vision pulled into focus she saw her
Sammie in front of her and her soul leapt out of
her body toward him. But her body stayed as inert
as wax.

Sammie was all tied up, his legs bound tightly together with clean white rope, his hands cinched behind
him. A piece of black electrical tape sealed his mouth.

He was lying on the floor, on his back, right in front of her. His head was turned to her and his wide-open eyes were drinking her in. Seeing her and finding her and pleading *mommy mommy mommy*. His eyes demanded that she cross the few feet between them and do her job and save him.

She watched him. Even her lids couldn't move, nothing about her was pliable except her brain, which saw and heard and felt everything.

She stared at her Sammie like an observer, a cool observer, he must have thought, passionless, uncaring, not the same mother whose need to help him would have been stronger than any rope. She was the same mother, that very mother, and she needed to help her son at that exact moment. Need. She was an open well of need. She sat propped against the curved inner wall of the reeking boat. She sat and she watched. Her body didn't flinch toward her son.

Sam's body twitched on the floor. Something else was wrong. Had the corn man given him some kind of shot too?

She heard the footsteps but this time they weren't coming for her. They were going to Sam. Her blood rushed to her heart and it engorged as fast as a helium-pumped balloon, about to burst out of her body. A pair of men's boat shoes, white, stood behind Sammie. The white pants began to bend and the knees appeared in her vision. The corn man sat himself down, cross-legged, right behind Sam.

And for the first time since she had been there she saw the corn man. And it wasn't him.

She felt her body stiffening. Her lungs filling with stone.

The man sitting behind her son was a total stranger,

even to her imagination. This monster who had kept her at the bottom of his boat like a dying eel. This freak who had hunted her child.

Sam's eyes shot off her face, up to the man just behind him. The man looked down and shook his head. For the first time she heard his voice, nasal, almost cranky.

"Didn't your mother ever tell you not to talk to strangers?"

Her body was racked with anger, pure hatred.

Sam's eyes slammed shut. So quiet, afraid. He was a single stone, sending shivers through a body of water larger than any imagination. One stone, sinking. Gone.

Every piece of her cascaded out of place.

The man shook his head at Sam like he was misbehaving and she would kill him she would destroy this monster with her bare hands. He looked at her and tilted his forehead to the side like he was wondering how to punish them.

"Let's take away his Pokemon cards, should we?"

She would obliterate him with her eyes.

"Games for Sam, books for David."

He knew their names.

"What about Mommy's favorite pastime?"

He got up, walked across the room, took something from a drawer and returned to sit back down in the same position. In the flat of his palm sat a strawberry pincushion pierced equidistantly by hundreds of straight pins.

The man's face was still and dead. He watched her.

All the fluids left in her body boiled, then froze.

The monster stared into her eyes.

"There's still time," the monster said in a strangely placid voice. "There's no rush." He stood and walked to the hatch. When he pulled it open, light rushed in and she was blinded. She heard his footsteps moving slowly up the ladder, the sound of the hatch closing, and his steps as he walked off the boat.

She blinked her eyes and struggled to grab Sammie with her vision, to focus into him. *My baby, let me hold you. Come safely into my eyes.*

Chapter 30

In Manhattan the world was a grid and all you needed was second-grade math to get yourself around. But here it was like a universe filled with crisscrossed threads. David didn't know where he was and now he was starting to wonder if Sam had been the smart one to stay behind. David was starting to think he should have planned it out a little better. Hidden himself a bicycle, taken along a backpack with supplies. It was hot and he was thirsty, getting hungry now too. At least he'd been sane enough to grab some of Dad's cash.

Dad would be ballistic just about now. David wondered what his punishment would be when he got home. If he ever got home. Maybe Dad and Grandma would take Sam and Maxi back to the city without him. Maybe they'd leave David and his mother here alone. Maybe he really would. David stopped a minute and sat on the grass at the side of the road and knew he'd made a big mistake. Dad would never leave the Cape without him. Dad would kill himself looking for him. It would be all David's fault, and they'd have no parents, and they'd have to live with Grandma, who couldn't even remember to give Maxi her medicine. They would become orphans all because David had been stupid enough to think he could find their mother better than Dad or the police or the FBI. Like some eleven-year-old kid could find someone who all the grown-ups put together couldn't even find. He had learned a lot in aikido about confidence and strength and fighting and not fighting and he had his brown belt but he hadn't learned how to be smart. Now everyone would know what an idiot he was. Dad knew. Grandma knew. Sam knew. Someday Maxi would know. Would Mom ever know?

His big plan had been to get to Stop & Shop and start looking for her there. He knew it was somewhere off Route 151 but that road ended an hour ago, then turned into Route 28, two 28s actually off a big rotary that was like a spinning wheel collecting up all the threads, spewing them out into more nowheres. David hadn't so much made a choice at that crazy intersection as kept going. Then 28 went on so long it started to look like it would never turn back into 151. And he was so hot and so thirsty.

Maybe it was the coolness of the breeze but when he sensed water he turned off onto the nearest road. Quinaquisset Avenue. He couldn't even pronounce it and that irritated him. He lost the breeze pretty quickly, and didn't like all the traffic on the avenue, so he took a quieter road with a name he could say. Simons Narrow Road. That was easier and a sign shaped like a swan told him that if he kept on going he'd get to a restaurant with a three-dollar-ninety-five-cents buffet lunch. Buffet was good because you could eat and drink as much as you wanted. He'd be smart and take a big to-go cup of water with him when he left, or maybe even buy himself a bottle if he had enough money.

David kept in the shade at the side of the road and walked and walked and walked. He passed houses and

kept going, just a kid old enough to be walking somewhere on his own. Looking for his mother. Sensei had
once told them they had an "inner compass" and if
they paid attention to it they would follow the "true
path." He was either following his inner compass to
his true path now or going nowhere. It didn't matter.
He was already on the road. He couldn't sit at Grandma's anymore like a dumb kid listening to the grown-
ups lie. All that time at the dojo learning not to be
afraid of other people, and he wasn't, but he was starting to feel afraid of himself and that was a brand-new
feeling. Walking down this loose end of a road he
didn't know anything anymore. He was looking for
another swan sign. He was looking for his mother.

He passed Yardarm Road and Spinnaker Drive
and finally just past Bryants Cove he saw a kind of
shack with the same swan-shaped sign hanging off a
set of chains in front. It said MUTE SWAN, LUNCH NOW
BEING SERVED. In Manhattan a place that looked like
that would be condemned, but here it was the kind
of place the grown-ups always wanted to go. It was
unbelievable how they changed their minds about
things.

David realized if he walked into a restaurant alone
it would look weird. Maybe if he pretended his parents
were waiting for him in the car. He opened the
wooden door and walked into a kind of lobby with a
glass display case under a counter and a cash register
on top. Blocks of fudge were stacked in the display
and David felt a spasm of hunger. He didn't want to
look obvious but he couldn't just stand there, so he
rang the little bell next to the cash register. He would
act normal. His parents were waiting for him in the
car.

A teenage boy came behind the counter. "You ring?"
David nodded. "Can I get the buffet take-out?"

The teenager shook his head. "We can wrap you up a sandwich or something though."

"Okay. Tuna fish?" He wanted a burger but it would take too long to cook it, he didn't want to wait, someone might notice him.

"White or whole wheat?"

"Whole wheat, I guess. And some water, please." David turned around and pretended to wave through the window at a red station wagon with a lady inside.

"Be right back." The teenager walked around the corner.

The restaurant was filled with people eating lunch and David didn't look at any of them. He stared into the display case crammed with the fudge and Beanie Babies and some local craft thing labeled scrimshaw, tiny drawings of boats and shells on something hard and creamy. It looked like bone. He was standing there waiting for his food and trying not to want the fudge when this girl came running over to look at the Beanie Babies. She was younger than Sam. She started to count all the Beanie Babies in the case.

"Twenty-seven," she said. "Not bad. Which one's your favorite?"

David ignored her.

"I love that tie-dyed one right there." She pressed her finger on the glass and David saw it: a silver charm bracelet just like his mother's on this little girl's wrist. She noticed him looking at the bracelet and twirled her wrist to show it off. "It's mine," she said.

Then David saw it wasn't just like his mother's bracelet—it *was* his mother's. It had to be. There were all the same charms. A heart, a swimmer, three babies, a coin, a cello, a sword.

"That's my mother's bracelet," David said.

"Oh no, it's *mine*." She held it up between them, as if that would prove it.

"Where did you find it?"

She looked at the bracelet, then at David, then at the bracelet, then back at David. It seemed like she was trying to decide what story to make up next. Little kids. It wasn't so long ago Sam was about her age and David hadn't forgotten.

"I'll pay you for it."

"Oh? How much?"

He dug into his pocket and counted out all his money. "Seven dollars and sixty-two cents."

"Deal!" She picked at the clasp but it wouldn't give. Funny, since it was always popping open and falling off his mother's wrist.

"Where did you find it?"

"That'll cost you more, mister."

"It's all I've got!"

"Sorry—"

"I'll let you keep it if you tell me where you found it." David realized the secret was worth more than the bracelet itself.

"For seven dollars that's all you want?" The girl pressed her hands into her hips and tried to look tough, but she didn't. She was just a little kid.

"And sixty-two cents."

"What's your name?"

"David. Where did you find it?"

"I'm Daisy. I can show you. It's right down there."

Daisy spun around and ran out of the restaurant. David heard footsteps coming toward the counter and he thought he better leave before the teenager got back with his food and he'd have to pay. He ran after Daisy, out of the Mute Swan, past all the parked cars, along more of Simons Narrow Road.

"Follow me!" Daisy called in a voice full of ping and echo.

She ran faster and he ran after her. He hoped she

was really taking him to the place where she found his mother's bracelet and not on a loser's game of hide-and-seek. They loved that, kids her age, playing games and trying to trick you. He was older than her, and faster, and if nothing else, he'd buy the bracelet off her skinny wrist. They ran to the end of the paved road and onto a dirt path that led them through a bunch of dried-up bushes, then onto the top of a grassy hill. The grass turned sandy at the foot of a bay filled with dark green water that brought David's thirst rushing to the top of his throat.

Chapter 31

Will pulled into the front parking lot at the police station. Sarah unbuckled Maxi, got out of the car and leaned back in to collect the limp, sleeping body. As Will waited he saw a squad car pull into the drive and head around back. An officer he didn't recognize was at the wheel and a black couple shared the backseat. Will thought about the first time he came to this police station, a mere two days ago, and now how badly familiar the place had become. He thought about Al Snow and how he wrote his name in blue on the dry-erase board on the fridge at home, the name of a stranger whose title—detective—indicated competence. He wondered what would have happened if Snow had acted sooner when Sarah had first reported Emily missing. Would there have been any evidence at the Volvo, before the rain? Had Roger Bell planned the storm? Had he planned Al Snow too?

Sarah stayed two paces behind Will as they walked into the lobby. The officer was bringing the black couple around to the front desk.

"Suellen, this is Ted and Marian Joyner. I'm going to get them some coffee. Then I'm going to find somewhere to take their report." The officer looked at Ted

Joyner. "There's a special investigation going on and we all loaned out our desks."

"We don't want any coffee." Marian Joyner was agitated.

"Just wait here and I'll be right back." The officer left the Joyners in the lobby and disappeared down the hall.

Sarah carefully sat down on one of the lobby chairs and positioned Maxi against her shoulder. Will paced. The Joyners stood together by the reception window, their eyes following him.

"Our daughter is missing," Marian said.

Ted reached out and stroked her arm. "Shh."

Will stopped pacing and stared at them. He had no idea what to say that wouldn't sound harsh. *Join the club. I'm missing three. Watch out for the cops here. They're useless.* He started pacing again. An entire constellation appeared in his mind: every cartoon he'd ever sketched for the children, all laughing at him now and pointing their line-drawn fingers. He pressed his hands against his eyes to rub them out.

"I'm sorry," Sarah whispered to Marian so she wouldn't disturb Maxi.

"What's the special investigation?" Marian's eyes flashed between Sarah and Will. "Does that have something to do with you?"

Sarah nodded, her voice was quiet. "My daughter."

"I saw the newspaper at the restaurant," Marian said, "while we were waiting for our lunch. We hadn't had any news all week. I was reading the newspaper and looked over and saw my Daisy talking to a boy. We read about the woman who's missing. My husband was just about to call about the bracelet when I noticed Daisy was gone." Marian stepped into Will's path. "My Daisy was showing the boy the bracelet she found, and then she disappeared. She found it on Monday when we were leaving for the Vineyard."

Will stopped walking.

"A silver charm bracelet," Marian said. "A heart, three babies, a swimmer, a sword, a cello, a coin."

Will remembered slipping the bracelet onto Emily's wrist; she had just given birth to David and was fast asleep. He could still feel her rush of delight when she woke up and saw it for the first time: the heart, swimmer, sword, cello and one baby. Then, with each new milestone, each new child, another charm.

"Daisy was showing this boy the bracelet," Marian said. "And then she was gone."

"The clasp was broken, Will," Sarah said, her voice rising. "It must have slipped off."

Will stepped close to Marian and held her shoulders. "The boy, what did he look like?"

"Ten, eleven years old," Marian said. "He looked like you."

Will was in the grip of understanding that Marian had just seen David, *alive,* when the front door of the station house swung open and footsteps clapped on the hard floor.

"Will!"

The snap of his own name pulled his gaze away from Marian, and for a split second he saw his mother standing ten feet away. It had been such a long, long time, and he missed her so very badly. Yearning rushed into his heart and his brain and his muscles and he felt her, saw her: her eyes exhausted against the white hospital pillow. Pale blue water emptying.

"Always trust yourself," she had said. "And remember, my sweetheart, that Mommy will never stop loving you."

And her eyes closing and her fingers falling open around his small hand.

His birthday, the very next day, without her.

He remembered.

"Will honey." Caroline rushed to him in her red sundress and wrapped him up in her arms. Like their mother, she had never lost her willowy body, and her skin was softer than soft. *Comfortable,* he had called it as a child; against his mother's skin had been the nicest place to be.

"We saw the news," Caro said. "We flew right back."

Will pressed his face into Caroline's short hair and smelled her summery perfume. Her husband, Harry, sat down next to Sarah and put his arm around her shoulders. Maxi was just now waking up.

Will whispered into Caro's neck: "The bastard's got Sammie." He pulled away and looked into his sister's endless, amber eyes, framed in lines of wisdom and love and memory. Then he turned back to Marian. "Where did Daisy find the bracelet?"

Ted stepped forward. "Come with me. I'll take you."

Chapter 32

Grass fell onto sand and sand fell into water. Stretched out into the bay was a splintery dock that looked like it might fall apart right then and there with its crooked legs pegged in wet sand. Only the end of the dock was in the water. That meant the tide was out. David knew about the tides, how they flowed in and out on schedule with the moon and the sun. At the ocean beach in the morning the sand was soaked through and ready for castling, foot digging, racing into the waves. Then at the end of the afternoon on the beach the water tried to steal your towel and it was time to go.

A white boat with a faded blue name and two white seats behind a windshield bobbed at the end of the dock.

"There." Daisy pointed straight ahead. "I found it right there."

"On the dock?"

"Give me my seven dollars and sixty-two cents, *please*."

"First show me exactly where."

"Oh *look*."

Daisy wasn't interested in the dock or the bay or the boat anymore. She had seen something better: the high flat nose of an ice-cream truck parked right there in the bramble.

She took off and ran toward it and David followed. "Come back!"

"We gotta check this out!" She sounded happy. Dumb kid. Didn't she understand there wasn't time for games?

He reached her at the truck; it was bashed in at one side and rusted out. She was trying to pull open the caved-in door and he grabbed at the waist of her shorts to yank her down.

"Hey!" She got up and ran to the other side of the truck, laughing.

David ran after her. "Daisy, show me where you found the bracelet."

"You can't catch me!" She took off around the nose of the truck.

But he was older and bigger and faster and he could catch her, easy. He grabbed her with both arms and stopped her short.

"Just show me where."

"You crazy?" She wasn't laughing anymore.

"Show me *now*."

He grabbed her hand and pulled her back down the path and into the bramble. They skidded down the grassy slope and Daisy fell onto her white shorts that were dirty and streaked with green and now she was crying.

"Let go of me!"

"Where? Show me *where*."

"There!" She was crying harder and pointing at the dock.

David ran onto the dock, to the end, and stood in front of the white boat. He saw a little door just across the deck. The boat pitched to the left and then stopped and just kind of rocked on top of the water.

David turned around to look at Daisy. She was running up the hill, not waiting for the money.

He heard a sound coming from the boat. Like an animal that was scared.

He leaned over and pulled on the rope that anchored the boat to the dock. He pulled as hard as he could and the boat inched toward him. A foot away and he stopped pulling, stood up and hopped aboard. He walked softly on his sneakers across the deck, quiet as a cat, just like when he needed to creep up on Sam and really take him by surprise.

He bent down to the half-size door and put his hand on the knob and wondered if it was locked and heard that sound again, the animal sound, and he was shaking and he didn't want to but he turned the knob because he had no choice. He turned the knob and pushed open the door.

David peered into the boat. It took his eyes a second to adjust to the darkness but then he saw her, his mother, at least her body. She looked like a dummy flopped against the wall of the boat, her face was stiff like a mask and her eyes were rolled back in her head. She was naked and he had seen her naked before but this was different because her skin was blue in some places and gray in others and she was sitting in a puddle of pee. It smelled like a sewer and there was his mother and he felt something bad twist through his brain.

"Mom!" David said.

He couldn't tell if she heard him or if she was even alive. She wasn't moving.

Then David heard the animal again but it wasn't an animal—it was Sammie. He was lying in front of their mother, all tied up.

David was shaking. Someone had brought Sam here this morning and it must have been that creepy Dr.

Bell: *I'm not a pirate. Would you like to get in my car?*
He must have picked Sammie up on the old Indian
road, after David heard a car and ran off to hide in
the woods. But the doctor wasn't here now; the boat's
cabin was small, just one room. David knew he had
to move fast.

The first thing he did was go to his mother and
quickly work to untie the rope binding her wrists. The
rope was damp and it smelled like mold. The knot
was tight but he picked at it until finally he could
unloop one part, then another; then he tugged it off.
He half expected her hands to reach up and hold him,
but they didn't even move; they just dropped down
on the floor. He kneeled in front of her and up close
saw that there were bruises at her temples and the
skin around her eyes was creased. Her eyes were wide
open but they were just bloodshot whites.

"Look at me, Mom!"

Her eyes didn't flinch.

He put his cheek to her face and felt the warm
pulse of breath at her nose.

He pulled at the corner of black tape at her mouth
and her skin pulled up too; he was afraid he'd hurt
her so he stopped. He'd work the rope off her ankles;
then he'd untie Sam. He didn't know how he'd get
them out of here but that was a problem he'd solve
later. First he'd just get them free, and if he could
wake Mom up, maybe they'd be able to walk out—
no, run—on their own.

He was picking at the rope around her ankles when
he thought he heard footsteps. He stopped working
and kept still.

Someone was walking across the boat, right over
their heads.

Chapter 33

The sound of a bell infiltrated Amy's dream, and only after a few long minutes did she realize it was her doorbell. She was on top of her covers, fully dressed. She had fallen asleep so fast she didn't even remember lying down. Forcing herself up, she went to her bedroom window and looked out on her front lawn. Snow's squad car was back. The doorbell rang again, and again. She went to the bathroom, brushed her hair, splashed some cold water on her face, and made a promise to herself to be civil to Al Snow.

She smiled at him when she opened her front door.

"They found the boat," he said. "I'm supposed to get you."

The smile vanished. "Where?"

He started down the path; she'd never seen him move so fast, hadn't known he could. She followed at a jog. He got in the driver's seat without looking at her and started the motor before she got in. As soon as she had her door shut, he backed out of the driveway and sped down Plum Hollow Drive toward the main route.

"Where?" She clicked her seat belt into place.

"Everyone's on their way."

"But *where*?"

The familiar frustration clawed at her but she wouldn't let it bite.

His eyebrows arched. "Forty minutes of sleep isn't enough, is it?"

She looked at her watch and was surprised to see that she had indeed been home for less than an hour.

"Tell me everything, Al, please."

His eyes stayed on the road and he didn't answer. Apparently he couldn't talk and drive at the same time. She pressed back her desire to take over the wheel.

"Drive faster," she told him, and immediately regretted it.

He slowed down. So he would perpetuate his grudge against her to the bitter end. She shouldn't have been born Portuguese and brought her mixed blood back to his snow-white island. She shouldn't have been promoted to his department. She should have refused his unmarked car when Kaminer assigned it to her. Or maybe she just should have had that romantic picnic on the beach with him like he'd wanted. Would that have scratched the itch for this loser? What did he want from her anyway?

She held her tongue until she realized they were headed in the direction of Popponesset Bay, where they had found Bobby Robertson.

"Here?" she said.

He shook his head and slowed for an oncoming turn.

She pressed back into her seat and waited. As long as he got her there, it didn't matter. He picked up speed on Spinnaker Drive and Amy saw her first glimpse of ocean ahead. They had to be close.

She was surprised not to see any other police heading to the scene. "Where is everyone?"

He shrugged.

That was it: when all was said and done, she'd have that talk with Kaminer. She couldn't tolerate Snow and she'd have to tell her boss exactly why.

They turned down Simons Narrow Road and stopped. There was no one there, just a dead end, a grassy knoll that spilled into a quiet bay—and a single boat.

"We made it here first," he said like he couldn't believe it.

She got out of the squad car and started down the hill. Snow was right behind her. Alone at a short sun-bleached dock was an unassuming white boat; but when she got closer she saw that the boat wasn't the SeaRay Sundancer they'd been looking for.

"This isn't Bell's boat." Amy stopped short and turned to look at Snow. "What's going on here?"

"This is where they sent me," he said. "Maybe they made a mistake about the boat."

She paused to watch Snow step down the hill carefully, so he wouldn't fall.

"Who sent you here, Al?"

"Got a message from dispatch, said to pick you up and bring you to Shoestring Bay. This is it."

"But you said I was home forty minutes. Didn't you get back to the station?"

He blinked. Kaminer had told him to stop back at Dunkin' Donuts and she could just see him parked on a stool at the counter, taking himself a break while he waited for the order to get pulled together. She looked at him and didn't know what else to say. Just then a breeze spun off the bay and caught Snow's comb-over by surprise, flipping it wrong-side over. He didn't even bother trying to slick it back in place. Amy felt a twang of pity for him.

She pulled her gun out of her holster. "Let's take a look."

Snow followed her as they crept across the deck. There was a small hatch. Amy tried the knob; it was unlocked. She turned it and pushed the hatch open into the darkness of a small cabin. She was hit by the reek of urine. It was awful. She jerked her head back and took a sharp breath of sea air.

"It's bad, Al. There's something in there."

"Want me to go first?" he asked.

She didn't bother answering. She felt around for a light switch but didn't find one. Across the cabin she noticed a set of curtains that was drawn together, with a small amount of light filtering through. She leaned in and her eyes began to adjust.

And she saw the still figure of a woman.

Amy's eyes gained focus and there she was, Emily Parker, naked, ankles bound, arms free, lying in her own waste. Her skin tone was bad and Amy didn't detect any breathing. Emily was possibly alive but more probably dead. In front of Emily was the younger boy, Sam, bound in rope.

"Police!" Amy called into the cabin.

Sam's body jerked at the sound of her voice.

She climbed down the ladder with her gun cocked. She could hear Snow rattling down behind her.

"Where are you, Bell? Come out! It's over."

She didn't hear anything, just the sound of Snow's footsteps moving slowly in her direction. He shouldn't have been following her; he was supposed to fan out in the opposite direction. She could see it was a small cabin but there were a few places Bell might be hiding.

"Al, check behind the galley." She felt his hesitation, his unwillingness to heed an order from the likes of her. "Please, just *do* it."

Chapter 34

From inside the hollow bench, crouched down next to a loop of hose, David listened as the footsteps pounded above on deck. It was hot in here, and dark, and the hose took up too much room, forcing him over to one side. He listened to the boat's hatch creak open and a voice, two voices talking. Then he heard the woman's voice say, "Police!" and he felt like crying.

It wasn't Dr. Bell, or any other bad guy; it was someone come to save them.

David started to push open the top of the bench. His eyes had to adjust to the murky light but it was better than the solid darkness of hiding inside. He could see the police through his inch-high opening. One of the cops ran right up to Mom but the other one just stood there. Something looked wrong. David kept still and quiet and watched.

The lady detective he'd met at Grandma's house and again at the police station—he remembered her name was Amy something—was leaning over Mom. David held his breath. He was so close to them he could have touched Amy's long hair as it fell over Mom's shoulder. Amy had two fingers around Mom's wrist, taking her pulse. Amy's eyes looked worried.

She seemed so relieved to have found Mom, like she would have cried if she hadn't been a cop. David wanted to cry too. He wanted to get out of the cramped dark bench and help Amy untie Sam.

Sam's head kept crashing on the floor and he kept making that sound. Amy moved over to him and looked right into his eyes and used her flat palm to wipe tears and sweat off his cheeks. She was wiping his face with one hand and pulling at the knot behind his back with her other hand.

Then David saw the other cop come right up behind her. A second ago David had heard her tell him to go check something, just *do* it. She'd sounded annoyed, but he hadn't budged; he'd just stood there, staring at her back. Now he started walking in her direction, quietly, like he didn't want her to hear him coming.

But she did hear him and she turned around.

"Al, I told you—"

Al was holding his gun by the barrel and he swung the handle down at Amy. She lifted her arm up to protect her face but it was too late. The butt end of Al's gun crashed against the side of her head and she pitched sideways, hard, against the bench David was hiding in. She fell right on top of her gun and lay there, still. His fingers ached, holding the top of the bench up just so, without moving it at all. If he moved it, Al might see.

Sammie started bucking against the floor harder than ever. Al stepped around Sammie and hunched over Amy and took another jab at her head with the butt of his gun. Al was breathing real hard now and sweating like rain; he was grinding his teeth and his eyes were slits. He was so close David could have spit on him. David could see the moles and hairs sprouting out of the back of the man's neck.

David understood. He understood everything. It was now or never.

His free hand reached out for the hose. There was no way not to make a sound. In one big movement he slammed the top of the bench up against the wall, hooked his other arm through the wreath of hose and brought it down hard on the back of Al's neck. Al fell forward under the weight of the hose, right over Amy. His gun went skidding along the floor and landed right next to Mom. Al grunted and pushed himself back up. The hose slid off his back and now the man was standing, looking right at David, who stood in front of him and didn't stop to think about what came next.

Harmonious ki. Blend with your attacker. But Sensei had always finished by telling them if they were in real trouble to fight back hard. Just fight.

Al lunged at David and reached out to grab his neck and almost got him but he was too fast; David stepped out of reach. He slid forward and snap-kicked at the front of Al's knees. Al buckled to the floor right next to Amy. David jabbed another kick at Al's shoulder.

Al jerked back up to his knees and tried to grab hold of David's leg. But David was fast; he spun behind Al, who kept reaching and fell by his own momentum. Al was jackknifed backward, bent at the knees, giving David a good clear shot at the crotch. They were taught to kick at the crotch and run for their lives but David had another idea. He'd weaken him with the kick at the crotch then knee him in the spot right under the jaw to knock him out.

He kicked and the cop moaned and then he kneed him. Al grunted, heaved forward and grabbed on to David's ankles. He pulled and David crashed to the floor. Al pitched his body in David's direction like he wanted to land on him, but David rolled away before the man hit the ground.

David ran to the other side of the boat and just like he wanted Al came for him. David fell into a crouch and braced as Al tripped over him and buckled to the floor.

Al struggled to his feet and David kept moving, pulling back for a snap-kick-punch-strike. But just as he came forward, the cop twisted to the side and grabbed something. A long knife. David felt the cold blade press into his neck.

Chapter 35

The little girl was running through the bramble, crying. Ted Joyner fell to his knees and she jumped into his arms.

Will hurled himself down the hill and leapt onto the dock. He took it in five long bounds, jumped across the water and landed on the deck of the boat. He kicked open the hatch and used his arms to vault himself into the cabin.

Crimson and panting and dripping with sweat, Detective Al Snow had a knife to David's throat. David's eyes twitched to Will's face and instantly filled with tears.

Al Snow.

Emily was wilted against the wall of the boat, her skin a frosty blue. Sam lay at her feet, his face twisted toward Will, terrified, every part of his body shaking against the rope he was tied in. Detective Cardoza lay just to the side, sprawled on the cabin floor.

It was all wrong, and Will felt an imminent shattering, like fissures speeding through glass.

Trust yourself.

"Drop the knife, Snow!"

Snow's face seemed to melt, a mask falling away, and what was left was raw and blistered by rage.

"Don't do it," Will said. "It's over."

Snow's mouth molted into the most hateful leer Will had ever seen as he tightened his grip on the knife's handle and pressed the blade into David's skin.

The moment opened in front of Will with the hopelessness of a chasm too wide to possibly leap, but you leapt anyway, because the ground beneath your feet was just then disintegrating. It was fly or fall. It was the moment that was never supposed to happen, when Will's limbs became the lethal weapons he was forbidden to use. It was the inevitable moment and it was right now.

No mind, no thought, pure reaction.

Will knew only one thing: he would save his family from this freak if he died doing it.

It took a split second of sheer force to propel himself at Snow and strike the edge of his hand against the side of Snow's face, twisting him back, hard. Will reached an arm up in a noose around the cop's neck and slid his other arm through Snow's elbow to reach the knife. David shrieked. Will squeezed Snow's wrist, forcing open his hand, and the knife fell to the floor. David slid down and away.

Will couldn't stop himself. Even though the knife was down, even though David was free, he tightened his grip on Snow's hand and jerked his arm down so hard he heard a bone crack. Snow didn't make a sound but Will felt the pause in his existence and jerked the arm again.

David took a step toward them.

"Get back!" Will shouted.

But David came forward and kicked at Snow's jaw. Will had never seen his son so enraged. He felt it too, but he wanted David clear of this.

"David, get back!" Will pleaded.

David kicked again.

Snow's body wilted. A long, pathetic moan seeped out; it was the sound of collapse, like the deflation of an air tunnel.

"I did it!" David was sweating, heaving for breath.

Snow crumpled to the floor. Will looked over at Emily and Sam and was overcome by the horror of what had been about to happen to them, what might have already happened to Emily. Her eyes were rolled back, her body was stone—her beautiful body, such stillness. Sammie beat against the floor and issued a high-pitched squeal. Will felt the boat sway and the sewer rankness brought his stomach to his throat. He was just moving toward Sam when David shouted:

"Dad!"

There was a loud scrape.

Snow was on his feet, holding the knife with his one good arm. The broken arm dangled by his side. His shirt was drenched and his pupils were dilated even in the dimness of the boat.

"You're fools," Snow hissed.

Will spun around. He would get to the broken arm and yank it down; he would curdle the monster with pain. But when he saw David charging at Snow, his impulse transformed and all he wanted was to keep his son out of danger.

He ran forward to intercept David. But he was too late.

Snow tripped David and grabbed a handful of his shirt, twisting him down to the floor. The knife had dropped beside them. David tried to pull away but Snow was fiercely strong. In a second he had David clamped between his knees. He picked up the knife and aimed it at exposed belly. Will hurled himself forward. The air seemed to turn gelatinous as the knife slipped through it, aimed at his own heart, barely protected in David's fragile body.

Then, a rush of footsteps thundered overhead, stopping time. Snow suspended the thrust of his knife briefly enough to listen. But as Will bore down on the killer's last chance, Snow's determination erupted. His face reddened and his fingers squeezed the knife's handle. He lifted it back as if to accelerate its ability to destroy.

Voices spilled through the open hatch and someone looked inside. Will recognized Officer Sagredo from the police station. Sagredo catapulted himself into the cabin, shouting, "Police!" Officers Landberg and Graves jumped in after. They were momentarily baffled as they took in the scene but in seconds got it right. In a refrain of mutual agreement, they aimed their guns at Snow's back.

"Al!" Graves shouted. "What the hell are you doing?"

"Put your guns down," Snow said, "or I'll kill the boy."

Sagredo's finger pulled against his trigger. "Don't make me do this, Al."

Snow's nostrils flared in defiance as the knife pierced David's skin just between his ribs.

Will felt a detonation of heat throughout his body and heard his own voice fly out: "No!"

There was a shot, and Snow's chest exploded. Blood spewed from a gash dead center in his front, like a target ripped open at the bull's-eye. Snow fell off David, a look of blank surprise dawning on his face. He rolled onto his back. Blood frothed from his mouth and nose.

David sobbed quietly, and Will held him, whispering, "Shh, it's over," and whispering it again. He looked up to see who had shot Al Snow, expecting Amy Cardoza to be on her feet, having leveled her best shot into a man who had briefly been her partner. But Amy was still sprawled on the floor, unconscious.

Instead, Will saw Emily.

She was on her knees, buckling in exhaustion, the gun falling from her loosened grip onto the floor in front of her. Her hands trembled as they reached up to catch her face, which dropped forward, pulling her fragile body into a curve. She dissolved onto the putrid floor, and wept without sound.

Chapter 36

John Geary stood under the SeaRay Sundancer's blue awning, next to his old friend Roger Bell, who manned the helm. It was Thursday evening, the cool end of a brilliant September afternoon. They made waves through Shoestring Bay, past Ryefield Point, and slowed down into a tidy outlet called Pinquickset Cove.

The cove was bordered by Crocker Neck, conservation land ending in a narrow channel that fed right into Fullers Marsh. Not a house in sight. At the end of the channel were abandoned cranberry bogs hidden by a tall curtain of reed. Egrets and blue herons stalked their prey, osprey hovered in the eerily quiet sky.

"I've been in here before," Roger said. "Saw a couple of paddlers once, but that's it."

Geary had rarely heard so much quiet in his long life. "Perfect," he said.

Turned out Al Snow really had known the Cape like the back of his hand, and as a lifelong fisherman he knew about Fullers Marsh. Once the Coast Guard had zeroed in on the area, they found it pretty fast. It took all of five minutes for the forensics team to locate fingers of engine oil slicking the surface of the quiet estuarial waters, evidence that a motor boat had recently strayed into the overgrown bogs. Residue of white paint was found on a few stalks of reed, and they all expected the lab would match it with Snow's boat.

This was where Snow had been hiding Emily Parker all week.

They would never know exactly why he'd accelerated his plan and motored back to the remote dock in Shoestring Bay on the fourth day instead of the fifth. Geary guessed it was because he saw them closing in. He had tempted fate a little too much, and maybe he even wanted to get caught, but he also wanted to finish the cycle one last time.

Once the tide had risen on the bay, he would have motored back into Fullers Marsh. It would have been late afternoon or early evening, right about now. He would be just starting his work on Sam Parker.

"Why was this nut so damn hard to crack?" Geary asked. "We hardly ever missed in the past."

"We were never sitting right next to our target before. You can't focus when what you're looking at is too close." Bell slowed the motor as it puttered farther along into the marsh. "Snow was one of the best we've seen, don't you agree?"

"He was up there." Geary breathed in the raw salt air. "I sure wish we had a chance to talk to him, though."

"As do I, but we'll have to satisfy ourselves with what little we know."

Geary had seen Al Snow's house for the first time that afternoon. It was one of those mobile homes not meant to travel, planted on a small plot of grass next to an identical plot in a row of plots laid out like graph paper. The house was sided in gray aluminum. There was a stumpy paved driveway, no garage. The

front door was flanked by windows too close together,
like beady eyes. Once the truth was out, it all looked
suspicious, but Geary knew that if he had seen Snow's
house before today, it would have blended in to his
assumption of the man as a harmless fool. The tiny
front lawn was crowded with busy gnomes holding lan-
terns, pushing wheelbarrows, tending deer. Inside, the
house was furnished in innocuous sets—living room
set, dining room set, bedroom set—that looked like
they'd been plucked from the pages of a sale cata-
logue. There was not a single photograph displayed in
the house, not even of Snow's daughter. Geary had
wandered the small rooms, tending his wounded ego,
berating himself for having slipped so ineffectively out
of retirement, while Amy Cardoza's team conducted
a thorough search for explanations.

Geary stood over Amy as she pulled open the flaps
of a cardboard box found on a shelf in the bedroom
closet. Her pale fingers hesitated as she seemed to
understand what she was seeing: Snow had kept trophies. But they weren't your usual trophies; no baseball statuettes, soccer plaques or commemorative
medals. Snow's trophies were personal, odd details
snatched from the scenes of his own crimes. A boy's
bathing suit crusted with sand, the scraped gold buckle
from a woman's shoe, a crushed foam coffee cup with
a blot of lipstick at the rim, the bloodied back closure
of a bra with the hooks neatly fastened, a black winter
cap with a lime green smiley-face button fastened to
the side, an old red pincushion with the pins pressed
in so deeply they'd been swallowed by puncture holes,
the keys to Emily Parker's car. The box was carted
back to the station house, where its contents were
carefully sorted and labeled.

When the box was empty, Amy oversaw the effort
to piece together Al Snow's history so she could con-

clude her report. Geary was impressed by her ability
to move forward. Not once had she mentioned the
fact that Snow had nearly killed her, and would have
if events hadn't colluded to bring Will Parker and the
police streaming to the boat. Geary knew that for all
his bravado, the fact was that lucky breaks solved
crimes as often as the most seasoned detectives and
profilers. He stared into the empty box, feeling emptied himself, wasted by time, exhausted by his own
efforts, when he saw something tucked into a seam
where four cardboard flaps overlapped at the bottom.
He reached in and nudged the white paper out with
his fingernail. It turned out to be the corner of a photograph. The black-and-white scallop-edged photo had
been torn and retaped in three different places. It
showed little Al Snow at the age of seven or eight,
standing apart from a steely-eyed woman. She wore a
paisley shift and the tendons on her neck were visibly
strained. It was a smileless moment in which two people appeared to have been captured against their will.
On the back a tight script identified the reluctant in-
habitants of that single memory: Eleanor Snow and
Son.

Local records filled in some of the details of their
lives. On Al's birth certificate, his father was listed as
unknown. The year after Al's birth, 1950, the Snows'
name was dropped from the roster of the DAR;
Daughters of the American Revolution did not give
birth out of wedlock. And old-line families, apparently, did not support them. Eleanor Snow, who had
grown up in one of the stateliest houses in Osterville,
had moved on to a series of shelters for wayward girls,
ending up in a trailer park listed by town and zip code
but no street address, just Wakeby Park. How she
made a living was unclear, but according to the town

hall she used the foster care system to help raise her son.

When Snow was seven years old, Eleanor pulled him out of foster care and brought him home. He was hospitalized five times that year alone, with injuries ranging from broken bones to burns on the soles of his feet and buttocks. The hospital record noted hundreds of pinprick-sized scars on his chest and stomach. Geary had read the description and it was severe, nothing like the scarring left behind by Roger Bell's dermatological outbreak as a child. Snow's map of ruin showed a war against love. What child would not conclude he was abhorred by his own mother?

Geary filled in the blanks. Snow must have been tormented by his mother's lack of love and empathy for him. He must have developed a craving for some glimmer of feeling—pain, guilt, regret—when she hurt him. He must have craved a look in his mother's eyes that he had never once seen. The record also showed that Eleanor Snow was brutally murdered twenty-eight years earlier—crime never solved. Geary took a wild guess that Snow himself had killed her. But not enough.

There was plenty of opportunity to repeat history. The world was full of mothers with seven-year-old sons.

Snow had figured out that in the course of five days he could reduce the mother physically through starvation and dehydration, and demoralize her by keeping her bound and blindfolded, in a puddle of her own waste. She would be alive yet significantly weakened and confused, which in combination with the muscle inhibitor would ripen her mind for a kind of mental implosion, given enough stress. The boy would be injected with an overdose of an antianxiety drug to excite his fear—Snow experimented with them over the years, trifluoperazine being his most recent selection. He figured that any mother watching her son die a slow, painful death in utter terror would die along with him. And they did, fully at first, then only mentally as Snow perfected the scenario. He shattered their minds by creating a state of perpetual, empathetic horror. He tested their love, watched it writhe, because he could.

Turned out Snow wasn't as dumb as he looked. He was keen, resourceful, and one of the most dangerous animals on the planet.

"Roger"—Geary cringed, but it had to be said—"I'm sorry I doubted you."

Bell's good eye cocked at him. "Guilty, are we?"

"Now you've really got a hammer for your old nail."

Bell laughed. "Yes, I do, and I'll die using it."

"Go right ahead. I'll take my penance."

"I don't fully understand how you could have suspected me, old friend." Bell's eye steadied ahead as he steered them into the narrowing passage.

"It was the Corvette. Why didn't you tell me you were buying it?"

Bell stopped the motor and the Sundancer came to rest in the marsh. Tall reed and cattails walled them off from the bog and cast a shadow over the boat. Bell stood up and dug his weathered hand into his shorts pocket. He showed Geary a key on a round plastic key chain with a red insert that read STEGNER MOTORS. The key chain didn't surprise Geary; Vera Ragnatelli had already confirmed that Ragnatelli's Vintage Automobiles hadn't had a Corvette on the lot in years.

"Happy birthday, John."

The gesture confounded Geary; it was too much, too fast, too late. "My birthday's in June."

"Better late than never."

Geary stared at the key dangling from Bell's hand. "Take it."

"Why?"

"You're starting over." Bell broke into that yellow-toothed grin of his, and Geary felt worse than before. "I thought this might sweeten the trip."

"Thanks, but no, thanks," Geary said. "Makes me feel like I'm sticking my hand in your retirement fund."

Bell shook his head and rigged a half smile. "I've had good jobs for decades, bestselling books, consulting fees. There's more than I'll ever need in my retirement fund. I've been alone all my life and it gives me pleasure to do this, John. You're my closest friend, and you owe me one. Take it."

But Geary couldn't. He'd worked all his life for the little he had; this would be like winning the lottery off your friend's ticket. "I haven't been the best friend to you."

"You looked at the facts," Bell said. "I'd do the same."

"So you could be convinced I'm a sociopathic killer?"

"Absolutely." Bell dropped the key into Geary's pants pocket. "It's paid for in full, by the way."

Geary felt the key rattling in his pocket like a hot rock; he didn't want it there but was afraid to touch it. Friendship came with obligations and if it meant that much to Roger, Geary would have to take the car. But he needed to get off the subject or he'd get maudlin and that wasn't his style.

"So, Roger, do you figure Snow saw you at the convention with the car? It was a sly move, working that into his story."

"Saw me? I gave him a ride, just this morning. He loved the car. He was like a child on a pony, I remember thinking he must have been a poor detective and certainly a foolish man." Roger shook his head. "I suppose he was thinking the same thing about me."

"He bought himself a little time, watched us spin our wheels," Geary said. "Turned us all into fools."

"So, John, after all these years, what do you think? Are psychotic sociopaths born to us, or do we breed them?"

"Wish I knew. I'd patent the gene and invest in the antidote."

"You'd become a wealthy man."

"He wore a white wig, you know," Geary said.

"Mr. Snow?"

"Cardoza found it in his house this afternoon."

"I'd have thought she'd be in the hospital."

"They brought her in unconscious, but the minute she woke up it was over for those doctors. She wanted to get out of there. What could they do, arrest her?" Geary chuckled. "She went straight from the hospital and joined the team at Snow's house. I drove her over there, stuck around for a little while."

"Looking for evidence after the fact?"

Geary shook his head. "Just answers. Looks like Snow had Bobby Robertson staked out, knew he'd be there every Monday like clockwork. Used the wig as cover when he drove the old Ford out of the lot. Called it in himself, the anonymous witness. I'd guess Emily Parker was just in the wrong place at the wrong time." An osprey glided over the bog. Geary watched the bird vanish into the tall grasses of Fullers Marsh. "Cardoza's back at the station now, finishing her report. Girl's got potential."

Bell's eyebrow arched sharply at the sound of that single word, *girl*. Geary took the cue like one of Pavlov's dogs and turned down memory lane under the long shadow of guilt. His whole life had nearly crumbled with that sexual harassment lawsuit; even now it gave him a jolt when he thought of it.

After all these years, he could still see Penny Aiken walking away. How could a girl look so good in a pair of those blue trousers Quantico issued to every trainee, male or female?

"It's Agent Aiken, sir," she told him, "not Penny."

He grinned. "Agent Aiken, interested in playing a little game?"

Her young face mustered up some respect. "What game, sir?"

"I'll tell you all about it later. We'll have a few drinks, talk about school."

"If I need to talk to you about school, sir, I'll come to your office." She stepped back at that point, and he stepped forward. That had been a mistake. Almost as bad as what he said next.

"I just thought it might be a little more comfortable away from campus, if you know what I mean."

He reached out and just managed to touch the blunt cut of her reddish hair as she turned around like a good junior agent and avoided the danger zone. He enjoyed watching her walk away, even thought it was a good sign she hadn't slapped his face. But he was dead wrong when he thought her cool walk meant she'd forget the proposition from the director of the BSU, her teacher, the program's founder and everyone's mentor. It took her twenty-four hours to file her complaint. It took him two years to fight it.

In the end, his biggest mistake in the whole mess was never coming clean with Ruth. He'd stuck hard to his story that Agent Aiken was a failing student who tried to exchange sex for grades and was striking out at him for refusing. With the great Dr. Roger Bell testifying that Special Agent Dr. John Geary was incapable of telling a lie, Ruth jumped right on the bandwagon and they rode into the sunset together, letting the case fade into history. Geary still wondered what Ruth had really thought, but at the same time doubted he would have the guts to take up her disapproval. Maybe someday he'd open her diaries. Or maybe not.

"I believe it was thirty years ago we were asked to stop calling them girls," Bell said.

"I heard it came back into style lately." Geary shrugged. "Go figure."

"Since when did you give a damn for style, John?"

"You know something, Roger?" Geary looked into the sky, sheer blue, that went on forever. "Sometimes I don't like the sound of my own voice, and that's the truth." Geary dug into his pocket, pulled out his wallet, flipped it open and took out a dollar bill.

"Of course." Bell laughed. "I won the bet. I know you too well, my friend. You were never going to be able to walk away from that case."

"Take it and don't gloat." Geary slapped the dollar onto Bell's open hand. "Cheapest car I ever bought."

DAY FIVE

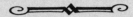

Chapter 37

Emily opened her eyes to darkness. Slowly, her brain shuffled pieces into place.

Sammie. My baby. *No.*

Speckles of light collected in a mist. There was no Sammie here. No one. She was all alone but not in the boat anymore. She took a deep, reflexive breath and waited for the footsteps. The corn man was not the corn man. A stranger. Don't talk to strangers.

He had a knife at David's chest.

Someone was going to die.

Oh, Sammie.

Her muscles jerked as if she had fallen off a cliff right before going to sleep. Her legs shifted on something soft. A bed. She was untied in a soft bed that smelled briskly clean.

Her brain reshuffled and she was in a hospital room. Alone. After David was born she had sworn never again to share a hospital room with someone she didn't know; for Sam then Maxi they paid for a private room. But now she hated it. She didn't want to be alone. She'd rather see an old, dying woman next to her, hear the calm flow of her breath, smell the suede richness of her skin. Watch her in a neighboring bed, thinking of the cycle of life, the turning wheel that drops one off and picks up another. Not the angry locusts that buzz in to eat you right off your branch.

She could move her arms and she could move her legs. Her eyes blinked freely. She stretched and looked around. Moonlight rippled across the ceiling, and outside she heard the hum of a car pulling away.

The air was dry, not spongy. She was over ground, not below sea level, submerged in water.

She took another deep breath.

The sharp, squealing noise. The pounding on the floor.

She didn't want to remember. *Go away.* She turned over onto her side and felt the tug of the IV taped onto her arm. Fluids, nutrition. Of course.

The corn man took off her blindfold and she saw Sammie on the floor.

And the corn man was not the corn man.

Go away.

She squeezed her eyes and turned onto her other side, carefully adjusting the IV tube. She gripped her toes and flexed her feet. Bent and straightened her legs. Turned onto her back and stretched her arms toward the ceiling. Someone must have washed her because the smell was mostly gone.

She looked around the room. White walls, industrial wood furniture, a phone on the bedside table. She picked it up and listened to the dial tone. Searching the walls she located a clock: it was ten past four in the morning. She dialed her mother's phone number and hung up before it rang. Let them sleep. Are they all safely home? *Go away.* Let them sleep. She would call at seven, tell her mother she was okay, remind her to give Maxi her medicine.

She couldn't lie there, couldn't keep still. She sat up and felt a little dizzy. Took a few deep breaths. Swung her feet over the side of the bed. Pressing her palms on the edge of the mattress, she eased herself down. The coldness of the linoleum floor shocked her bare feet. She stood, wobbly, and kept still while a wave of dizziness ebbed. A deep breath and she could do it, one step forward and then another. She just needed to walk. It had either been the worst dream or the longest night in history.

The IV stand wheeled easily along, clattering but not resisting. Her door was open, and when she entered the hallway it was like sunrise. The salmon-colored floor and cream walls were soaked in fluorescent light and small room monitors blinked behind a U-shaped nurses' station. But no one was there to witness the emptying of her bed, her slow creep out, the abandonment of her lurid nightmare.

She pushed her IV around a bend in the hall that led to a set of double doors just before another turn. The doors swung open and a youngish Asian woman in a white lab coat hurried through. Her name tag read MARY LAO, M.D., PEDIATRICS. Dr. Lao looked surprised when she saw Emily, and stopped right in front of her.

"Mrs. Parker, you're out of bed!"

Emily couldn't think of what to say.

Dr. Lao smiled and hugged a clipboard to her chest. "How do you feel?"

"A little woozy," Emily said. "I felt like walking."

Dr. Lao seemed to search Emily's eyes, like she was conducting an unauthorized examination of her being, like she needed to know more than the fact that her body was alive.

"Where are you going?" she asked.

"Nowhere, just walking."

"Let me help you with this." Inserting herself between the IV pole and Emily, Dr. Lao held the pole with one hand and laced her free arm through Emily's so she could lean if she needed to. They walked slowly, carefully, until they reached the double doors. Dr. Lao pushed them open and maneuvered Emily through. They were on the pediatrics ward, with its sky blue walls bordered with puffs of cloud. A hand-drawn rainbow arched over a bulletin board crowded with photos of newborn babies.

Dr. Lao stopped in front of the collage and pointed to a picture of a baby in the upper right corner. "That's my daughter, Samantha. She's seven months old now but the nurses keep her picture here to humor me." She touched the miniaturized cheek of her baby, then looked at Emily.

"She's adorable," Emily said. "It must be hard not to be with her all the time."

Dr. Lao nodded. "Exactly."

She took Emily's arm and guided her halfway down the hall, then stopped in front of an open door. Emily looked in and saw a bed and a cot. Will was on the cot, fully clothed, unshaven, deeply asleep. Sammie lay on the bed, tossing in his sleep, with his own IV tube dangling into his arm.

"The IV's just to hydrate him. I gave him something to help him sleep."

Tears burned into Emily's eyes at the sight of Sam and Will, sleeping, safe.

"Where are my other children?"

"They're at home with your mother and your sister-in-law."

"Caro's here?" Emily didn't understand; Caroline was in Italy.

"She was here until just after midnight. She took care of all the paperwork and waited until David was released. I checked him over myself and he's in excellent condition. Your brother-in-law took Sarah and the baby home earlier. Little Maxi is doing great, by the way."

"She has an ear infection," Emily said.

"Yes, I know. It's healing up nicely."

Emily felt the cool wash of relief; all that worry for nothing.

"How long was I gone?"

"Including today? Five days."

"That long."

Dr. Lao squeezed Emily's arm. "It's over now."

"Can I go in?"

"Why do you think I brought you here?"

Dr. Lao helped her over to Sam's bed and parked her IV stand on the side opposite his. She lifted the covers off his body and smiled. "Don't get your tubes tangled up."

Emily slid in next to Sammie and smelled the salty mold of the boat in his hair. She kissed the crown of his head, and both eyelids and his nose, and one cheek, and the other, and his chin. When she looked up, Dr. Lao was gone.

Sammie took a long, deep breath and threw a leg over Emily's, just like he did at home when they snuggled and read. She slipped one arm under his neck, wrapped the other one around him, and pulled him close.

His eyes fluttered open. "Mommy."

"I love you, Sammie." She kissed the tender fold of his ear.

His small hands pressed into her back in a refusal to let her go, as if she had somewhere better to be. She didn't, and never would.

"Tell me a story, Mommy."

The shadowy room and Will's slow breathing brought back words Emily had long forgotten. She leaned her head into Sam's pillow so their foreheads touched, and let him feel her breath on his ear as she whispered a story he'd loved since he was two. *In the little wood, slept a big bear. On the big bear, slept a little mouse. And in his dreams, the little mouse danced on great big clouds.* . . . . Sam listened as she spun the story precisely as she always had: the clouds forming a wall, a hole opening in the wall, the mouse running through the hole into a kitchen, finding a plate of cheese and peanut butter and cookies, then discovering a way out into a warm field, that led into a shady little wood, in which slept a big warm bear, in whose soft fur the little mouse nestled and fell asleep and dreamed.

Sam's eyes were wide open. She kissed him, and had no idea how to lull him back to sleep, how to influence his mind to relax and slide into gentle dreams, how to convince him monsters weren't real and lurking everywhere. Worse, maybe, that you couldn't identify them. She had been unnerved in the store by the corn man, but hadn't even noticed the person she had really needed to fear. Even now, when she recalled that recent day, she couldn't see him anywhere.